Beneath the Retreat's Veil

By

Arthur Patterson

Retreat to Deception

In the heart of New York City, as the summer's warmth reluctantly surrendered to the encroaching embrace of autumn, the atmosphere became a symphony of transition. The city streets, usually bustling with the ceaseless rhythm of urban life, now bore witness to the gradual metamorphosis of nature. Each step along the sidewalks scattered a mosaic of golden leaves, their descent a testament to the changing tides of the seasons. A soft breeze from the cooling temperatures wove through the towering buildings, whispering tales of transformation and renewal. The city, adorned in the vibrant palette of autumn, stood as a canvas where the passage of time painted its subtle strokes. As pedestrians moved through this dynamic urban landscape, they sensed the inevitability of change, and the promise of a new chapter echoed in the gentle breeze that carried the fragrance of autumn in its embrace.

As the autumnal shift unfolded, the alliance of friends found themselves drawn into a ritual that had become an unspoken tradition among them. The preparations for the weekend retreat at Tranquil Haven Spa were not merely practical tasks; they were a shared experience that held the weight of history, a ritual that had woven itself into the fabric of their friendships.

The genesis of this ritual could be traced back to a moment when the group, feeling the gravitational pull of their individual responsibilities and the relentless pace of city life, yearned for an escape. Five years prior, amidst the concrete jungle of New York, the friends found solace in the idea of retreating to the serene embrace of the Catskill Mountains. What began as a spontaneous weekend getaway morphed into an annual tradition, an unspoken pact to hit pause on the incessant demands of their bustling lives.

As the years unfolded, this ritualistic meeting grew in significance, transcending its initial purpose. It became more than just a break from the routine; it evolved into a sacred space where friendships were nurtured, and the complexities of their intertwined histories were unraveled. The journey to Tranquil Haven Spa was not just a physical escape but a symbolic pilgrimage, a collective endeavor to confront, reconcile, and celebrate the intricate tapestry woven by the threads of their lives.

Tranquil Haven Spa became more than a mere backdrop for their annual gathering; it transformed into a vessel of introspection, ferrying them away from the urban clamor to the stillness of nature. The verdant mountains and the secluded spa, embraced by the crisp mountain air, acted as a cocoon where the intricacies of their relationships could be examined with a newfound clarity.

Within the sanctuary of the Catskill Mountains, the ritual was more than an escape; it was a deliberate act of self-discovery and connection. As they entered this haven, the noise of their everyday lives dissipated, allowing them to hear the echoes of their shared laughter and the subtle vibrations of their unspoken words. The tranquility of the mountains acted as a mirror, reflecting the nuances of their friendships and the unresolved tensions that lingered beneath the surface.

In this space of reflection, the friends could pause, free from the city's distractions, and breathe in the rejuvenating mountain air. The sanctuary they created amidst the peaks and valleys became a sacred ground where they navigated the intricacies of their relationships. Here, laughter carried the weight of shared memories, and the mountain air seemed to hold the whispers of spoken and unsaid conversations.

With each recurring visit, the spa emerged as a silent observer, chronicling the metamorphosis of their connections. It became a repository of memories, witnessing the profound shifts in their relationships, mirroring their friendships' growth, struggles, and dynamic evolution.

As they immersed themselves in the serenity of the spa, the ebbs and flows of their collective journey were laid bare. With its whispers of wisdom, the mountain air seemed to embrace the uncharted territories of their relationships, providing a canvas for the unspoken narratives that unfolded in the company of close friends. Standing as an eternal testament to their shared history, the spa held the echoes of their laughter and the gentle sighs that accompanied the unburdening of their hearts.

In the embrace of the tranquil haven, time seemed to slow, allowing the friends to sift through the layers of their connections with intention and care. With its serene ambiance, the spa bore witness to their vulnerabilities, celebrations, and the complexities that defined their camaraderie. In these moments of reflection, the mountain air whispered unspoken truths, creating a mosaic of memories etched in the fabric of their collective narrative.

Olivia's penthouse, perched high above the city's skyline, was an opulent testament to her elevated status, a reflection of the success she unabashedly flaunted. The aura of affluence was palpable as the friends gathered within its sleek confines, from the gleaming marble floors to the expansive floor-to-ceiling windows offering a panoramic view of the city below. The penthouse had become the yearly planning vessel for the upcoming Spa adventure.

The penthouse itself, a sprawling sanctuary of luxury, boasted modern aesthetics with clean lines and minimalist decor. Plush, designer furniture adorned the living spaces, inviting comfort in a setting that seemed more curated than lived-in. The neutral color palette, dominated by shades of ivory and charcoal, accentuated the air of sophistication that Olivia had meticulously cultivated.

In the heart of the penthouse, the meeting unfolded around a meticulously crafted glass table, its surface reflecting the ambient glow of contemporary chandeliers overhead. The friends, seated in designer chairs, were surrounded by abstract art pieces that adorned the walls, perhaps chosen more for their price tags than any emotional resonance.

The penthouse's open layout facilitated the exchange of ideas, yet its grandeur also carried an inherent distance. The pristine atmosphere seemed to amplify the unspoken tensions that lingered beneath the surface of their friendships. As Olivia orchestrated the symphony of their gatherings, her penthouse became both the stage and the throne from which she presided over the delicate dance of camaraderie.

As the friends navigated the complexities of their relationships, the penthouse bore silent witness to their highs and lows. The dust settling on the metaphorical mantle was not just a metaphor; it manifested in the subtle undercurrents of competition and unspoken comparisons that Olivia's success had unwittingly fueled.

Amidst the laughter and shared memories, the friends found themselves treading carefully, mindful of the unspoken hierarchy that Olivia's penthouse subtly enforced. The space, while a neutral ground for their annual ritual, couldn't escape the undertones of

Olivia's success, a dynamic that would prove to be a silent accomplice in the unraveling of their friendships as the weekend unfolded.

Olivia's penthouse's atmosphere shimmered with excitement and an underlying tension as each friend arrived, adding their unique energy to the mix. As the planning session for the retreat commenced, it quickly became apparent that the friends had specific desires and reservations, setting the stage for potential conflicts.

With her meticulous executive mindset, Mia came armed with a detailed agenda for the weekend. She requested a more structured program outlining specific activities and team-building exercises to maximize their time at the spa. However, her precision clashed with Diane's more free-spirited approach, sparking an early debate on the balance between planned activities and spontaneous relaxation. Mia, however, could not be deterred, her meticulous schedule was to be followed.

Emily, seeking a respite from her troubled marriage, expressed a desire for individual counseling sessions with the spa's wellness experts. Mark, however, seemed uncomfortable with the idea, and the tension between their differing needs cast a shadow over the room. Unspoken glances and tightened shoulders hinted at the complex dynamics simmering beneath the surface.

Having recently gone through a divorce, Ava looked forward to the retreat as a time of reflection and renewal, for healing from the deep wounds of a failed relationship. The loneliness she experienced to be quieted by the friendships forged over the years.

Sophia, although positioned on the periphery of the group, possessed a deep desire to infuse the retreat with her artistic vision. Sophia yearned to elevate the retreat beyond a mere gathering, envisioning it as a canvas for artistic expression, self-discovery, and communal bonding, a desire for an immersive and transformative experience.

Richard, Olivia's husband, soon found himself caught between her ambition for success and Sophia's artistic vision for the retreat. Richard's discomfort grew palpable as the women articulated their preferences, torn between his loyalty to Olivia and his desire to support Sophia's creative endeavors.

Initially meant to foster unity, the planning session inadvertently exposed fault lines within the group. The clash of preferences, desires, and unspoken tensions created a charged atmosphere, and the subtle dance of compromise and assertion set the tone for a weekend that would prove to be more tumultuous than tranquil. As the friends navigated the delicate negotiation of their individual needs, the penthouse witnessed the fragile intricacies of their friendships, setting the stage for the unraveling drama that awaited them at Tranquil Haven Spa.

The annual meeting, a precursor to their spa retreat, was a delicate dance of camaraderie and concealed complexities. Over the years, the friends had honed the art of projecting an image of harmony while veiling the intricacies that colored their individual lives. Each gathering presented an opportunity to navigate the labyrinth of their intertwined relationships, setting the stage for a weekend that promised both tranquility and unforeseen revelations.

The dynamics within the group had evolved, becoming a sophisticated tapestry of shared experiences, unspoken tensions, and carefully crafted facades. Behind the laughter, shared memories, and seemingly casual exchanges lay a network of intricate connections, each friend balancing their own desires, secrets, and personal struggles.

As they masked the complexities of their lives with practiced smiles and surface-level conversations, the penthouse became a microcosm of their relationships—fraught with untold stories and suppressed emotions. The seemingly routine ritual was a delicate dance on the precipice of revelation, a prelude to the storm of truths that would disrupt the tranquility they sought.

Little did the friends know that within the carefully orchestrated planning session, the threads of their friendships were already unraveling, weaving a narrative that would expose the hidden corners of their lives. Once a simple tradition, the annual meeting had transformed into a pivotal moment that would redefine their bonds and shatter the illusions of tranquility they had carefully maintained.

After the meeting concluded in Olivia's penthouse, the friends departed to complete their individual preparations for the impending weekend at Tranquil Haven Spa. The air, thick with the weight of shared histories and unspoken truths, lingered in the wake of their departure. Each friend, armed with a forced smile and an air of composure, retreated into their private worlds. The veneer of tranquility they presented to the world masked the underlying tensions within their relationships. Behind each smile, beneath each polite exchange, simmered the unresolved complexities that would inevitably surface during the retreat. As they dispersed to their respective corners of the city, the anticipation of the upcoming weekend hung in the air—a palpable tension that would echo in the mountains and transform their idyllic escape into a crucible for the unspoken truths that bound them together.

With its unspoken rules and subtle negotiations, the ceremonial meeting allowed the friends to synchronize their expectations for the upcoming retreat. It served as a communal canvas where they could collectively paint the vision of their tranquil haven in the Catskill Mountains. However, in the process of laying the groundwork for a weekend of serenity, they unwittingly set the stage for the unraveling drama that awaited them at Tranquil Haven Spa.

Preparing the Canvas

In her Upper East Side apartment, Emily Rodriguez, the pinnacle of success, navigated the space with an air of poise and sophistication that mirrored her professional demeanor. The soft glow of muted sunlight filtered through the luxurious curtains, casting a warm and inviting ambiance over her meticulously curated surroundings.

The apartment, an embodiment of modern elegance, boasted a seamless blend of contemporary design and timeless accents. Crisp white walls served as a canvas for an eclectic mix of artwork, each piece carefully chosen to reflect Emily's refined taste and appreciation for the aesthetic. Polished wooden floors gleamed beneath the ambient light, inviting a sense of warmth into the space.

The living room, adorned with plush furnishings in subtle hues, exuded an understated opulence. Soft, textured throw pillows adorned the sofa, offering a comfort without compromising the room's immaculate design. A sleek coffee table adorned with art books and a carefully arranged floral centerpiece served as a focal point in the room.

Emily's personal touches were evident throughout the living space. Framed photographs captured moments frozen in time—smiles from memorable vacations, snapshots with friends, and achievements that spoke volumes of her professional prowess. The apartment was not just a residence but a curated reflection of Emily's journey, a living testament to her achievements and the relationships that had shaped her.

The muted sunlight played upon carefully chosen decor elements as Emily glided through the rooms. The air held a subtle fragrance, an olfactory symphony of soft vanilla, and hints of lavender that added a layer of tranquility to the sophisticated atmosphere. The sound of distant city life, muffled by the double-paned windows, hinted at the bustling world beyond, a world where Emily navigated boardrooms with the same grace she displayed in her home.

Her bedroom, an oasis of serenity, continued the theme of restrained luxury. The bed, adorned with high-thread-count linens and an array of plush pillows, invited rest and relaxation. A vanity adorned with neatly organized cosmetics and fragrances hinted at self-care rituals that punctuated Emily's busy life.

In her Upper East Side sanctuary, Emily Rodriguez seamlessly blended the demands of her successful legal career with the comforts of a meticulously curated home. Every detail, from the carefully chosen artwork to the subtle interplay of light and shadow, contributed to an atmosphere that spoke not only of sophistication but also of a life lived with intention and discernment.

Against a backdrop of neutral tones, Emily meticulously packed her bags, each item carefully chosen and folded with precision. The wardrobe selection was a strategic array of casual elegance, belying the tension beneath her composed exterior. The scent of lavender-scented sachets permeated the air, an attempt to infuse a sense of tranquility into the imminent journey.

As Emily stole fleeting glances at her husband, Mark, a figure of affluence in the world of high-powered investment banking, she couldn't help but observe the intensity with which he engaged in a phone call that seemed to carry the weight of the world on its shoulders. Mark's animated gestures and the furrowed lines on his forehead painted a vivid picture of the demands and pressures inherent in his high-stakes career, a world that often demanded his undivided attention.

The plush living room, an emblem of their shared success, bore witness to the stark contrast between Emily's poised exterior and the silent discontent that lingered beneath the surface. The room, adorned with tasteful decor and affluent accents, provided a backdrop to the complexities of their intertwined lives.

Mark, oblivious to the contemplative glances from his wife, was immersed in a conversation that demanded his immediate focus. The ambient light accentuated the sharp angles of his features, revealing a man dedicated to navigating the tumultuous currents of the financial world. While seemingly tranquil, the air in the room carried an undercurrent of unspoken tension.

In this snapshot of marital dynamics, Emily harbored a quiet dissatisfaction that lay dormant beneath the facade of contentment she wore for the outside world. The finely crafted exterior of their Upper East Side apartment mirrored the meticulous precision of their professional lives, yet it failed to shield the subtle fractures that had developed within the framework of their marriage.

The dynamics between Emily and Mark were an intricate dance of shared successes and unspoken struggles. An accomplished lawyer, Emily navigated the complexities of her legal career with the same grace she brought to her role as a wife. Mark, the quintessential high-powered banker, juggled the demands of a career that often spilled over into the sacred spaces of home.

As the distant hum of city life permeated the apartment, Emily's introspective glances hinted at a desire for more, a longing for a connection that transcended the boundaries of their respective careers. The room, despite its opulence, couldn't conceal the complexities of their relationship, and Emily grappled with the question of whether the life they had built together was truly fulfilling or merely an illusion of success.

As she zipped up her suitcase, the bustling city life outside her window served as a poignant contrast to the unspoken tensions within. The sounds of honking horns and the muffled chatter of passersby created a symphony that accompanied the underlying unease in Emily's heart.

The reflection in the bedroom mirror betrayed a woman of outward elegance, yet her eyes told a different story – a narrative of unvoiced desires and the yearning for something more. The changing seasons mirrored the shifting dynamics in Emily's life, and the weekend at Tranquil Haven Spa loomed on the horizon as a potential catalyst for the transformation that lingered in the autumn air.

In the expansive embrace of her SoHo loft, Sophia Harris found herself surrounded by an environment as eclectic and vibrant as her illustrious journalism career. The loft, a canvas of creativity and personality, embraced the essence of Sophia's multifaceted life. The expansive floor-to-ceiling windows served as portals for natural light, casting a warm, golden glow upon the exposed brick walls that showcased an array of avant-garde art pieces, each telling a story of its own.

The loft, a sanctuary for creative expression, resonated with the scent of freshly brewed coffee, the rich aroma wafting through the air and blending seamlessly with the subtle undertones of aged leather emanating from well-worn books that lined the shelves. The fusion of these sensory elements created an ambiance that reflected Sophia's intellectual curiosity and passion for storytelling.

With her innate sense of style, Sophia had curated a space that served as both a haven and an extension of her dynamic personality. The open layout invited exploration; every corner held a treasure trove of memories and inspirations. The loft was not just a living space but a testament to a well-lived life where creativity and intellect converged.

As Sophia navigated the loft's open spaces, her thoughts meandered through the various facets of her life. An accomplished and award-winning journalis known for her incisive reporting, Sophia was unapologetically single, a status she embraced with a sense of liberation. Lately, her social calendar had seen a flurry of activity, with Sophia casually dating several men and women, each adding a different hue to the canvas of her personal life.

The loft's blend of modern aesthetics and vintage charm mirrored Sophia's ability to navigate the complexities of her professional and personal worlds. It was a space where ideas flowed freely, the clinking of coffee mugs echoed alongside the tapping of keys on a laptop, and a symphony of creativity reverberated within the walls.

Amidst the curated chaos of books and art and the subtle drone of city life filtering through the windows, Sophia found solace and inspiration. The loft wasn't just a physical space but an extension of her identity. It reflected the woman who thrived on the ceaseless pursuit of truth and the ever-evolving tapestry of her life and relationships.

While preparing for the upcoming weekend retreat, Sophia found herself irresistibly drawn to the gravitational pull of her journalistic pursuits. A sleek laptop adorned with stickers representing various prestigious news outlets claimed its place on a modern desk, seamlessly blending with the loft's industrial-chic aesthetic. An array of notebooks, their pages filled with the handwritten intricacies of her investigative mind, sprawled across the desk, each one a testament to the depth of her commitment to the craft.

As a prominent journalist contributing to "City Chronicles," a publication renowned for its immersive explorations into the intricate layers of New York City's complex tapestry, Sophia's latest project had become a lodestar guiding her thoughts. The loft, with its exposed beams and a decor that harmonized modernity with an industrial edge, stood witness to the birth and evolution of her journalistic endeavors.

The laptop, a conduit to a world of information and stories waiting to be unearthed, beckoned Sophia to delve into the labyrinthine narratives that defined the city's underbelly. One folder stood out among the scattered notes on her desk, marked with purposeful strokes of a red pen. This folder encapsulated the preliminary sketches for an upcoming exposé, a meticulous plan to expose the covert dealings of a powerful figure entrenched within the city's political landscape.

Within the confines of those meticulously organized files and notes lay the potential to unravel a web of corruption, laying bare the clandestine connections between influential people, politicians, business leaders, and community supporters. The story, conceived and nurtured within the loft's artistic enclave, held the promise of shaking the very foundations of the city's power structure.

As Sophia prepared for the retreat, the juxtaposition of her creative haven and the pressing urgency of her investigative work created a symphony of inspiration and determination.

However, beneath Sophia's professional exterior lay a personal history entwined with complex emotions. The longstanding grudge against Emily Rodriguez stemmed from a betrayal during their college years. Sophia had confided in Emily about a personal struggle, trusting her with a vulnerability that proved misplaced. Instead of offering support, Emily had inadvertently exposed Sophia's secret to the broader social circle, leading to a cascade of consequences that left lasting scars on their friendship.

As Sophia gathered her notes and prepared for the weekend at Tranquil Haven Spa, the loft bore witness to the convergence of her professional ambitions and personal vendettas. The polished surfaces of her journalism career contrasted against the raw, exposed elements of her loft mirrored the duality that defined Sophia's life—a dichotomy that promised to unravel further amidst the serenity of the upcoming retreat.

Amid her studio apartment's chic and sunlit ambiance, Ava Turner confronted the aftermath of a recent divorce that lingered in the air like the mingling scents of fresh paint and the remnants of emotional upheaval. The apartment, a canvas for Ava's journey toward healing, bore witness to the unique olfactory tapestry that unfolded within its walls.

The aroma of the newly applied pigment that permeated the air served as a metaphor for the transformation and renewal that Ava sought in the wake of her divorce. The walls echoed the resilience and strength required to paint over the emotional complexities left in the wake of a broken marriage.

Large windows adorned the space, offering panoramic views of the city skyline that starkly contrasted the intimate struggle playing out within the confines of Ava's personal sanctuary. The bustling city beyond served as a visual backdrop to the inner workings of her heart and mind, emphasizing the juxtaposition between the external world and the internal journey toward self-discovery.

In this sunlit haven, Ava grappled with the echoes of her past, each beam of light that streamed through the expansive windows illuminating not only the physical space but also the emotional terrain she navigated. The city skyline, distant yet ever-present, became a silent observer to Ava's introspective moments, a reminder that life outside continued its relentless pace while she sought solace within.

The studio apartment, with its sunlit corners and the scent of renewal, became a sanctuary for Ava—a place where the remnants of emotional upheaval mingled with the promise of a new beginning. The journey toward healing desperately trying to unfold against the backdrop of the city, encapsulated the resilience and transformation that marked this chapter in Ava's life.

The divorce, a chapter closed only a few months ago, had inflicted upon Ava emotional scars still tender to the touch. Her marriage, once a hopeful union, unraveled under the weight of incompatible dreams and the burden of unmet expectations. In the wake of this dissolution, a poignant sense of loss clung to her like an ever-present shadow, casting its influence on every corner of her being.

The spacious apartment, once witness to a couple's shared dreams and aspirations, now echoed with the residual echoes of arguments and the haunting silence that followed. Each room bore traces of emotional upheaval, and the walls seemed to resonate with the memories of a relationship that had reached its breaking point.

Amid the remnants of a life once shared, Ava stood resilient, confronting the emotional scars of her past while embracing the opportunity for growth and renewal. The spaciousness of her apartment mirrored the vast possibilities that lay ahead, inviting her to embark on a journey of self-discovery and reclaiming her individual identity outside the constraints of a dissolved marriage.

As Ava prepared for the retreat at Tranquil Haven Spa, she stood before the mirror in her chic studio apartment, her gaze fixed on the reflection that stared back at her. Dark eyes, tinged with the residue of heartbreak, held a depth of emotion that spoke of her challenges. The mirror became a silent witness to the journey of self-discovery and healing that Ava embarked upon in the aftermath of her recent divorce.

The act of preparing for the retreat became a ritual of self-care and renewal. Ava acknowledged the complexities of her emotions and her transformative journey as she gazed into the mirror. Each stroke of the brush, every adjustment to her appearance, was a conscious step toward reclaiming her sense of self and embracing the therapeutic solitude promised by Tranquil Haven Spa.

The mirror, reflecting her physical appearance and the evolving landscape of her emotions, witnessed Ava's quiet strength and resilience. In that moment, she stood poised on the threshold of a new chapter, ready to confront the challenges of the retreat and, ultimately, to find solace and healing amidst the tranquil haven that awaited her in the Catskill Mountains.

Ava's unconventional pursuit of art was at the core of Sophia's disapproval. Ava had boldly forged a unique path into the realm of abstract expressionism, using unconventional mediums and techniques to convey the raw emotions that so often eluded verbal articulation. Her loft served not only as a living space but also as both sanctuary and canvas, a testament to the collision of chaos and creativity that defined her artistic journey.

Firmly grounded in investigative journalism, Sophia found herself grappling with the abstract nature of Ava's creative endeavors. The therapeutic release that Ava discovered in each brushstroke and the chaotic beauty that emerged from her unconventional methods—these aspects remained elusive to Sophia, who was more accustomed to the structured pursuit of truth in her own field.

In a previous confrontation during an intimate gathering of friends, Sophia couldn't conceal her displeasure. Amidst the camaraderie of the group, she expressed her reservations about Ava's art, unable to fully comprehend Ava's profound connection with her creations. The verbal clash of perspectives highlighted the divergence in their respective approaches to life and creativity, setting the stage for a tension that would simmer beneath the surface of their friendship.

With a raised eyebrow and a thinly veiled smirk, Sophia dismissed Ava's art as a frivolous pursuit—an escape that, in her eyes, lacked the intellectual depth necessary for creative endeavors. The disapproval manifested in subtle jabs and veiled criticisms, creating a palpable tension whenever the topic of Ava's art arose within their close-knit group of friends. Despite Sophia's disdain, Ava steadfastly clung to her artistic expression as a lifeline, a source of solace and self-discovery.

Though masked behind a facade of sophistication, Sophia's critiques carried the weight of judgment, challenging Ava's chosen path in the realm of abstract expressionism. The clash of perspectives between Sophia's pragmatic, investigative mindset and Ava's emotionally charged, freeform approach set the stage for ongoing discord. The loft, which Ava considered both a haven and an evolving masterpiece, became a battleground for the clash of their worldviews.

This clash of creative philosophies would become a focal point, a thread of unresolved tension woven into the intricate fabric of their friendship.

As Ava prepared for the retreat at Tranquil Haven Spa, she carried with her the hope that the serene environment would offer a respite from the judgment she faced among her well-meaning but opinionated friends. The mountainside retreat held the promise of both personal reflection and an opportunity to navigate the complexities of friendships that had, over time, become entangled with unspoken critiques and creative differences.

In the spacious penthouse overlooking Central Park, the accomplished fashion designer Olivia Barnes reveled in the glow of her recent achievements. The panoramic view of the city served as a fitting backdrop to her success, the floor-to-ceiling windows allowing the city lights to dance with the sparkles in her champagne flute. The room echoed with tasteful elegance, adorned with minimalist decor that spoke to Olivia's refined taste.

Her recent achievement, a critically acclaimed runway show showcased her latest collection at New York Fashion Week, had garnered widespread acclaim. Olivia's designs seamlessly blended classic aesthetics with avant-garde twists, earning her a coveted spot among the industry's elite. The penthouse, adorned with mood boards and fabric swatches, bore witness to the creative process leading to this success.

As Olivia poured herself a glass of champagne, the effervescence mirrored the excitement bubbling within her. The golden liquid cascaded into the crystal flute, the soft pop of the cork releasing a symphony of celebration. Her husband, Richard, a well-known architect, entered the room, attempting to join in her excitement.

However, "tried to join" was a nuanced expression that hinted at a disconnection beneath the surface. Richard, a supportive presence in Olivia's life, couldn't help but feel a growing frustration as he navigated the labyrinth of high fashion alongside his wife. Olivia's success, while admirable, cast a shadow over their relationship, creating an unspoken tension. The intricacies of the fashion world seemed like an impenetrable fortress to Richard, and despite his genuine efforts to understand and engage, he often found himself on the outskirts, unable to grasp the nuances of Olivia's triumphs. The divide between their worlds widened, leaving Richard with a silent frustration that he kept carefully concealed within himself.

Beneath the façade of Olivia's accomplishments lay a troubled past that haunted her. Raised in modest circumstances, she had fought tooth and nail to establish herself in the cutthroat world of fashion.

The memories of early struggles dismissed dreams, and relentless competition lingered in the shadows of her success.

The web of envy and discontent within the group was palpable, but Olivia felt it most acutely. The accolades she garnered stirred a mixture of admiration and resentment among her friends. Some admired her tenacity and talent, while others harbored unspoken envy, yearning for a taste of the success that eluded them. The penthouse symbolizing Olivia's triumph became a focal point for the group's complex emotions.

During gatherings, congratulatory smiles masked a simmering jealousy that threatened to boil over. Unbeknownst to Olivia, her success cast a shadow over the aspirations of her friends, creating a delicate balance of admiration and rivalry within the group. The celebratory champagne in Olivia's hand was both a toast to her achievements and a harbinger of the discontent that would come to a head during the weekend at Tranquil Haven Spa.

In the sleek, high-rise office of a prestigious advertising firm, a high-powered executive, Mia Johnson, commanded a corner suite with floor-to-ceiling windows offering panoramic views of the city skyline. The sunlight streamed through the expansive glass, casting a warm glow over the meticulously arranged space. As the Senior Vice President of Marketing and Strategic Partnerships, Mia navigated the competitive world of corporate strategy with finesse and determination, her every move reflecting a carefully honed skill set and a keen understanding of the industry.

Mia's desk, a polished expanse of rich mahogany, stood as the epicenter of her domain. Adorned with industry accolades and a meticulously arranged array of productivity tools, it mirrored the gravitas of her position within the advertising firm. The skyline-inspired nameplate, a nod to her unwavering commitment to her craft, constantly reminded her of the heights she had reached in her career.

The air in Mia's office carried a sense of purpose, each element meticulously chosen to enhance her professional persona. The carefully curated artwork on the walls spoke to her creative flair. At the same time, the sleek, modern furniture seamlessly blended with the corporate aesthetic. Mia's office was not merely a workspace; it was a testament to her journey, a tangible representation of the milestones she had achieved in the competitive advertising world.

As Mia prepared for the upcoming retreat at Tranquil Haven Spa, she left behind the fast-paced rhythm of the corporate realm, seeking peace and solace in the serene mountainside setting. The contrast between her high-rise office and the tranquil retreat mirrored the dual facets of Mia's life—the demanding world of corporate strategy and the desire for personal reflection and connection with friends. The retreat held the promise of a temporary escape from the relentless demands of her professional life, providing a space to unravel the complexities that lurked beneath the surface of her seemingly seamless success.

The decision for Mia to organize the retreat wasn't arbitrary; her meticulous nature and knack for handling logistics made her the natural choice. Beyond her executive prowess, Mia was known for orchestrating flawless events, seamlessly blending luxury with efficiency. The retreat at Tranquil Haven Spa, with its carefully curated experience, was a testament to Mia's ability to craft unforgettable moments while concealing her own secret.

However, Mia's knack for planning wasn't without its nuances within the group. While her organizational skills were unmatched, her insistence on detailed schedules and meticulously arranged activities created a subtle tension among her friends. Some found comfort in predictability, appreciating Mia's ability to eliminate any room for uncertainty. Others felt a sense of restriction as if the carefully planned itinerary left little room for spontaneity and genuine connection.

The planning sessions in Olivia's penthouse often became a battleground of preferences, with Mia ardently defending her structured approach to ensure every moment was optimized for relaxation and self-discovery. Unbeknownst to the friends, Mia's need for control stemmed from her own struggles with unpredictability and the fear of facing the uncharted territories of her personal life.

As Mia delved into the intricate details of each friend's preferences, her determination to provide a flawless experience occasionally clashed with the more laid-back attitudes of some friends. The tension bubbled beneath the surface, an unspoken undercurrent that threatened to disrupt the idyllic serenity they sought at Tranquil Haven Spa.

Little did they realize that Mia's desire for meticulous planning reflected not just her professional acumen but a shield she wielded to safeguard the vulnerability she concealed. The upcoming retreat, with all its carefully plotted activities, would not only unveil hidden tensions within the group but also force Mia to confront the unspoken complexities that lingered in the shadows of her own life, and would change the group forever.

The coworker with whom Mia shared the clandestine affair was Emily, a charismatic and ambitious colleague. The synergy between their professional lives spilled into something more intimate, and the discreet encounters in hidden corners of their shared workspace became a thrilling escape from the demands of their high-powered careers.

With her captivating presence and the allure of her enigmatic personality, Emily drew Mia into a world where the boundaries between personal and professional were blurred. The clandestine affair was a refuge, a clandestine oasis in the midst of the corporate hustle, where incredible passion and desire momentarily eclipsed the pressures of their ambitious careers.

Their liaisons were shrouded in secrecy, conducted in the quiet corners of the sleek high-rise office, where the city skyline bore witness to their hidden connection. The allure of lust and forbidden and secretive intimacy added a layer of excitement to their professional camaraderie, a dangerous dance that heightened the stakes with every stolen moment.

As Mia meticulously organized the retreat at Tranquil Haven Spa, the weight of the affair lingered in the air, invisible yet palpable. The unspoken tension between Mia and Emily, a delicate thread woven into the fabric of their shared secrets, added a layer of complexity to the upcoming weekend. Little did the friends know that the meticulously planned escape to the tranquil mountains would expose their struggles and unravel the hidden connections that bound them together.

Diane and Sophia's relationship transcended the bounds of friendship; they were confidantes, soulmates who shared an unspoken understanding that went beyond the conventional ties of marriage. Although Diane was married to Mia, their connection went far deeper than mere labels could define.

Navigating the complexities of love and connection, Diane and Sophia found solace in the quiet corners of their shared experiences. The intricacies of their relationship extended beyond the comprehension of those who perceived it through the lens of societal norms. In a world that often struggled to embrace the diversity of love, Diane and Sophia's bond faced the challenges that came with being a part of the LGBTQ+ community.

Their connection was a testament to the resilience required to forge relationships beyond society's conventional expectations. Diane, committed to Mia in the eyes of the world, found a different kind of commitment in the moments shared with Sophia. The secrecy surrounding their relationship added a layer of complexity, a delicate dance between the authentic expression of their feelings and the need to navigate a world that wasn't always accepting.

As they approached the annual retreat at Tranquil Haven Spa, Diane and Sophia carried the weight of their hidden connection. The retreat, ostensibly a sanctuary for friendships, would also become a stage for the unveiling of their truth, a truth that existed in the spaces between societal norms and personal authenticity. Little did they know that the weekend in the Catskill Mountains would force them to confront the challenges of their relationship and the broader complexities of love and acceptance in a world that was still learning to embrace diversity.

In the intricate dance of relationships, a affair unfolded between Mia and Emily, two individuals entangled in a web of secrecy and hidden desires. What Mia believed to be her well-kept secret was not lost on Diane. As an astute observer of human nature, Diane had sensed the subtle shifts in Mia's behavior, the lingering glances, and the unexplained absences. While Mia assumed her affair was concealed, Diane, wise to the nuances of their complex dynamic, saw through the facade.

Recognizing the need for guidance and an outlet for her own emotions, Mia turned to Sophia, laying bare the intricate details of her affair with Emily. In Sophia, she found a confidante and a source of wisdom. Empathetic and understanding, Sophia listened without judgment, offering advice and solace in the face of Mia's internal turmoil. The weight of their shared secret became a bond that strengthened the ties between Diane and Sophia, creating a unique triangle of trust and understanding amidst the complexities of their intertwined lives.

Amid the backdrop of Mia's carefully constructed corporate facade, Diane played the blissfully unaware partner, the emotional pain ever swelling inside. Diane, a respected professor of psychology at a renowned university, dedicated herself to the intricacies of the human mind. Her lectures, delivered with a captivating blend of intellect and empathy, earned her admiration from students and colleagues alike.

Juggling her personal and professional lives required a delicate balance that Mia executed with practiced precision. The retreat planning provided the perfect cover for her secret liaisons, with late-night calls and covert rendezvous seamlessly woven into the tapestry of organizational details. Mia's dual existence was a testament to her ability to compartmentalize, each compartment shielded from the prying eyes of those who believed they knew her best.

As Mia meticulously arranged spa treatments, dining experiences, and team-building activities for the upcoming weekend, the dichotomy of her life became more pronounced. Initially conceived as a respite from the demands of work, the retreat would unwittingly become the stage for the revelation of Mia's hidden truth. The delicate balance Mia had maintained between her professional prowess and the clandestine affair would face its most significant test during the retreat at Tranquil Haven Spa, leaving ripples that would alter the dynamics of the group forever.

The journey to Tranquil Haven Spa unfolded as a symphony of individual narratives, with each group member navigating the winding roads leading to the Catskill Mountains in their own unique way. The distance from the city to the spa was measured not only in miles but in the complex emotions that accompanied the group, transforming the picturesque drive into a tapestry of anticipation and reflection.

Emily and Mark: The atmosphere carried an air of deceptive tranquility within the cocoon of their luxury sedan. The plush leather seats, though seemingly inviting, masked the underlying tension that permeated the confined space. As Emily and Mark embarked on the scenic route to Tranquil Haven Spa, the changing landscape outside the window mirrored the shifting dynamics within the car.

Emily, her exterior meticulously composed, gazed pensively at the passing scenery. Her contemplative stare betrayed the storm of dissatisfaction brewing within, a tempest that raged silently as the miles rolled by. The mountainside journey became a metaphor for the twists and turns of her emotional landscape, each bend in the road amplifying the complexities of her discontent.

Engrossed in a phone call, Mark remained oblivious to the subtle shifts in his wife's demeanor. The divide between them, unspoken but palpable, stretched like an unseen chasm within the luxurious confines of the sedan. While Emily grappled with internal turmoil, Mark's attention remained tethered to the outside world, the distant voice on the other end of the line overshadowing the unspoken rift between husband and wife.

As Mark concluded the call, Emily couldn't contain her curiosity any longer. The air inside the car seemed to thicken with tension as she turned toward him, her eyes searching for answers. "Who was that, Mark?" she inquired, her voice betraying a mix of concern and suspicion. Mark, caught off guard, tried to reassure her, "Just work stuff, Em. You know how it is." But Emily, sensing something amiss, pressed on, "You've been taking a lot of these mysterious calls lately. Is there something you're not telling me?" Mark, feeling the weight of her scrutiny, attempted to deny any wrongdoing, but the conversation lingered in an uncomfortable silence, leaving the growing distance between them unaddressed.

As the winding roads unfolded, the couple traveled in silence, the scenic beauty outside contrasting with the quiet turbulence within. The sedan moved through the landscape, each turn accentuating the emotional twists that Emily navigated, creating an atmosphere of disquiet beneath the veneer of luxury and comfort.

Sophia: Amidst the cocoon of her compact car, Sophia embarked on the solitary journey, the rhythmic hum of the engine providing a backdrop to the internal dialogue that unfolded within her mind. The expansive views that unfolded outside the car's windows offered a temporary reprieve, a fleeting distraction from the persistent weight of a lingering grudge against Emily.

As the winding roads stretched before her, Sophia found a metaphorical resonance in each twist and turn. The sinuous path became a visual representation of the intricate web of emotions she carried – a tapestry woven with threads of resentment, hurt, and unresolved tensions. With every bend in the road, the complexity of her feelings mirrored the labyrinthine journey that lay ahead.

Though momentarily soothing, the panoramic vistas could not entirely mask the emotional turbulence that resided within Sophia. With its steady propulsion forward, the car served as both a vessel for physical travel and a conduit for Sophia's introspective journey. Tranquil Haven Spa awaited on the horizon, its promise of serenity contrasting with the emotional tumult that accompanied Sophia on her drive. The journey became more than a physical passage; it became a symbolic exploration of the intricate landscapes of the human heart.

Ava: Within the confines of her trusty pickup truck, Ava embarked on the open road, the worn exterior of the vehicle mirroring the weathered edges of her recent divorce. The hum of the engine served as both companion and confidant, resonating with the raw emotions she carried as she traversed the rough-hewn terrain that stretched before her.

The landscape outside the window became a visual metaphor for the renewal Ava sought. Each mile passed served as a marker of resilience, a testament to her determination to navigate the twists and turns of life's unpredictable journey. The open road, stretching endlessly before her, offered a canvas for reflection and renewal.

Ava deliberately chose the therapeutic solitude of the drive, an intentional separation from the echoes of a failed marriage. The solitude became a balm for wounds still healing, providing a respite from the judgment and expectations that often accompanied the presence of a significant other. In the cocoon of her truck, Ava found a sanctuary where she could confront her emotions head-on, unburdened by external influences.

As Tranquil Haven Spa loomed on the horizon, Ava's journey became more than a physical commute; it transformed into a symbolic passage toward personal rejuvenation. With its twists and turns, the road mirrored the complexities of her emotional landscape, and each mile brought her closer to the promise of solace and self-discovery that awaited at the retreat.

Olivia and Richard: Olivia and Richard shared the journey, but not on the same wavelength. Olivia's recent success, marked by champagne toasts, cast a glittering facade over the landscape. The supportive partner, Richard, tried to bridge the gap between their worlds, but the disconnection lingered like an unsolved puzzle. The decision to bring Richard stemmed from a desire to share her triumph, but the divide between their worlds remained palpable.

As the sleek SUV sliced through the early morning mist, Olivia's eyes were fixed on the horizon, a vision of ambition and accomplishment. She exuded an air of superiority that permeated the confined space, her recent success a shimmering crown that rested on her head. Olivia reveled in the echo of champagne toasts and accolades, the sounds of her triumph playing like a symphony in her mind.

Conversely, Richard occupied the passenger seat with a demeanor that mirrored the landscape passing by—obscured, distant, and shrouded in uncertainty. The journey to Tranquil Haven Spa was more than just a drive; it was a navigation through the complexities of their relationship. Richard, the supportive partner, sat in the shadow of Olivia's triumph, a realm he struggled to fully comprehend.

The air inside the SUV crackled with unspoken tension, the divide between Olivia's soaring success and Richard's more grounded reality becoming increasingly apparent. Olivia's every movement and word seemed to underscore the vast difference in their worlds.

Yet, Richard, earnest and pleading, attempted to bridge the gap. He urged Olivia not to make too big a deal out of her success, sensing the strain it placed on their connection. The confines of the car became a microcosm of their relationship dynamics. As the miles rolled by, the disconnection persisted like an unsolved puzzle, casting a subtle shadow over the triumphant journey to Tranquil Haven Spa.

Mia and Diane: The high-performance sports car sliced through the winding roads, its engine's purr harmonizing with the picturesque landscape around them. While navigating the journey with the precision befitting an executive, Mia wore a mask of composure that belied the emotional turbulence swirling beneath the surface. Behind the wheel, she grappled with the weight of a secret affair, a snare entangled in the recesses of her thoughts.

Beside her, Diane, absorbed in the cocoon of her academic musings, tried to appear blissfully unaware of the tempestuous currents within the car. Mia's decision to include Diane in the trip was a calculated move, an attempt to cloak the truth in the guise of a loving couple. The carefully orchestrated facade extended beyond the car's exterior, intertwining the scenic journey with the intricacies of personal deception.

As they navigated the scenic route toward Tranquil Haven Spa, the relationship between Mia and Diane became a complex dance of appearances and hidden truths. The verdant landscape and open road, seemingly symbols of freedom, served as a contrasting backdrop to the concealed emotions and unspoken tensions within the confines of the sports car. The Spa awaited them like a haven of secrets, and the journey unfolded as a prelude to the enigmatic interplay of relationships that would define their time at Tranquil Haven.

As the friends arrived at Tranquil Haven Spa, the tension that had traveled with them lingered in the air. Greetings were exchanged on the manicured grounds with forced smiles, the mountain air amplifying their unspoken conflicts. The promise of a tranquil weekend now hung in the balance, the idyllic setting masking the storm of emotions brewing within the group. The friends, each carrying their own burdens, stepped into the serene surroundings of the spa, unaware that the weekend would unravel the carefully woven threads of their lives. The air thickened with anticipation as the group entered a retreat that would force them to confront their hidden truths amidst the picturesque backdrop of the Catskill Mountains.

Tranquil Prelude

The afternoon sun cast a warm glow over the manicured grounds of Tranquil Haven Spa as the friends dispersed to explore the idyllic retreat. Nestled within the embrace of the Catskill Mountains, the spa exuded an air of tranquility, its lush foliage and serene architecture promising an escape from the chaos of city life.

The spa's main building, adorned with ivy-clad walls and large, arched windows, stood as a beacon of relaxation. A cascading waterfall, strategically placed near the entrance, added to the ambiance, its soothing sounds echoing through the air. The scent of pine mingled with hints of lavender, creating an olfactory symphony that enveloped the friends as they embarked on various activities.

As each guest arrived at Tranquil Haven Spa, the meticulous orchestration of the weekend's activities unfolded under the discreet yet authoritative command of Mia Johnson. In the spa's elegant meeting room, Mia worked with meticulous precision, ensuring that every detail of the weekend reflected a seamless blend of relaxation and tailored experiences for each friend.

The meeting room, adorned with soft hues and natural textures, served as the nerve center for Mia's careful planning. She discreetly reviewed notes, carefully cross-referencing preferences, allergies, and aversions while maintaining a facade of normalcy. The tables were adorned with carefully arranged spa brochures, and the scent of vanilla-infused candles wafted through the air, creating an atmosphere of tranquility.

Mia's composed exterior belied the tension in her shoulders as the friends filed in. The weight of her hidden affair bore down on her, a heavy burden concealed beneath the tailored blazer she wore with professional precision. Her gaze, however, remained focused on the task at hand—ensuring that the weekend unfolded flawlessly for her friends.

The guests entered the meeting room one by one, greeted by Mia's welcoming smile that masked the complexities within. She engaged in polite small talk, seamlessly navigating the delicate balance between personal and professional demeanor. Behind the scenes, the undercurrent of her hidden affair pulsed through her actions, adding a layer of complexity to the composed executive.

Each friend's preferences were considered with a level of detail that spoke to Mia's organizational prowess. From dietary restrictions to preferred spa treatments, she had gathered a trove of information, transforming the spa experience into a personalized haven for each guest. The air in the meeting room held the subtle tension of unspoken secrets. Yet, Mia skillfully maintained the illusion of seamless hospitality.

As the group gathered in the meeting room, Mia's outward composure masked the intricate dance of emotions within. The stage was set for a weekend of seemingly idyllic serenity, but beneath the surface, the friends were unaware that the carefully woven threads of their lives were already beginning to unravel.

Amidst the tranquil ambiance of the meeting room, Olivia, the maven of sophistication, orchestrated a moment that would soon resonate with echoes of tension and veiled competition among the friends. The air was filled with anticipation as Olivia, adorned in an ensemble that mirrored her luxurious taste, produced elegantly wrapped cosmetic cases, one for each group member.

The cosmetic cases, crafted from polished titanium, gleamed with an otherworldly sheen as Olivia prepared to present them to her friends. Each case bore an air of opulence, the weight and smoothness of the metal hinting at the luxurious contents within. Engraved with delicate patterns, the cases were a testament to Olivia's taste for the finer things in life. With a flourish, Mia handed Olivia the personalized cases containing meticulously curated beauty products to present.

Upon opening the cases, the friends discovered a new line of cosmetics designed by Olivia herself. The colors were a striking departure from the conventional, boasting shades not found in the typical palettes. Olivia took pride in explaining the exclusivity of her creations, emphasizing that these cosmetics were a preview of a line not yet available to the public. The friends, though initially enchanted by the lavishness of the gifts, couldn't shake the feeling that this gesture was more than just generosity; it was a subtle display of Olivia's dominance in the world of beauty and fashion.

A unique silk wrap accompanying each case was another stroke of Olivia's design prowess. Sourced from a small village in Italy, the silk exuded a rare quality, further enhancing the allure of the cosmetic cases. Little did the friends know that this seemingly benevolent gift would later become a focal point, entwining itself with the unfolding mystery that would alter the course of their relationships.

The men received tailored selections catering to their grooming needs, while the women were treated to an array of high-end cosmetics. Olivia's gestures carried an air of ostentation, the cosmetic cases more than mere gifts – they were declarations of her success, her status, and an unspoken competition that rippled through the room.

As the cosmetic cases were distributed, Olivia couldn't resist a subtle brag, weaving tales of the exclusivity of the products and the bespoke nature of the silk wrap that accompanied each case.

The friends, though appreciative, couldn't shake the undercurrent of discomfort that threaded through the room. Olivia's display of extravagance, coupled with the unspoken comparisons it invited, cast a shadow over the weekend that had initially promised serenity.

After the meticulous planning in the spa's meeting room, the friends slowly made their way out, eager to immerse themselves in the carefully crafted activities awaiting them. The air outside carried the promise of serenity as they embarked on the day's agenda, blissfully unaware of the intricate dynamics simmering beneath the surface. The spa's grounds beckoned with the allure of rejuvenating treatments, scenic walks, and the soothing embrace of nature. Each step toward enjoyment was a tentative journey into a weekend with the potential for relaxation and revelation.

Emily and Mark wandered along the meandering paths of Tranquil Haven Spa's expansive gardens, the crunch of gravel and the rustle of leaves beneath their feet creating a symphony of natural sounds. The spa's gardens, adorned with vibrant flowers and interspersed with cozy nooks, offered a picturesque escape. Yet, the beauty of the surroundings couldn't mask the growing tension between the couple.

The late afternoon sun filtered through the branches, casting dappled shadows on the path ahead. Emily, the poised lawyer with an air of sophistication, maintained a composed exterior. Her perfectly crafted image, however, belied the storm of dissatisfaction brewing within. Mark sensed the undercurrent of tension but struggled to pinpoint its source.

As they strolled, Emily's gaze wandered across the landscape, her mind burdened by unspoken concerns. The air between them crackled with unexpressed emotions, and the once-serene gardens became a backdrop for a conversation veiled in ambiguity.

"Mark, have you ever felt like something is missing?" Emily finally broached the subject, her words measured but laced with a vulnerability she tried to conceal.

Engrossed in the natural beauty surrounding them, Mark took a moment to register the weight behind Emily's question. "Missing? I thought things were good, Em. What's on your mind?"

The unease in his voice mirrored the unease in the atmosphere. Emily hesitated, her eyes flitting between the vibrant flowers and the path ahead. "It's just... work, life, everything. I feel like I'm at a crossroads, and I'm not sure which way to go."

Mark's brow furrowed, concern etching lines across his face. "You're not alone in this, Em. We'll figure it out together. What's been bothering you?"

The tension deepened as Emily grappled with her inner turmoil, torn between the desire to confide in her husband and the fear of burdening their relationship. The delicate dance of words continued, each sentence a careful step on the tightrope of vulnerability.

"It's just that... I've been questioning if this is the life I want, the life we've built. The routine, the expectations. I feel like there's more out there, but I'm not sure how to reach for it without... without shaking everything up," Emily admitted, her voice almost lost in the rustle of leaves and the distant murmur of the spa's activities.

Mark listened, his supportive demeanor attempting to bridge the emotional gap between them. The once-peaceful stroll now mirrored the complexities of their relationship. The gardens, lush and inviting, became witness to a conversation laden with unspoken truths, a conversation that held the potential to reshape the course of their lives.

As the couple continued their walk, Emily's dissatisfaction hung in the air, an unspoken tension wrapped in the beauty of Tranquil Haven Spa's gardens. The path ahead, both literal and metaphorical, remained uncertain, and the tranquility they sought seemed elusive amidst the swirling emotions of the moment.

Meanwhile, Sophia, nursing her longstanding grudge against Emily, indulged in a solitary yoga session in the state-of-art yoga studio overlooking a serene pond. The rhythmic flow of her movements belied the turmoil within as her mind replayed past grievances, adding fuel to the simmering resentment.

Sophia's yoga mat was unfurled and bathed in the soft glow of the late afternoon sun. The serene ambiance of Tranquil Haven Spa offered a stark contrast to the tempestuous emotions swirling within Sophia as she began her yoga session. The rhythmic flow of her movements was a deceptive facade, a carefully orchestrated dance that belied the chaos in her mind.

The yoga studio provided a panoramic view of the pond, its still waters reflecting the surrounding greenery. Yet, the tranquility of the setting failed to penetrate the storm of emotions within Sophia. Each pose she assumed held the weight of past grievances, and every stretch seemed to echo the unresolved conflicts that had fueled her longstanding grudge against Emily.

As Sophia moved through the yoga sequence, her breath synchronized with the undulating rhythm of the pond below. The rhythmic inhales and exhales became a meditative mantra, a feeble attempt to calm the tempest within. Yet, with each breath, the replay of past interactions with Emily flickered in her mind like an unwelcome movie reel.

The longstanding grudge Sophia harbored was rooted in a tapestry of perceived slights, unspoken rivalries, and a history of unaddressed grievances. A tangled web of misunderstandings and miscommunications had woven itself into the fabric of their friendship, leaving Sophia nursing wounds that time had failed to heal.

As Sophia moved from downward dog to warrior pose, her body betrayed the tension within. Muscles tensed and released, mirroring the ebb and flow of resentment coursing through her veins. Yoga, usually a haven for introspection and serenity, now bore witness to the silent struggle unfolding in Sophia.

In the solace of her yoga practice, Sophia's mind revisited moments when she felt overshadowed, unheard, or dismissed by Emily. The long-suppressed memories resurfaced with each stretch.

The occasional rustle of leaves outside, stirred by a gentle breeze, echoed Sophia's sighs of unresolved grievances. Her solo yoga session became a cathartic release, an attempt to channel the chaos within into a semblance of order. The picturesque pond, a symbol of stillness, mirrored the external calm that Sophia presented to the world, concealing the storm raging beneath the surface.

Sophia, her lithe form moving gracefully through yoga poses in the serene studio, couldn't escape the undercurrents of tension that threaded through her thoughts. As her body contorted into various postures, her mind wrestled with conflicting emotions, and her focus shifted to Olivia, the epitome of success and ambition.

Olivia's accomplishments in the fashion world loomed large in Sophia's mind, creating a complex tapestry of envy and admiration. Once parallel, the gulf between their paths had widened into a chasm of unspoken competition. Sophia, a former graphic designer turned journalist, grappled with the choices that had led her down a different road.

The whispers of self-doubt mingled with flashes of resentment as Sophia pondered the divergent trajectories of their lives. Olivia's success cast a shadow over Sophia's more modest pursuits, igniting a spark of longing for the recognition and glamour that seemed to accompany Olivia's every step.

Amidst the quiet confines of the yoga studio, Sophia confronted her insecurities, the echo of Olivia's achievements reverberating through the space. The rhythmic flow of her movements mirrored the ebb and flow of emotions, creating a silent dance of conflict within her.

Sophia's internal struggle continued as the yoga session unfolded, the tranquil exterior belying the storm of emotions beneath. The reflective surfaces of the studio captured the complexity of her sentiments, painting a poignant portrait of a woman caught in the crosscurrents of ambition, success, and the relentless pursuit of self-discovery.

In the relaxed haven of the yoga studio, Sophia's movements seamlessly transitioned from one pose to another, but her inner world remained entangled in a web of emotions. As the rhythmic cadence of her breath synchronized with the ambient sounds, Sophia's thoughts shifted to another figure in her life – Ava.

Ava, the impressionist artist with a spirit as vibrant as her canvases, presented a canvas of conflicting sentiments for Sophia. The echoes of past disagreements and subtle clashes resurfaced in Sophia's mind, complicating the serene atmosphere of the yoga studio.

Ava's free-spirited nature sometimes clashed with Sophia's more grounded approach to life, and she found herself grappling with the contrast between her disciplined daily routine and Ava's spontaneous creativity. The hues of their interactions painted an intricate picture of friendship strained by divergent perspectives.

As Sophia moved through the yoga postures, the energy of her struggles manifested in the controlled strength of her poses. The echo of unspoken grievances and unresolved conflicts reverberated through each breath, creating an emotional undercurrent that wove its way into the very fabric of the space.

The mirrored walls of the studio reflected not only the physical grace of Sophia's yoga practice but also the intricate dance of emotions that unfolded within her. Amidst the calming ambiance, Sophia faced the challenge of reconciling the complexities of her relationship with Ava, each movement a silent plea for resolution.

As the sun dipped below the horizon, Sophia concluded her yoga session, the room now bathed in the soft hues of the afternoon. The longstanding grudge, nurtured over time, remained a silent companion, an ever-present undercurrent in the tranquil surroundings of Tranquil Haven Spa. The rhythmic flow of her movements may have brought temporary physical relief, but the emotional storm within continued to cast shadows over Sophia's attempts at finding serenity amidst the unresolved conflicts of the past.

Sophia's evening yoga session had been both therapeutic and contemplative, a solitary pursuit to clear her mind. As the final notes of a calming melody resonated in the studio, she eased into the stillness of her savasana, basking in the tranquility that yoga often bestowed upon her tumultuous thoughts. The muted lighting and soothing ambiance were meant to be a sanctuary, a brief escape from the complexities of her troubled friendships.

As she gradually emerged from the meditative state, Sophia sensed a shift in the atmosphere. A subtle awareness tingled at the back of her neck, and she became cognizant that she was not alone. Startled at first, her eyes widened, searching for the intruder. Then, recognition softened her features as she identified the shadowy figure, a friend she hadn't expected.

Relieved, Sophia released a breath she didn't realize she had been holding. "You scared me," she admitted with a smile, the corners of her eyes crinkling. The unidentified friend reciprocated with a nod, an unspoken understanding passing between them.

However, the tranquil moment took a dark turn when, in an unexpected twist, the shadowy presence moved with deliberate intent toward the security camera. Sophia's eyebrows furrowed in confusion, and she couldn't help but question, "What are you doing?"

Before she could receive an answer, the room plunged into darkness as the camera lens was covered with fabric. Panic surged within Sophia as she registered the sudden shift. "Wait, why are you doing this?" she demanded, her voice tinged with fear.

The ensuing struggle was brief but intense, the echoes of muffled sounds and the rustle of fabric reverberating in the dimly lit space. Then, an unsettling stillness settled over the yoga studio, the once-serene atmosphere shattered by an unforeseen and tragic event. Sophia's lifeless body lay on the mat, a stark contrast to the peaceful setting that had enveloped her only moments before. The camera, now obscured, held the secrets of that fateful encounter, its silent witness to a crime that would send shockwaves through the circle of friends.

With a calculated caution, the killer carefully removed the fabric that obscured the camera, intending to erase any trace of their presence. However, in the haste of the moment, a few stray fibers clung to the edges of the camera, unseen by the naked eye.

Once satisfied with their attempt at concealing the crime, the killer, cloaked in shadows, moved swiftly toward the back door of the studio. Aware of the surveillance cameras in the hallways outside, the killer skillfully avoided their watchful gaze. The dimly lit corridors became a clandestine path, allowing the killer to slip away undetected, leaving behind only the lingering echoes of the heinous act committed within the confines of the yoga studio. The obscured camera, now a silent witness, held the key to unraveling the mystery that lay shrouded in darkness.

As the day unfolded, the friends engaged in spa treatments, meditation sessions, and leisurely dips in the rejuvenating hot springs. Conversations were punctuated by forced smiles and veiled tensions, with the picturesque backdrop of the Catskill Mountains serving as a serene yet deceptive canvas.

Unbeknownst to them, the shadows of their past and the intricacies of their relationships cast a lingering tension over the spa. The promise of a tranquil weekend hung in the balance, concealing the storm of emotions brewing within the group. Each friend, carrying their own burdens and navigating the delicate dance of camaraderie, remained unaware that the picturesque spa held the potential to unravel the carefully woven threads of their lives.

In the heart of Tranquil Haven Spa, the chic lounge area unexpectedly came to life in the early evening. The contemporary allure of the space, defined by clean lines and muted tones, became an impromptu setting for Olivia Barnes to host an evening gathering. The ambiance, usually reserved for tranquil moments, now buzzed with the clinking of champagne glasses and the harmonious hum of conversations. Plush seating and strategically placed artwork adorned the walls, creating a sophisticated backdrop for the event that was supposed to be the highlight of everyone's day.

Olivia, a vision of refined elegance, orchestrated the gathering with practiced ease. As the clinking of champagne glasses echoed through the lounge, guests, their silhouettes cast in the ambient glow of subdued lighting, gathered around Olivia. She shared her recent achievements in the fashion world, transforming the lounge into a stage for a celebration that had spontaneously emerged amid the spa's serenity.

As Ava Turner joined the group, her entrance seemed to go unnoticed amidst the celebratory atmosphere. Ava, the recently divorced artist, wore an air of quiet contemplation. Her unconventional pursuits in art, somewhat edgy and avant-garde, stood in stark contrast to the polished fashion world surrounding her. Ava's art, a reflection of her emotional journey and defiance of societal norms, often incorporated unconventional materials and daring concepts.

Her private studio for the weekend, was nestled discreetly on-site at Tranquil Haven Spa, offered a sanctuary for her creative expression. The studio's entrance, marked by a unique metal sculpture, hinted at the eclectic world within.

Upon entering Ava's studio, a burst of vibrant colors and a symphony of textures greeted the observer. Canvases adorned with bold strokes and sculptures crafted from repurposed materials adorned the space.

As Olivia recounted her triumphs, the contrast between the fashion designer's polished success and Ava's unconventional art became palpable. Hidden insecurities within the group, simmering beneath the surface, were catalyzed by Olivia's achievements. The lounge, now a microcosm of their intertwined lives, became a stage for the subtle web of envy and discontent to unfurl.

Amidst the clinking glasses and congratulatory words for Olivia, Ava's thoughts lingered on her own artwork in the studio, a tangible representation of her emotional landscape. The tension within her, a mix of admiration for Olivia's success and a yearning for her own artistic path to be acknowledged added complexity to the emotions coursing through the impromptu gathering.

The lounge, bathed in the glow of subdued lighting, became a silent arena where the interplay of success and creative expression unfolded. Olivia's achievements acted as a silent trigger, setting off a chain reaction of introspection and unspoken desires among the group. As Ava grappled with the contrasting worlds of fashion and avant-garde art, the lounge at Tranquil Haven Spa transformed into a canvas for the subtle intricacies of envy and the quest for individual recognition.

As the friends gathered for the initial cocktail hour, a palpable anticipation hung in the air. The luxury resort's ambiance provided an elegant backdrop for the reunion, but beneath the surface, unspoken tensions simmered.

Diane, clad in an ensemble that Sophia had personally helped her choose, took a sip of her martini and glanced around the room. The absence of Sophia, usually the center of their gatherings, was keenly felt. Diane, eager to dispel any concerns, offered a reassuring smile. "Sophia sends her regrets; she's doing a private yoga session tonight and will join us tomorrow. You know how committed she is to her yoga and serenity."

The news seemed to alleviate some of the unease among the friends, but subtle glances and hushed conversations hinted at an undercurrent of unresolved issues. Emily exchanged a strained smile with Mark, their recent tensions lingering beneath the surface. Meanwhile, Richard observed Olivia, the dissonance in their relationship temporarily masked by the social pleasantries.

As the night unfolded, laughter and clinking glasses filled the air, but the absence of Sophia cast a shadow over the festivities.

As the carefully orchestrated gathering in the lounge hosted by Olivia wound down, the atmosphere shifted subtly. Glasses clinked in a final toast, and guests exchanged polite smiles as they made their way back to their respective significant others. Olivia, maintained her poise, but a discerning eye could catch glimpses of the complexities hidden beneath her elegant facade.

The interplay between the characters and their husbands or significant others carried nuances of unspoken tensions. Partners exchanged pleasantries; their conversations laced with the subtle undercurrents of the day's interactions. Mark, Emily's husband, sought to decipher the source of his wife's unease, while Richard, Olivia's husband, attempted to bridge the emotional distance that lingered beneath their celebratory facade.

Amidst the elegant lounge setting, Mia Johnson exchanged a subtle glance with her partner, Diane, as Olivia's impromptu gathering drew to a close. The façade of normalcy that Mia had carefully crafted throughout the evening began to crack, revealing the hidden tensions beneath the surface of their relationship.

Diane met Mia's gaze with a knowing look. The unspoken communication between them carried the weight of unresolved issues and the strain of Mia's concealed affair. The lounge, once a haven for relaxation, now became a battleground for the subtle interplay of emotions.

Mia and Diane found themselves momentarily alone as the group dispersed, their private world encroached upon by the complexities that had long lingered in the shadows. Mia's shoulders, burdened by the weight of her hidden affair, tensed further as she navigated the delicate dance of maintaining composure in the presence of her partner.

Attuning to the undercurrents in their relationship, Diane broke the silence that hung heavily in the air. "Mia, we need to talk," she said, her voice carrying a mix of concern and resignation.

Mia, ever the high-powered executive adept at managing crises, felt a bead of sweat form on her forehead. The lounge, with its plush surroundings, became a crucible for the tensions that had simmered between them. "Can it wait, Diane? We're here to enjoy the weekend with our friends," Mia deflected her words, a fragile shield against the impending confrontation.

Diane's expression remained stoic, betraying the hurt and frustration she had long harbored. "No more deflections, Mia. Something's been off for a while now, and it's time we address it. What are you hiding?"

The lounge, once a camaraderie scene, now witnessed a relationship unraveling. Mia's carefully crafted world threatened to collapse as Diane pressed for honesty. The plush surroundings absorbed the whispers of a conversation fraught with unspoken grievances and the fragile threads holding a partnership on the brink.

As the evening progressed, the group retired to their rooms for the night, tension lingering in the air from earlier interactions. Bedrooms became isolated chambers where the friends grappled with their thoughts and the intricacies of the relationships surrounding them. The tranquility promised by Tranquil Haven Spa now seemed fragile, a thin veil over the unresolved conflicts and simmering emotions within the group.

Plans for an early morning activity and breakfast were made, each friend contemplating the day ahead with a mix of anticipation and trepidation. The idyllic setting of the spa held the promise of a refreshing start, but the unspoken undercurrents threatened to cast shadows over the morning's tranquility.

As the friends settled into their rooms, the night held the last vestiges of peace before the impending demise that would alter the course of their retreat. The morning sun would rise on a day that would change everything, marking the beginning of a chilling mystery that would shatter the fragile serenity of Tranquil Haven Spa.

The Labyrinth of Lies

The early morning sunbathed Tranquil Haven Spa in a gentle glow, promising a day of serenity and relaxation. The guests gathered at the communal breakfast table, an air of anticipation hanging over them. The agenda for the day, meticulously prepared by Mia Johnson, awaited them, promising a series of rejuvenating activities and spa treatments.

As the friends settled into their seats, the conversation flowed with a mix of excitement and curiosity. The successful fashion designer Olivia Barnes raised her glass in a toast, celebrating the recent achievements that had brought them all together. Glasses clinked, and polite smiles adorned each face, masking the complex web of emotions beneath the surface.

"Have you all seen the schedule Mia put together?" The poised lawyer, Emily Rodriguez, inquired, her eyes scanning the printed agenda. "It looks like we're in for a day of pure indulgence."

Ava Turner nodded with a hopeful smile. "I could use some indulgence after the chaos of the past few weeks," she admitted, her gaze briefly meeting a chair reserved for Sophia that remained vacant before looking away.

Sophia's absence was noted but initially dismissed as the group immersed themselves in discussions about the day ahead. Mia Johnson, the organizer of the retreat, skillfully directed the conversation toward the planned activities, diverting attention from the underlying tension.

"I've arranged for a guided nature walk this morning," Mia announced, her eyes subtly avoiding the empty chair. "It's a great way to connect with each other and with the beautiful surroundings."

Olivia's husband, Richard, tried to engage the group in light banter, bringing a momentary reprieve from the unspoken unease. However, the absence of Sophia lingered in the air, a subtle undercurrent that none could ignore.

As the group continued their breakfast, the tranquil setting of the spa's dining area masked the labyrinth of lies that circled beneath the surface. Each friend played their part, their conversations echoing the complexity of relationships and the concealed truths that bound them together.

The elegant breakfast came to a close, and the guests dispersed, leaving the chic lounge area with the promise of an exclusive memorable trip scheduled by Mia Johnson. The clock ticked toward 10 a.m., the anticipated rendezvous time for the next adventure. As the group assembled at the designated meeting point, a subdued atmosphere hung in the air, marred by Sophia's continued absence.

Mia, the meticulous planner, greeted the friends with a warm smile, her eyes subtly searching for any sign of Sophia. "I hope you all enjoyed breakfast," Mia began, her tone betraying a hint of concern. "We have a special excursion planned, and I'm sure you'll find it delightful."

Ava Turner shifted uncomfortably, casting a glance toward the empty chair that should have been occupied. Emily Rodriguez, the poised lawyer with a simmering grudge, exchanged a knowing look with Ava, their unease growing.

As the group waited, the perturbation caused by Sophia's absence became palpable. Olivia Barnes glanced at her watch, her impatience evident. Her husband Richard offered a reassuring smile, attempting to ease the tension.

"I'll give Sophia a call," volunteered Ava, pulling out her cell phone. She dialed Sophia's number, but the repeated rings went unanswered. The unease deepened.

Now visibly perturbed, Olivia suggested, "Maybe she's lost track of time. I'll go check on her." With a quick nod from Mia, Olivia excused herself from the group, disappearing into the serene surroundings of Tranquil Haven Spa.

Minutes passed, and Olivia returned with a furrowed brow. "Her room is empty, and there's no sign of her. Something's not right."

Concern etched across their faces, the group huddled, grappling with the unsettling reality of Sophia's disappearance. Ava, Emily, and Olivia exchanged worried glances, each contemplating the implications of their friend's mysterious absence.

"I'm going to the front desk. Maybe they've seen her," Mia suggested, her attempts to maintain composure betraying an underlying worry. With a sense of foreboding, the friends awaited Mia's return, the idyllic backdrop of Tranquil Haven Spa now overshadowed by the looming mystery of Sophia's disappearance.

Ava exchanged a worried glance with Emily, the poised lawyer nursing a longstanding grudge. The unease in the group deepened as Ava spoke up, "I'll check the yoga studio. Maybe she decided to go back for another session."

With a nod from Mia, Ava made her way to the yoga studio as Mia went to the front desk. The atmosphere among the remaining friends became increasingly tense as they awaited Ava's and Mia's return. The tranquil haven that once promised relaxation now echoed with an undercurrent of anxiety, setting the stage for the unsettling discovery that awaited them at Tranquil Haven Spa.

Mia returned from the front desk, her expression a mix of confusion and concern. The friends, gathered in a small huddle near the entrance, looked at her expectantly. The tranquility of Tranquil Haven Spa seemed to waver as Mia delivered the unsettling news.

"The front desk hasn't seen Sophia. They don't have any record of her leaving or any scheduled activities for her this morning," Mia explained, her voice tinged with worry. "It's as if she vanished."

The realization settled over the group like a heavy fog. Ava Turner had gone to check the yoga studio, and now Mia's confirmation that Sophia had not been spotted at the front desk heightened the sense of unease. Emily exchanged a glance with Olivia, both sensing that the situation was taking a dire turn.

"Could she have decided to explore the spa grounds on her own?" Richard Barnes, Olivia's husband, suggested, attempting to inject a note of optimism into the conversation.

Olivia's response was cautious, "She might, but she's never been one to wander off without telling someone. And why wouldn't she join us for the special trip Mia had planned?"

The minutes ticked by, and Ava had yet to return from the yoga studio. The suspense lingered, each passing moment amplifying the underlying tension within the group. The spa, once a haven of serenity, now echoed with the uncertainty of Sophia's disappearance.

Finally, Ava stumbled back into view, her complexion drained of color. The group turned to her, a collective hush falling over them as Ava, ghost-white and visibly shaken, struggled to find the words.

"I found her... I found Sophia," Ava stammered, her voice barely above a whisper. The weight of her discovery hung in the air, and the once-tranquil spa retreat now stood as the haunting backdrop to a chilling mystery that would redefine the lives of these friends forever.

Shattered Serenity

"I found her... I found Sophia," Ava stammered, her voice barely above a whisper. The weight of her discovery hung in the air, and the once-tranquil spa retreat now stood as the haunting backdrop to a chilling mystery that would redefine the lives of these friends forever.

A heavy silence settled over the group, broken only by the soft rustle of leaves outside. Ava's words lingered in the air, each syllable revealing the grim reality they now faced. Emily Rodriguez, with a longstanding grudge against Sophia, felt a surge of conflicting emotions—shock, sorrow, and a trace of something darker.

Olivia exchanged a horrified glance with her husband Richard. The once-elegant surroundings of Tranquil Haven Spa now bore witness to an unfolding tragedy that shattered the illusion of serenity.

Mia took a step forward, her composed exterior momentarily faltering. The organized world she meticulously constructed now crumbled in the face of a grim truth.

Richard Barnes, ever the voice of reason, broke the silence. "Where is she, Ava? What happened?" he asked, his concern etched across his face.

Ava, still visibly shaken, managed to convey the grim discovery. "She's in the yoga studio. I... I didn't want to disturb anything. It looks like..." Her voice trailed off, the unsaid words hanging heavily between them.

Olivia's hand flew to her mouth, her eyes wide with disbelief. The reality of the situation began to sink in, and the once-tranquil spa now echoed with the piercing silence of a crime scene.

Taking charge despite the shock, Mia instructed, "We need to call the police. Richard, use your phone." As Richard fumbled for his phone, Mia turned to the group. "I know someone on the force, Detective Eleanor Harper. She's experienced. She'll know what to do."

The friends, now united in the face of tragedy, gathered their thoughts. The serene haven they sought had transformed into a chilling crime scene, and the once-promised weekend of relaxation now became a journey into the dark recesses of their shared history. As they waited for the arrival of Detective Harper, the group stood at the precipice of a mystery that would forever alter the course of their lives.

As Richard dialed the emergency number, the friends gathered in the lounge area, the weight of the situation palpable. Conversations were hushed, a mix of shock, disbelief, and quiet speculation echoing through the room. Emily exchanged a wary glance with Olivia, each grappling with the enormity of the tragedy that had befallen their once-tranquil retreat.

Ava, still visibly shaken from her discovery of Sophia's lifeless body, sat apart from the group. Eyes cast downward, she clutched her trembling hands, hesitant to recount the haunting scene she had stumbled upon in the yoga studio. Mia approached Ava with a gentle touch on her shoulder.

"Ava, can you tell us what you saw?" Mia asked, her voice filled with concern. The friends gathered around, their faces a mosaic of dread and curiosity.

Ava took a deep breath, summoning the strength to recount the grim details. "I went to check the yoga studio, thinking Sophia might be there. The door was slightly ajar, and when I entered, I found her... on the floor. She wasn't moving. It looked like she..." Her voice faltered, the unsaid words lingering in the heavy silence.

Emily, ever the sharp observer, pressed for details. "Was there anyone else in the studio? Anything out of place?" Her lawyer instincts kicked in, and the group turned their attention to Ava's account.

Ava shook her head, her eyes haunted by the image she had witnessed. "No, no one else. The room was quiet and peaceful, just like it should be. Sophia was alone."

Emily, her keen eyes narrowing slightly, continued her inquiry. "Did you notice anything unusual, Ava? Any signs of a struggle or, perhaps, something that seemed out of place?"

Ava hesitated, grappling with the haunting images etched in her memory. "It was hard to focus, but it looked like... it looked like she had been strangled, but there was so much blood," she finally admitted, her voice trembling. "It looks like she was hit in the head, too," revealed Ava. The revelation sent a shiver through the room, and the friends exchanged uneasy glances.

"Strangled? Bludgeoned?" Richard interjected; his brow furrowed with concern. "Are you sure, Ava?"

Ava nodded; her gaze fixed on a distant point. "The marks on her neck...the blood… it was horrifying. I didn't stay long. I ran to get you all."

As the room hung heavy with unanswered questions, Emily's mind raced with thoughts that remained unspoken. Unbeknownst to the others, a seed of suspicion had taken root within her—a suspicion that would only grow as the investigation unfolded. For now,

Emily played the role of the concerned friend, masking the hidden motives that lurked beneath her composed exterior. The chilling truth behind Sophia's death loomed over them, and the once-close group of friends found themselves thrust into a mystery that would unravel the carefully woven fabric of their relationships.

The minutes dragged on as they awaited the arrival of the police, and tension simmered beneath the surface. Whispers circulated among the friends, raising questions and unsettling suspicions. Olivia leaned in toward Richard, her words barely audible. "Could this be related to our past, Richard? The secrets we thought were buried?"

Though visibly disturbed, Richard replied, "I don't know, Liv. We left that behind us, didn't we?" Their shared history, once buried beneath the veneer of their friendships, now resurfaced like a specter.

Mia, sensing the unease, addressed the group. "Let's not jump to conclusions. The police will handle this, and we should cooperate fully. Detective Harper will get to the bottom of it."

Olivia, who had been listening in stunned silence, whispered, "But why? Why would anyone do this to Sophia?"

Mia, trying to maintain a semblance of order, interjected, "Let's wait for the police to arrive. They'll conduct a thorough investigation and figure out what happened. Right now, we need to focus on supporting each other."

Mark stood by, a mix of shock and grief etched on his face. "Sophia... strangled? How is that even possible? She was here with us just last night. Are you sure, Ava? I mean, maybe she just... passed away. It doesn't have to be a murder."

Ava's eyes conveyed the horror she had witnessed, "No, Mark, it was deliberate. The blood was everywhere. Someone did this to her."

Diane stood frozen for a moment, her eyes fixed on the floor as the weight of the news settled in. Sophia had been a significant part of her life, and the shock of her sudden and violent death was overwhelming. The room seemed to blur as Diane's mind grappled with the reality that Sophia was gone.

Tears welled up in Diane's eyes, her hands trembling as she covered her mouth in disbelief. Her breath caught, and a stifled gasp escaped as she finally spoke, her voice wavering. "No, no, this can't be happening. Sophia..." Her words trailed off into a choked sob.

The friends exchanged glances, unsure of how to interpret Diane's reaction. Olivia glanced at Richard, her expression questioning.

"Is she genuinely distraught, or could she be involved somehow?" Olivia whispered to Richard, her eyes still on Diane.

Ever the voice of reason, Richard responded cautiously, "It's hard to say, Liv. Let's not jump to conclusions. We'll have to wait for the police to sort this out."

Diane looked around the room, absorbing the weight of the situation. "This is unreal. Who would want to hurt her?" Mia, taking charge, approached Diane. "We'll find out, Diane. The police are on their way. We need to cooperate fully with their investigation."

As the group continued to grapple with the shock of Sophia's death, Diane's grief became a focal point, an enigma that added an unsettling dimension to the already tense atmosphere. The impending investigation would delve into the intricacies of the relationships within the group. As Detective Eleanor Harper arrived, the once-close friends found themselves on the precipice of a mystery that would force them to confront not only the truth behind Sophia's murder but also the hidden complexities of their shared history.

The serenity of Tranquil Haven Spa had shattered. In its place, a chilling mystery unfolded, casting a long shadow over the lives of those who once sought refuge within its seemingly tranquil walls.

The distant wail of sirens grew louder, signaling the arrival of the police. The flashing lights of police cruisers illuminated the night, casting an eerie glow on the spa's serene facade.

The once-tranquil haven of Tranquil Haven Spa now stood at the center of a chilling mystery, and the friends braced themselves for unraveling hidden truths that would redefine their lives.

Detective Harper, the embodiment of methodical determination, stepped onto the scene, her expression unreadable. Behind her was a team of crime scene investigators, each a silent guardian of justice armed with forensic tools and a commitment to unveil the truth.

The spa's manager, visibly shaken, guided Harper and the forensic team through the hallowed halls toward the yoga studio. Yellow crime scene tape unraveled like a cautionary ribbon, sealing off the entry and marking the beginning of an investigation that would unravel the threads of deception woven through the once-tranquil haven.

Inside the studio, the forensic team donned their sterile white suits, a stark contrast to the muted hues of the yoga mats. Carefully, they documented the scene, capturing every detail before the sanctity of the space was forever altered.

As Harper conferred with the lead investigator, the coroner arrived, a solemn figure prepared to perform the grim duty of removing Sophia's lifeless form. Clad in professional detachment, the coroner approached the scene, her expertise a necessary component in this macabre puzzle.

In the cold silence of the yoga studio, the aftermath of Sophia's brutal attack painted a chilling tableau. Her once serene sanctuary had become a crime scene, bearing witness to the unfathomable violence that unfolded within its tranquil confines.

Sophia's lifeless body lay sprawled on the yoga mat, a stark contrast to the peaceful setting. Visible marks around her neck bore the grim testimony of strangulation, revealing the ferocity of the assault. The cold, merciless grip of the assailant left a haunting imprint, a morbid signature of their intent.

Yet, the violence didn't stop there. A deep gash on Sophia's forehead, evidence of a forceful blow with a solid object. The contours of the wound indicated that the weapon was substantial, a revelation that would later prove vital.

Blood, once the vital force coursing through Sophia's veins, now pooled around her lifeless form. The head injury had caused a substantial loss, adding a macabre dimension to the tragedy. The crimson stain on the yoga mat mirrored the brutality of the act, a stark reminder of the shattered tranquility that once enveloped the spa.

As investigators meticulously combed through the scene, every detail became a piece of the puzzle, and the injuries inflicted upon Sophia became a haunting narrative etched into the very fabric of the crime that had unfolded in the once-sacred space.

The air grew heavier as the coroner prepared to transport Sophia from the yoga mat that had witnessed her final moments. A respectful hush fell over the investigators and Spa staff, a poignant acknowledgment of the tragedy unfolding in this space. With practiced precision, the coroner carefully lifted Sophia's body onto a gurney, enveloping her in a sterile shroud that spoke of finality.

As Sophia was wheeled away from the crime scene, the spa's tranquility hung in the balance, disrupted by the violence that had stained its walls. The investigation had begun, and the once-sacred space became a nexus of questions, where answers would be sought in the silence of forensic analysis and the pursuit of justice.

The solemn procession of the coroner, accompanied by Sophia's lifeless form on a gurney, passed through the midst of the hushed friends. The air in the spa seemed to constrict, and the weight of the tragedy hung heavy in the atmosphere.

Olivia, the epitome of composed elegance, couldn't conceal the flicker of sorrow in her eyes as she watched the coroner wheel past. Richard, her husband, maintained a stoic exterior, but the furrow in his brow betrayed the sadness etched into his heart.

Mia, her usually vibrant spirit subdued, looked away, unable to bear the somber sight. Her weariness now etched deeper, Diane stared into the distance, lost in her thoughts of what might have been.

Ava, the impressionist artist, painted a facade of indifference, her gaze fixed on a distant point, concealing the turmoil beneath. Mark betrayed a fleeting expression of guilt as he avoided eye contact with the passing gurney.

Emily, caught in a web of guilt and uncertainty, stole a glance at Mia, a silent acknowledgment of the complexities that unraveled among them. Harper, the detective orchestrating the unraveling mystery, observed the diverse reactions with a keen eye, noting the nuances that hinted at the tangled threads connecting each friend to Sophia's demise.

As the coroner and Sophia's still form retreated from the spa, the echo of the gurney's wheels against the tiled floor reverberated through the hearts of the friends. The sanctuary that once cradled their shared laughter and secrets now bore witness to the painful departure of a beloved companion. The aftermath of tragedy lingered in the air, leaving the friends to grapple with the harsh reality that had shattered the tranquility of their haven.

Murder Unveiled

As the friends grappled with the emotional maelstrom following Sophia's shocking demise, the distant wail of sirens continued. A hushed anticipation enveloped the room, and it seemed as if the air held its breath as the Detective stepped into the spa's lounge.

Detective Harper, an enigmatic figure shrouded in the gravity of her profession, entered with an air of unyielding authority. Framed by a cascade of jet-black hair, her steely gaze surveyed the friends gathered in the lounge. Dressed in a perfectly tailored, charcoal-gray coat accentuating her commanding presence, she exuded a quiet intensity that left an indelible mark on the atmosphere.

A woman of few words, Detective Harper, allowed a deliberate moment of silence to linger, heightening the weight of her scrutiny. Her keen eyes, the color of stormy seas, navigated the room with unwavering precision, capturing the subtle nuances of each individual's reaction. The friends, caught in the crossfire of her penetrating gaze, exchanged furtive glances that betrayed a mix of nervous anticipation and guarded apprehension.

Olivia exchanged a nervous glance with her husband, Richard, as if seeking reassurance in the face of Detective Harper's formidable presence. Emily, harboring her own secrets, maintained a composed exterior that concealed the labyrinth of hidden motives lurking within. The Detective's arrival had cast a spotlight on the intricate web of relationships and emotions that now lay exposed in the wake of Sophia's tragic end.

As Detective Harper took her place at the center of the room, the spa's once-inviting lounge transformed into a stage for an unfolding drama. The Detective's demeanor, a fusion of professionalism and quiet authority, hinted at a depth of experience transcending the mere solving of crimes. The friends, now under the scrutiny of this formidable investigator, stood on the precipice of a mystery that would challenge not only their understanding of each other but also the very fabric of their intertwined lives.

Breaking the heavy silence that hung over the room, Detective Harper took command of the situation with a measured tone that cut through the tense air. "I understand that you've experienced a traumatic event. I need each of you to cooperate fully with the investigation. I'll be asking questions, and I expect honest answers. Let's get to the bottom of what happened here."

The friends, their faces etched with shock and sorrow, nodded in acknowledgment. The room remained charged with an unspoken tension as Detective Harper began her meticulous inquiry. Her sharp and penetrating gaze moved from one person to the next, seeking the nuances in their reactions.

"Let's start with the basics," Detective Harper began, directing her attention to Emily Rodriguez, "Can you tell me what each of you was doing before the discovery of Sophia's body? How would you describe your connection with her?"

Emily hesitated for a moment, her composure momentarily flickering. "Sophia and I go way back. We were college roommates and shared a lot during those years. But, over time, life took us on different paths."

Detective Harper leaned forward, sensing there might be more to the story. "Different paths? Can you elaborate?"

Maintaining her calm demeanor, Emily elaborated, "Sophia pursued her passion for yoga and holistic living, while I went into law. We remained friends, of course, but our interests diverged."

The Detective continued, probing, "And how would you characterize your relationship now, leading up to this retreat?"

"We've stayed friends, but there's always been a subtle tension between us," Emily confessed. "She disapproved of the corporate world I work in, and I sometimes felt judged for not embracing her lifestyle."

Detective Harper sensed a motive brewing beneath the surface. "So, there was tension between you and Sophia. Can you recall any recent disagreements or conflicts?"

Emily paused, carefully choosing her words. "We had our differences, especially when she left her job as a graphic designer. But, recently, her disapproval of my career choices added strain."

Detective Harper, keenly attuned to the nuances of human relationships, sensed there was more beneath the surface. Before Emily could elaborate further, Mark, Emily's husband, interjected with a tinge of frustration. "Sophia always had a way of meddling. Remember when she insisted on that art show, Em? It caused a lot of tension."

The obvious strained relationships between Emily, her husband Mark, and Sophia flooded Detective Harper's mind, prompting her to delve deeper into the past to unearth the roots of the tension that had simmered beneath the surface.

In a vivid flashback, Emily found herself in the midst of a heated argument with Sophia. The spa's tranquil surroundings stood witness to their clash of ideologies. Clad in serene yoga attire, Sophia confronted Emily about her career choices.

"I don't understand why you're wasting your talents in that corporate jungle," Sophia chided, frustration evident in her expressive eyes.

Emily, dressed in the polished attire of the corporate world, shot back, "Not everyone wants to abandon their ambitions to meditate all day, Sophia. Some of us have to make a living."

The tension between them escalated as Mark, attempting to mediate, found himself caught in the crossfire. "Can't you two just get along? We're here to relax, not fight," he implored.

Sophia, undeterred, responded with a cutting remark, "Maybe if you had more passion for something meaningful, Emily wouldn't have to bear the burden of providing purpose for both of you."

The flashback dissolved, returning Detective Harper to the present. The vivid scene of discord hinted at a complex dynamic that extended beyond the seemingly serene surface of Tranquil Haven Spa, adding another layer of intrigue to the already tangled web of relationships.

As the Detective probed further, Emily's husband, Mark, interjected, "We were just trying to escape the stress of our daily lives with this weekend retreat. Emily's career has been demanding, and we thought Tranquil Haven would be a sanctuary."

Detective Harper shifted her focus to Mark. "And what is your role in all of this, Mark? Do you share the same tensions with Sophia as Emily does?"

Mark sighed, "Not to the same extent, but yeah, there were moments. Sophia and I never fully connected. I think she always wanted Emily to have a different life, one more aligned with her own."

Detective Harper noted the complexities within the relationships. "So, Emily, during the time leading up to the incident, where were you? Can anyone vouch for your whereabouts?"

Emily thought for a moment before responding, "We were strolling through the spa grounds, enjoying some fresh air. It was a peaceful activity to unwind."

Mark added, "It was just the two of us. A moment of solace before everything turned upside down."

Detective Harper continued to scrutinize the details, her sharp gaze focused on Emily and Mark as they recounted their alibi. "Strolling through the spa grounds," Emily had said, a seemingly innocent activity. However, Harper knew that even the smallest details could hold significance in a complex web of relationships and suspicions.

"So, you were alone during this stroll?" Harper inquired; her tone measured.

"Yes," Emily replied, exchanging a glance with Mark, who nodded in agreement. "Just the two of us. We wanted some time away from the group to enjoy the fresh air and clear our minds."

Detective Harper's next question probed deeper into the specifics, "Did anyone see you while you were strolling?"

Emily hesitated, glancing at Mark before responding, "It was a secluded area. We didn't encounter anyone else during our walk. It was supposed to be a private moment."

Mark interjected, "We headed back to our room after that. We didn't cross paths with anyone from the group until the next scheduled gathering."

Harper took mental notes of their responses, aware that the solitude of their stroll could be both a strength and a weakness. A moment away from prying eyes yet lacking the corroborating alibi of a witness. The Detective made a mental note to cross-reference their timeline with other potential witnesses to ascertain the credibility of their alibi. The intricate dance of relationships within the spa had taken a complicated turn, and Harper aimed to unravel the threads that concealed the truth.

Detective Harper jotted down the alibi: "Thank you for your cooperation. I might need to circle back later if I have further questions."

As Emily and Mark exchanged wary glances, the Detective continued her meticulous inquiry.

Detective Harper's gaze shifted to Olivia Barnes, "Olivia, tell me about the gathering you hosted in the lounge area. What was the atmosphere like, and what interactions stood out to you?"

Still somewhat shaken by the recent turn of events, Olivia recounted, "It was an impromptu gathering in the early afternoon. I wanted to share my recent achievements with everyone. We were celebrating, and champagne was flowing."

Richard, Olivia's husband, chimed in, "It was a toast to Olivia's success. A moment to revel in her accomplishments. Little did we know..."

Detective Harper noted the hint of bitterness in Richard's voice and decided to explore further. "Tell me more about the dynamics within the group during this gathering. Any tensions or conflicts that might have surfaced?"

Olivia hesitated, exchanging a quick glance with Richard. "Well, the group dynamics are complex. We've been friends for a long time, and with that comes a certain level of competition and comparison."

Detective Harper pressed, "Competition? Can you elaborate?"

Olivia sighed, "We all have our successes, but mine have been more prominent lately. It's not something I flaunt, but I can sense the envy sometimes."

Richard, seemingly supportive, added, "Olivia has worked hard for her success. But success can be a double-edged sword. It brings joy but also triggers insecurities."

Detective Harper delved into personal dynamics. "And how about your relationship with Sophia, Olivia? Any dynamics or tensions there?"

Olivia hesitated, choosing her words carefully. "Sophia and I had our differences. Like most people, she admired my success but sometimes questioned the choices that led me there. It was a subtle tension, but it existed."

Detective Harper maintained a focused gaze on Olivia, sensing that beneath the polished exterior of the successful fashion designer, there were layers of nuanced emotions and untold stories.

"And how would you characterize your relationship now, leading up to this retreat?" Harper pressed, aiming to uncover the intricacies that might have played a role in Sophia's demise.

Olivia took a moment, recalling a recent encounter that had left an imprint on her memory. "We had a disagreement not long ago. Sophia disapproved of a bold design choice I made for an upcoming collection. She thought it was too avant-garde and might not resonate with our clientele. I valued her opinion, but in that instance, I decided to follow my instincts."

Detective Harper listened intently, recognizing the clash of artistic vision and corporate sensibility. "So, there was tension between you and Sophia. Can you recall any recent disagreements or conflicts?"

Olivia nodded, her expression thoughtful. "That disagreement lingered, but we didn't let it escalate. We agreed to disagree. Despite our differences, I never imagined it would lead to... this."

Harper acknowledged the complexity of their relationship and filed away this recent conflict as a potential piece of the puzzle. The subtle tension that Olivia described hinted at the layers of strain beneath the surface. Detective Harper remained fully determined to unveil the truth concealed within the intricacies of their connections.

Detective Harper, sensing a potential motive, continued, "During the time leading up to the incident, where were you, Olivia? Can anyone vouch for your whereabouts?"

Olivia thought momentarily, then responded, "After the gathering, I took a moment to myself in the lounge. Richard joined me. We were discussing plans for the evening."

Richard chimed in, "That's right. We were making plans for a quiet dinner and maybe a late-night stroll. A typical evening for us."

Detective Harper focused on Olivia, gauging her response for any signs of deception. "And during this quiet evening, where did you have dinner?"

Olivia shared with a confident yet measured tone, "We dined at the spa's restaurant. It was a lovely setting, and we enjoyed a delightful meal with a bottle of champagne."

Detective Harper raised an eyebrow at the mention of champagne, an element that could be crucial in the unfolding investigation. "Champagne, you say? Was it a special occasion?"

Richard, Olivia's husband, answered, "Not particularly. We just enjoy indulging in the finer things during our getaways. It was a way to unwind and make the evening memorable."

The Detective made a mental note of the detail. Dinner and champagne—seemingly innocent components of a typical evening, yet Harper understood the importance of scrutinizing every detail. As the friends' relationships revealed intricate layers, Harper knew that seemingly ordinary events could hold the key to understanding the extraordinary tragedy that had unfolded at Tranquil Haven Spa.

Detective Harper made a note of their alibi but sensed an undercurrent of unresolved emotions. "Thank you for your cooperation. I might need to revisit this if more questions arise." Olivia and Richard exchanged knowing glances as the Detective moved on.

Detective Harper shifted her focus to Ava Turner, the recently divorced artist with an air of vulnerability. "Ava, you mentioned you were in your art loft earlier. Can you provide more details about what you were doing and your whereabouts leading up to the incident?"

Ava took a deep breath, her nervous demeanor evident. "I needed some time alone, away from the group. I retreated to my loft to work on my art, trying to channel my emotions onto the canvas. It's a therapeutic process for me."

Sensing an emotional undercurrent, Detective Harper probed further, "Tell me more about your emotions during that time. Anything specific on your mind?"

Ava hesitated, choosing her words carefully. "The recent divorce has left its mark. I carry emotional scars, and this retreat was a way to escape the judgment and expectations of my friends, especially Sophia. She never understood my unconventional approach to art."

Detective Harper explored this dynamic. "You mentioned Sophia. What was her stance on your art, and were there any unresolved tensions between you two?"

Ava sighed, "Sophia disapproved of my art. She had a more traditional view, and my unconventional pursuits didn't align with her expectations. It created a rift, and her disapproval weighed heavily on me."

Detective Harper, noting the potential motive rooted in the strained relationship, continued, "During the time leading up to the incident, were you alone in your room? Can anyone vouch for your whereabouts?"

Ava nodded, "Yes, I was alone. I had no plans to socialize that evening. I was lost in my art, trying to find a semblance of peace."

Detective Harper acknowledged Ava's statement, noting her emotional vulnerability and the potential motive stemming from the unresolved tensions with Sophia. As Ava's alibi formed, the Detective understood that behind the delicate strokes of Ava's art lay a canvas of emotions that might hold the key to the mystery.

Detective Harper shifted her attention to Mia Johnson, the high-powered executive with a knack for managing complexities. "Mia, as the organizer of this weekend, can you walk me through the arrangements and your role in the events leading up to now?"

Maintaining a composed exterior, Mia began to elaborate on the meticulous planning. "I ensured that each friend's preferences were considered, organizing activities and accommodations. It's my job to make sure everything runs smoothly."

Detective Harper, keenly observing Mia's body language, delved deeper. "Beyond the organizational aspect, were there any personal dynamics or tensions you were aware of within the group?"

Mia hesitated, her eyes momentarily betraying the underlying tension. "Well, you know, friendships can be complex. Everyone has their own history and relationships, but I try to ensure everyone has a good time."

The Detective probed further, "And your personal life, Mia? Any challenges or conflicts that might have influenced the dynamics of this weekend?"

Mia took a measured breath, "My personal life is separate from the group. I strive to maintain a balance between my work and relationships. My wife, Diane, is a professor, and we both have demanding careers."

With her keen eye for unraveling personal intricacies, Detective Harper delved deeper into Mia's personal life. "Tell me more about your marriage to Diane. Any challenges or conflicts?"

Mia sighed, her shoulders slightly slumping under the weight of unspoken troubles. "Diane and I have our share of challenges. We're both busy with our careers and finding time for each other can be difficult. Lately, it feels like we're drifting apart."

Harper nodded, sensing there might be more beneath the surface. "Have you tried to address these issues and seek solutions?"

Mia hesitated before responding, "Diane has been talking to Emily about our marriage. She believes Emily can provide some insights and help us navigate the challenges we face."

Detective Harper's interest piqued at the mention of Emily's involvement. The dynamics within the group were becoming increasingly intricate, with personal relationships and conflicts weaving a complex tapestry. As Mia revealed the challenges in her marriage, Harper wondered if the threads of these personal struggles could be connected to the tragic events that unfolded during the spa retreat.

Sensing a delicate balance, Detective Harper continued, "Speaking of relationships, Mia, was everyone accounted for during the incident? Can you provide alibis for yourself and Diane?"

Mia nodded, "Yes, we were together in our room. Diane and I spent the evening enjoying the spa's amenities. We had no reason to leave or be involved in anything outside our private space."

Detective Harper acknowledged Mia's statement, recognizing the intricacies of her dual life as an executive and a spouse. The Detective understood that a web of connections and potential motives lay beneath the polished exterior, adding another layer of complexity to the unfolding mystery.

Finally, Detective Harper directed her inquiries to Diane, "Diane, you share a history with Sophia. Can you tell me about your relationship and the dynamics between you leading up to the retreat?"

Visibly distraught, Diane shared fragments of their past, exposing the emotional complexities of their history. Detective Harper delved deeper into Diane's tumultuous relationship with Sophia, recognizing the emotional complexities of their shared history. "Diane, can you share more about how you and Sophia met?"

Diane took a deep breath, recounting the early days of their connection. "Sophia and I met during college. We were both exploring our identities, and our friendship developed into something more. Our relationship was groundbreaking for both of us, but over time, we faced challenges that we couldn't overcome."

Detective Harper, observing Diane's expressions keenly, asked, "Did anyone within your social circles or the group express any discomfort or disapproval regarding your relationship with Sophia, especially considering your LGBTQ+ status?"

Diane paused, recalling the judgments they faced. "Yes, there were times when we encountered prejudice. Some friends were supportive, while others distanced themselves. It strained our relationship, but we persevered until the tensions became too much. But no one in this group of friends knew of our relationship"

Detective Harper continued, "Leading up to the incident, did you sense any prejudice or negative attitudes within the group regarding your relationship with Sophia?"

Diane hesitated before responding, "There were moments when I felt an undercurrent of discomfort, but nothing overt. I hoped this weekend would allow us to put those judgments behind us and move forward as friends."

The Detective then focused on Diane's whereabouts during the incident. "Can you provide more details about your activities in your room during that time?"

Diane composed herself, stating, "I was alone, reflecting on our past and the effort to rebuild our friendship. I hadn't left my room when whatever happened occurred. I needed some time away from the group dynamics."

Detective Harper absorbed the information, recognizing the layers of complexity within Diane's history with Sophia. As the Detective continued questioning, the intricate web of relationships within the group unraveled, each revelation adding new dimensions to the unfolding mystery.

As Detective Harper concluded the initial round of questioning, the spa's lounge held an air of palpable tension. Each member of the group felt the weight of the Detective's scrutiny, and the once-secluded retreat had transformed into the epicenter of a chilling investigation.

The Detective, with a measured nod, acknowledged the group. "Thank you for your cooperation. I will continue to explore the circumstances surrounding Sophia's death. Please remain available for further questioning, and if any of you remember additional details, don't hesitate to come forward."

The friends exchanged glances, their expressions reflecting a mix of unease and curiosity about the unfolding investigation. Detective Harper rose from her seat, her gaze lingering on each person in the room before she made her way toward the exit.

As the Detective left, the friends were left to grapple with the reality of the situation. The once-tranquil spa had become a crime scene, and the search for answers would lead Detective Harper to explore the hidden corners of Tranquil Haven. Little did they know that beneath the seemingly serene surface, the spa held secrets that would soon come to light.

Unraveling Threads of Tranquility

Detective Harper navigated through the spa's pristine corridors, her steps echoing in the hushed ambiance. Tranquil Haven Spa, nestled within the embrace of the Catskill Mountains, had long been regarded as a retreat from the chaos of the outside world. The exterior boasted manicured gardens with meandering paths that wound through vibrant floral displays. The spa's architectural design seamlessly blended with the natural landscape, creating an idyllic haven.

As Detective Harper approached the yoga room, the exterior belied the turmoil within. Yellow crime scene tape cordoned off the area, indicating the boundaries of the investigation. Uniformed officers stood guard, ensuring the sanctity of the scene. The Detective noticed a quiet murmur of conversation among the law enforcement personnel, a collective effort to piece together the puzzle of Sophia Turner's demise.

Inside the yoga room, the atmosphere hung heavy with a mix of lingering incense and the palpable energy of the investigation. The room was bathed in a soft, diffused light, casting an ethereal glow on the hardwood floors. The mats, once arranged for a tranquil session, now lay undisturbed as part of the preserved crime scene.

Detective Harper observed forensic experts meticulously at work. Crime scene investigators donned gloves, carefully collecting evidence that could potentially unravel the mystery. Fingerprint dust shimmered in the air as they methodically combed through surfaces. Cameras on tripods captured every angle, documenting the state of the room and preserving it as a frozen moment in time.

As the Detective surveyed the surroundings, her keen eyes sought out any anomalies. Were there signs of struggle? Was there a misplaced object that could hold significance? Were there security cameras within the room, and if so, did they capture the events leading up to Sophia's death?

The yoga room, once a place of serenity, had become a canvas for forensic scrutiny. Detective Harper's meticulous exploration aimed to unravel the threads that bound Tranquil Haven Spa to a web of secrets, laying the foundation for the truth to emerge.

Detective Harper approached the CSI technicians, a dedicated team known for their meticulous work in crime scene investigations. The lead technician, seasoned and methodical, was named Detective Angela Rodriguez. Her two assistants, specializing in forensics and digital evidence, were Olivia "Liv" Marshall and Ethan Barnes. Liv was skilled in analyzing physical evidence, while Ethan's expertise lay in unraveling the complexities of digital clues. Together, they formed a formidable team, ready to delve into the intricacies of Tranquil Haven Spa's enigmatic crime scene.

Detective Harper: “Were there any signs of a struggle, any indication of forced entry?”

Detective Angela Rodriguez: “No signs of forced entry, Detective. The perimeter appears undisturbed.”

Detective Harper: “What about the security cameras? Have we reviewed the footage?”

Olivia "Liv" Marshall: “Yes, Detective. We've got footage up until a certain point. The camera lens got covered at some stage, creating a gap in the recording.”

Detective Harper: “Covered? Deliberately?”

Olivia "Liv" Marshall: “It seems so. The lens was obstructed by what looks like a yoga outfit, a towel, or some sort of clothing. We're working on enhancing the frames around that period.”

Detective Harper: “Keep me posted on that. Did we find anything else unusual?”

Ethan Barnes: “We discovered a torn piece of fabric near the camera. It doesn't match the surroundings. It's from a different material.”

Detective Harper: “Let's get that analyzed. Any sign of a struggle on the yoga mats?”

Detective Angela Rodriguez: “Not that we can see. The mats are undisturbed, with no signs of a scuffle.”

Detective Harper: “Sophia was working out, right? Did the video show her interacting with anyone?”

Olivia "Liv" Marshall: “She was alone for most of it. At one point, there's a brief interaction with another guest, Emily Rodriguez.”

Detective Harper: “What was their interaction like?”

Ethan Barnes: “It’s difficult to say. It was in the studio, and partially out of the camera’s view. Then Emily left.”

The obscured camera footage, capturing Emily leaving Sophia's yoga session with Sophia still alive, raised more questions.

Detective Harper: “Thank you for letting me know. We'll review the footage closely.”

Detective Harper's keen eyes narrowed slightly at the mention of Emily's visit to Sophia's yoga session. Emily had failed to mention the visit during questioning.

Detective Harper, armed with newfound information about Emily's unmentioned visit to the yoga room, decided to seek answers directly. She left the studio and headed directly to Rodriguez’s room. Knocking on the door of Emily and Mark's room, Harper maintained her composed demeanor as the door creaked open, revealing the couple within.

"Emily, Mark, may I come in? I have a few more questions," Detective Harper requested, her tone carrying a sense of determination.

The room, adorned in subdued spa decor, emanated an air of tranquility that sharply contrasted with the tension now filling the space. Soft, ambient lighting cast a warm glow over the room, creating an illusion of serenity that clashed with the dark turn of events.

Emily and Mark, sitting on the edge of the neatly made bed, exchanged a glance that betrayed a hint of unease. "Of course, Detective. Please, have a seat," Emily gestured toward a small seating area by the window.

Taking a measured seat, Detective Harper began, "I've learned that you visited the yoga room earlier today, Emily. Interestingly, you and Mark didn't mention that during our earlier conversation."

Emily's gaze momentarily flickered, and Mark shifted in his seat uncomfortably. "Yes, we did stop by. It was a brief visit. We didn't think it was relevant," Emily explained, her composed exterior revealing little.

Detective Harper pressed further, "It's essential that we have all the details. Can you tell me why you chose to visit the yoga room and why it wasn't deemed relevant during our initial questioning?"

Emily hesitated before responding, "We were passing by and noticed the door was slightly ajar. Curiosity got the better of us, and we peeked in. But truly, there was nothing noteworthy."

Mark added, "We left shortly after and saw Olivia in the hallway outside the yoga room."

Detective Harper filed away this new piece of information. "Interesting. And Olivia, did you speak to her? Did she enter the yoga room after you left?"

Emily shook her head, "No, we exchanged a few words, and that was it. We didn't see her go into the yoga room."

Mark chimed in, "We continued down the hallway towards our room after the brief interaction."

Detective Harper nodded, her gaze narrowing slightly as she contemplated the unfolding puzzle. "Thank you for your cooperation. I might have more questions as the investigation progresses. Please don't hesitate to reach out if you remember anything else."

As the Detective left their room, the air thickened with unresolved tension. Harper refrained from directly accusing Emily, allowing the puzzle pieces to fall into place. The obscured camera lens opened a window of doubt, leaving room for the possibility that someone else, possibly Olivia, could have entered after Emily's departure.

Leaving Emily and Mark's room, Detective Eleanor Harper felt a subtle undercurrent of tension lingering in the air. The unspoken details surrounding Emily's undisclosed visit to the yoga room added another layer of complexity to the unfolding mystery. As she navigated the spa's corridors, Detective Harper's keen instincts led her outdoors, where the well-maintained gardens beckoned with the possibility of hidden truths. The morning sun cast a gentle glow on the landscape, yet Detective Harper saw beyond the picturesque facade. The gardens, once a backdrop for the friends' leisurely strolls, now held the potential to unveil crucial evidence. With each step, she embarked on a meticulous exploration, determined to sift through the natural beauty and uncover the threads that connected the friends to the enigma surrounding Sophia Turner's death.

Each path winding through the manicured lawns seemed to hold secrets, and every flower bed and bench became a potential repository of clues that could unravel the mystery concealed within the spa's walls.

The Detective, accompanied by a forensics team, moved purposefully through the outdoor crime scene. The fragrance of blooming flowers lingered in the air, providing a stark contrast to the tension that clung to the atmosphere. Footprints imprinted in the soil, a discarded item inconspicuously tucked away, or the slightest disturbance in the carefully landscaped grounds—all promised to become crucial pieces of evidence in the ongoing investigation.

Once a serene backdrop for the friends' leisurely walks and conversations, the garden's ambiance now transformed into a tableau of hidden secrets. Olivia Barnes, the friend mentioned by Emily and Mark, had reportedly been in the vicinity after the visit to the yoga room. Detective Harper, attuned to the nuances of the environment, considered the possibility that the gardens might hold a missing link—a detail overlooked during the initial questioning that could shed light on the mysterious events leading to Sophia Turner's tragic demise.

Detective Harper and the CSI team meticulously combed through the spa's gardens, examining the landscape for any signs of disturbance or overlooked clues. The ambiance, once serene, now carried an air of suspicion. As they scrutinized the flower beds, pathways, and tranquil nooks, the Detective's sharp eyes caught a subtle trail of footprints leading from the yoga room area. The prints seemed to deviate from the friends' usual paths, raising questions about who else might have been in the vicinity.

The garden revealed additional anomalies—a discarded champagne glass, its contents now evaporated in the morning sun, hinted at a clandestine gathering. Cigarette butts near a secluded bench suggested an illicit meeting. Olivia Barnes, mentioned by Emily and Mark, now emerged as a figure of interest due to her proximity to the yoga room during the crucial time frame. Detective Harper pondered the significance of these findings, realizing that the garden held more than mere beauty—it concealed a canvas of hidden alliances and potential suspects, complicating the unraveling of Sophia Turner's tragic fate.

The discarded champagne glass was nestled inconspicuously behind a decorative shrub near the yoga room's entrance. Detective Harper's eyes narrowed as she examined the finding and noted the absence of other glasses in the immediate vicinity. The CSI team carefully collected the evidence, carefully preserving any potential fingerprints.

Upon closer inspection, the footprints revealed an interesting detail—the distinct impression of heels. Detective Harper's instincts on high alert considered the possibility of a female presence near the crime scene. A trail of such footprints seemed unusual, given the friends' casual footwear during their walks. The

Detective instructed the CSI agents to intensify their search, exploring the garden for more clues.

As the investigation unfolded, Detective Harper decided to confront Olivia Barnes directly. The champagne glass, she believed, could be a pivotal link to Olivia's involvement. A faint, almost imperceptible lipstick stain on the rim heightened Harper's suspicion. The Detective, having observed Olivia's beauty routines and penchant for bold lipstick colors during initial questioning, recognized the shade as one Olivia favored.

Detective Harper wasted no time in seeking out Olivia, determined to get to the bottom of the mysteries shrouding the spa. Olivia was discovered in an unusual place—the spa's art studio where Ava had settled in, surrounded by the tools of her trade and the vibrant hues of her creations. Harper, entering the space with a purposeful stride, found Olivia engrossed in her work, her hands moving deftly over a canvas.

Observing Olivia in the art studio, Detective Harper was genuinely surprised to find the fashion designer immersed in a realm usually reserved for friends who identified as artists. The Detective, curious about Olivia's presence, questioned, "Olivia, what brings you to the art studio? You're a fashion designer, not a painter."

Olivia, momentarily flustered, gestured towards a table strewn with color swatches and fabric samples. "I'm working on a new line, and I find inspiration in the vibrant colors of art. It helps me create unique color palettes for my designs."

"Olivia," Detective Harper's voice cut through the creative atmosphere, causing Olivia to startle. The Detective's gaze was unwavering, her piercing eyes meeting Olivia's with a mix of suspicion and determination. "We need to talk."

Caught off guard, Olivia set her paintbrush down, her eyes flickering nervously as Detective Harper entered the art studio. Holding the champagne glass as evidence, Harper couldn't help but notice the momentary lapse in Olivia's usually confident demeanor. The Detective wasted no time explaining the findings and the lipstick stain that implicated Olivia.

Olivia's initial denial, though shaky, rang through the art studio. "I gave beauty products to all my friends. That glass could have been used by anyone," she protested, attempting to dismiss the incriminating evidence. Detective Harper, unfazed by the deflection, pressed for more details.

"So, Olivia, mind if I see your lipstick containers? Just to cross-check, you know," Harper inquired, expecting cooperation.

Olivia, however, became evasive, hesitating before responding. "Well, I have so many, and they're all mixed up. It might take a while to find the exact one."

Detective Harper, leaning against an easel, observed Olivia closely. The tension in the room was palpable, the once vibrant studio now a backdrop for a different kind of creation—the unraveling of a mystery. The Detective probed deeper, asking Olivia about her whereabouts during the critical time, attempting to discern any inconsistencies in her story.

Detective Harper, determined to unravel the intricate relationship web, continued questioning. "Olivia, can you share more about your relationship with Sophia? Any past problems or conflicts that might help us understand what happened?"

Olivia hesitated, her eyes darting away briefly before meeting Harper's gaze. "Sophia and I were friends, but like any friendship, we had our ups and downs. Nothing serious, though. We were here to reconnect and put everything behind us."

Detective Harper, not easily swayed, pressed further. "And your husband, Richard? Where was he the night of the murder?"

Olivia's response was swift and decisive. "We had a late-night dinner and took a stroll. He was with me the whole time."

Harper, sensing potential motives in tangled relationships, probed deeper. "How did Richard feel about Sophia?" she inquired.

Olivia's response carried a note of hesitation. "Richard always felt that Sophia might be jealous of my success. He thought she could undermine my achievements, but it was just protective talk, you know?"

The Detective filed away Olivia's words, recognizing the intricate dynamics within the group. Richard's perceived protective stance and the underlying tension within the friendships added another layer to the complex narrative that now unfolded within Tranquil Haven Spa.

Detective Harper's keen eyes subtly shifted downward, briefly fixating on Olivia's shoes. As she observed, she noted a peculiar detail—a small smudge of dirt on Olivia's otherwise impeccably fashionable footwear. The incongruity struck Harper as odd, considering Olivia's meticulous fashion sense. Harper made a mental note of this unexpected detail, recognizing that even the slightest discrepancies could become crucial in untangling the web of events leading to the tragic demise of Sophia Turner.

As Detective Harper delved deeper into the intricacies of the investigation, she encountered a subtle undercurrent of reluctance in Olivia's responses. The designer's evasive answers and the unexpected detail of a dirt smudge on her fashionable shoes added layers of complexity to the mystery surrounding Sophia's death. Harper, ever attuned to the nuances of human behavior and the significance of even the tiniest discrepancies, made a mental note to revisit this line of inquiry.

The puzzle of Tranquil Haven Spa's secrets was far from complete, and each encounter with the friends revealed more threads waiting to be unraveled. Harper's determined gaze hinted at the relentless pursuit of truth, promising that the elusive answers would eventually come to light.

The Detective left Olivia, momentarily, to her work, but the champagne glass and its damning lipstick stain lingered as a pivotal piece of evidence in the ongoing investigation at Tranquil Haven Spa.

Detective Harper's phone vibrated, pulling her attention away from the enigmatic art studio. As she answered the call, Mia's voice resonated with urgency on the other end. "Detective Harper, I need to discuss something with you in private. It's about the events leading up to Sophia's death."

Harper's sharp instincts tingled with interest and suspicion. The unexpected call from Mia, the detailed orchestrator of the weekend's activities, hinted at the possibility of hidden truths waiting to be unveiled. While she maintained her professional composure inwardly, Harper acknowledged the gravity of Mia's revelation. The Detective knew this private conversation could possibly hold the key to understanding the intricate relationships surrounding Sophia's demise. The intricate puzzle was growing more complex, and Mia's insights might be the missing piece that would bring clarity to the chilling mystery.

Detective Harper, guided by the need to unravel the intricate web of relationships within the group, met Mia in a private room separate from her wife, Diane. The choice of the meeting location raised an eyebrow, hinting at an underlying tension in the air. Mia, usually composed and authoritative, appeared visibly distressed as she invited Detective Harper in.

Seated in a quiet corner, Mia took a deep breath, the weight of unspoken truths hanging in the air. She decided it was time to lay bare the complexities of her marriage to Diane. In a moment of vulnerability, Mia shared a revelation that startled Detective Harper — her marriage was over. The revelation was unexpected, given the façade of unity the couple had presented to the world.

The night of Sophia's tragic murder, Diane confronted Mia with a revelation of her own. Mia's affair with Emily, once considered a well-guarded secret, had been laid bare. Diane, aware of the infidelity, disclosed that Sophia had urged her to end the marriage.

The news struck Mia like a lightning bolt, igniting a furious internal conflict. Driven by her professional image and the fear of the scandal affecting her executive standing, Mia grappled with the consequences of her choices.

Detective Harper, absorbing the revelation of Mia's crumbling marriage and the exposed affair, knew that the dynamics within the group were more intricate than they initially seemed. Seated in the quiet room, Harper sought to understand Mia's emotions and motivations in the wake of Sophia's murder.

"Can you tell me more about your relationship with Emily?" Detective Harper inquired; her tone measured but empathetic.

While grappling with the weight of her confessions, Mia met Harper's gaze. "Emily and I... It started as a connection, a shared understanding of the challenges we faced in our marriages. It was supposed to be a comfort, an escape from difficulties. But now, with everything that has happened, it feels like a mistake."

Harper nodded, encouraging Mia to continue. "What about Diane? How did she find out about the affair?"

Mia's eyes lowered, a mix of guilt and regret etched on her face. "Diane found some messages between Emily and me. She confronted me on the night of Sophia's murder. It was explosive. Sophia, apparently, had encouraged Diane to end our marriage."

Detective Harper processed the information, realizing the complex web of relationships that had unraveled within the group. "How did you react to Diane's revelation about Sophia's advice?"

Mia sighed; a heavy burden evident in her words. "I was furious and hurt. Sophia was a close friend and the idea that she played a role in urging Diane to end our marriage... it's overwhelming."

Looking further into the intricate dynamics, Harper asked, "What about Emily's husband? Is he aware of the affair?"

Mia hesitated before responding, "No, he doesn't know. Emily and I have been careful to keep it hidden. It adds another layer of complexity to this mess."

As Harper delved into the intricate tapestry of relationships, she could sense the threads of betrayal, secrets, and tangled emotions weaving a complex narrative. The unraveling personal lives of the friends hinted at motives that might extend beyond the surface, making the investigation more challenging and the truth more elusive.

Detective Harper, absorbing the revelation of Mia's crumbling marriage and the exposed affair, knew that the dynamics within the group were more intricate than they initially seemed. Seated in the quiet room, Harper sought to understand Mia's emotions and motivations in the wake of Sophia's murder.

Still visibly distressed, Mia expressed a mix of conflicting feelings toward Sophia. Their long history of conflict had been marked by deep-rooted resentments, and Mia admitted to confronting Sophia about her interference in her personal life. The confrontation had taken place earlier on the day of the murder, creating an additional layer of tension within the group.

Diane, Mia's wife, was not present during this revelation. Harper sensed that Diane's knowledge of the affair and the impending end of their marriage had created a delicate situation. The absence of Diane in the room left room for speculation about her own role in the unfolding drama.

Detective Harper, bearing the weight of the newly revealed complexities in the relationships among the friends, made her way to the room that had once been occupied by Mia and Diane. A discreet knock on the door preceded Harper's entrance.

Diane, already aware that Mia had spoken to Detective Harper, greeted her with a mix of anticipation and apprehension. Harper, maintaining her calm demeanor, relayed the recent conversation with Mia. The Detective's words hung in the air; the room seemingly charged with unspoken tension.

Diane, wrestling with the unraveling threads of her marriage, listened as Harper delved into the intricacies of Mia and Sophia's conflicts. The Detective sought to understand Diane's perspective on the events leading up to Sophia's murder and how her knowledge of Mia's affair might have influenced the dynamics within the group.

Detective Harper, sitting across from Diane in the now-hushed room, observed the conflicting emotions etched on Diane's face. The Detective, adept at reading subtle cues, acknowledged the gravity of the situation. Diane, having sobbed so intensely upon learning of Sophia's death, now faced Harper's questions with a mix of sorrow and introspection.

Harper, delving into the complexities of Diane and Sophia's friendship, broached the topic of Sophia's advice regarding Diane's decision to seek a divorce from Mia. "Diane, in light of recent events, can you share your feelings about Sophia's guidance in your personal life? Did you have any reservations about following her advice?"

Grappling with Sophia's memories and the weight of the decisions she had made, Diane took a moment before responding. "Sophia was my confidante. She understood the intricacies of my relationship with Mia. I trusted her advice, and she played a pivotal role in my decision to seek a divorce. However, in the aftermath, I can't help but wonder if there were aspects of her guidance that I might have misunderstood."

Diane sighed, revealing a mix of emotions. "I never expected this revelation. Emily and Mia having an affair... it adds another layer to the challenges we were already facing. As for my feelings about Emily, well, we all have our complexities, but she's been a friend. I can't say I'm pleased about the affair, though."

Harper, ever observant, continued her line of inquiry. "Did you notice any issues between Emily and her husband, Mark, during your time at the spa?"

Diane paused, contemplating her response. "Emily and Mark have their challenges, like any couple. I've seen moments of tension, but the details of their relationship are their own. I can't claim to know the ins and outs of their marriage."

Detective Harper, noting the subtle nuances of Diane's emotions, continued her questioning, seeking to unravel the layers of the friendships that had become entangled in Sophia's demise. The once-secluded room echoed with echoes of truth and deception, the shadows of the past converging in a chilling dance that would eventually reveal the intricate motives behind the murder at Tranquil Haven Spa.

Detective Harper's keen eyes scanned the room that once bore witness to the intricacies of Diane and Mia's relationship. The atmosphere was fraught with tension, mirroring the complexities that had come to light. As Harper observed the details within the room, she couldn't help but notice a subtle discrepancy that set off a faint alarm.

Amid personal effects and scattered belongings, only one cosmetic case caught Harper's attention. It was an anomaly, given Olivia's claim that she had gifted each friend with a similar case. Mia's room, too, had lacked evidence of such a cosmetic case.

This incongruity raised questions in Harper's mind. Was Olivia being deceptive about the cosmetic gifts, or was there a possibility that these cases were being hidden? The lipstick-stained champagne glass served as a breadcrumb leading Harper into the intricate labyrinth of friendships, betrayals, and hidden motives that surrounded Sophia Turner's tragic fate.

Detective Harper, her instincts honed by years of investigation, approached Diane with the subtle question, "Is this your cosmetic case?" Her gaze fixed on the lone case that stood out in the room.

Diane, her eyes still swollen from grief, shook her head, denying any ownership of the cosmetic case. "No, that's Mia's," she replied, her voice tinged with a mix of sorrow and resignation.

Harper carefully opened the cosmetic case, revealing its contents. Nestled inside, she discovered an open lipstick container, its color perfectly matching the shade found on the champagne glass. The Detective's sharp eyes took in this critical piece of evidence. This revelation could potentially tie Mia to the scene of the crime.

Diane, her eyes fixed on the open lipstick container in Mia's cosmetic case, hesitated for a moment before speaking. "Detective, I couldn't wear cosmetics even if I wanted to. I'm deathly allergic to most kinds. It's one of the reasons Mia and I got along so well—she never had to worry about me using her makeup."

Detective Harper absorbed this information, her expression remaining neutral. She made a mental note to verify Diane's allergy claim with medical records, recognizing the potential significance of the lipstick's presence in the case. The investigation was reaching a critical juncture, and each revelation brought the detective one step closer to unraveling the truth behind Sophia's tragic demise.

As Detective Harper navigated through the emotional minefield of Diane's reactions, the once-secluded room became a silent witness to the shattered bonds that defined the friends' relationships. The revelations continued to unfold, leaving behind a lingering sense of unease as Harper probed deeper into the interconnected lives of those entangled in the web of suspicion and betrayal.

Diane, starting to sob again, asked Detective Harper for privacy. Detective Harper, respecting Diane's request, nodded and began to leave the room. As she glanced back before closing the door, she caught a glimpse of Diane tossing the open lipstick container into a nearby garbage can. The action struck her as odd since Diane had claimed to be deathly allergic to cosmetics. A sense of intrigue lingered in the air. Harper made a mental note to retrieve the discarded container discreetly for further examination, recognizing that even the smallest detail could hold a crucial piece of the puzzle.

Detective Harper left Diane's room, her mind buzzing with the various threads of the investigation. As she walked down the corridor, she noticed Ava storming out of the room Emily had been staying in, her expression a mix of distress and anger. Harper attempted to engage her in conversation, but Ava briskly passed by, muttering a curt "Not now."

Curiosity piqued; Harper decided to check on Emily. A knock on her door yielded no response. The Detective then set out to find Ava, initially losing track of her movements. Eventually, Harper located Ava in the spa restaurant, seated at a table with Mark, Emily's husband. The Detective approached them, noting the atmospheric charm of the restaurant with its soft lighting and tranquil ambiance.

"Is it alright if I join you?" Harper inquired, her voice a mix of professionalism and casual curiosity. She pulled out a chair, observing the intricate dynamics happening at the table. Ava, the impressionist artist with a history of issues with Sophia, and Mark, Emily's husband in a strained relationship, were the only occupants present, leaving Emily as the elusive missing piece in the unfolding puzzle.

Detective Harper settled into the chair, her gaze shifting between Ava and Mark. "I saw you leaving Emily's room just now. What were you two discussing?"

Ava hesitated, her eyes flickering as she searched for a response. "We were just talking, trying to make sense of everything that's happened."

Harper observed the subtle exchange between Ava and Mark. "Is everything okay, Ava? You seem upset."

Ava glanced at Mark; her discomfort evident. "It's just a lot to process. Sophia's death, the investigation... It's overwhelming."

Mark, silent until now, spoke up. "We're all feeling the weight of it. It's just hard to wrap our heads around."

Detective Harper nodded, sensing there was more beneath the surface. Detective Harper leaned in, her focus shifting to Mark. "Mark, can you shed some light on the strained relationship between Emily and Sophia? Did they have any recent conflicts or unresolved issues?"

Mark sighed, his shoulders slumping slightly. "It's complicated. Sophia and Emily have clashed in the past, mainly about Emily's demanding career. Sophia thought Emily wasn't prioritizing their relationship."

Harper cut to the chase; her gaze focused on Mark. "I recently learned about the affair between Emily and Mia. Did you have any knowledge of this before?"

Mark's eyes widened in surprise. "An affair? No, I had no idea. Emily and I have our issues, but I didn't expect something like that."

Detective Harper leaned forward, studying Mark's reaction with a scrutinizing gaze. The spa restaurant, once a haven of tranquility, now crackled with unspoken tension as Harper delved into the intricate dynamics of the relationships.

"Emily and Mia were having an affair," Harper reiterated, watching Mark's expressions closely.

Mark, a cocktail of surprise and disbelief written across his face, stammered, "Emily and Mia? I find that hard to believe. We've had our problems, but infidelity?"

Detective Harper maintained her composed demeanor. "You seem genuinely surprised. Are you telling me you had no inkling of this affair, Mark?"

Mark hesitated, the weight of the revelation settling in. "I swear, Detective, I had no idea. This is... it's shocking."

Sitting beside Mark, Ava remained silent, her eyes focused on the table. Detective Harper redirected her attention to Ava, "And you, Ava? Any insights into Emily's relationship or any knowledge of this affair?"

Ava's silence hung in the air, and Mark interjected, "Ava is a friend. We've been supporting each other through tough times. I can vouch for her innocence in this matter."

Detective Harper continued to probe, "Mark, given this revelation, do you have any suspicions about why Emily might be having an affair with Mia?"

Mark ran a hand through his hair, grappling with the unfolding reality. "We've been distant, but this? I need to talk to Emily and get some answers. It's hard to believe she'd do something like this."

Ava, her gaze avoiding Harper's eyes, responded, "I had no clue about that. I'm just here to clear my head after the divorce."

Harper, adept at reading between the lines, pressed further. "Given the recent revelations, do you have any insights into Emily's relationship with Mark? Any tensions or conflicts that you've observed?"

Glancing uncomfortably at Ava, Mark replied, "Our marriage has been strained, but I didn't think Emily would resort to having an affair. As we've both said, Ava is a friend. We've been supporting each other through tough times."

Sensing an undercurrent beneath their responses, Harper continued her questioning. "Ava, did you witness any conflicts between Emily and Mark during your stay here?"

Ava hesitated before answering, "There were moments, but relationships are complicated. I didn't think it was my place to pry."

Ava sighed; her gaze momentarily distant as she recollected the recent events at Tranquil Haven Spa. "But there was this one evening a bit ago," she began, her voice tinged with hesitation. "We were all in a lounge, and the atmosphere was already charged with tension. Emily and Mark had been having arguments—nothing too loud or overt, but you could feel it in the air."

Detective Harper leaned in, her interest piqued. "What happened that evening?"

Ava continued, "Emily was talking about her demanding job and the pressure, and Mark was trying to be supportive. But you could sense the strain. Sophia, being the mediator she always tried to be, suggested they take a walk, maybe clear their heads. It seemed like a reasonable suggestion at the time."

Harper's expression remained neutral, encouraging Ava to reveal more.

"They left together, and we assumed they were going to sort things out," Ava recounted. "But when they returned, the tension hadn't lifted. Emily looked even more agitated, and Mark seemed frustrated. It was as if the walk had escalated their disagreement instead of resolving it. Isn't that true, Mark?"

Mark, listening intently, said nothing.

Detective Harper considered Ava's account, recognizing the significance of the evening and its potential connection to the underlying tensions within the group. "Did you notice anything unusual during their walk or when they returned?"

Ava hesitated before responding, "Not during the walk, but when they returned, Emily went straight to the lounge, and Mark disappeared into his room. It felt like something had shifted, like an undercurrent of unresolved issues was pulling them apart."

Harper thanked Ava for her insight, realizing that the evening stroll might hold more clues than initially apparent.

Harper turned her attention to Ava. "Ava, Olivia mentioned giving all of you a cosmetic case. Did you receive one, and what did you think of it?"

Ava nodded. "Yes, I got one. Being an artist, I appreciated the unique array of colors. Olivia has a great eye for aesthetics. The lipstick, especially, had some intriguing shades."

Detective Harper observed Ava closely and couldn't help but notice the vibrant lipstick shade the artist was currently wearing. "Ava, do you always wear Olivia's lipstick, or is this a recent addition?"

Ava touched her lips, a faint smile playing on her face. "Actually, I decided to try it out today. It's such an intriguing shade, and I thought it would be a nice change. What do you think?"

Harper's mind raced as she compared the lipstick on Ava's lips to the sample found on the champagne glass. The unique array of colors Olivia had gifted seemed to have a distinctive mark, and Harper was determined to follow this lead in the intricate investigation unfolding at Tranquil Haven Spa.

As Ava excused herself from the table, her hand grazed Mark's shoulder with a subtle, practiced ease. Detective Harper, ever attentive to details, couldn't help but notice the nuanced interaction. A fleeting touch, almost imperceptible, left the Detective pondering the nature of the relationships within the group. Harper filed away the observation, adding a new layer of complexity to the web of connections surrounding Sophia's untimely demise.

As the sun dipped below the horizon, casting long shadows across the tranquil spa grounds, Detective Harper concluded the intense round of questioning. The tangled web of relationships and hidden tensions had been laid bare, each revelation deepening the mystery surrounding Sophia Turner's tragic demise.

Leaving Tranquil Haven Spa temporarily, Detective Harper returned to the CSI building, determined to sift through the evidence collected from the crime scene. The yoga room, once a serene sanctuary, now held the key to unlocking the secrets of that fateful night. Harper's mind buzzed with the fragments of conversations, the subtle contradictions, and the potential motives that had emerged during the interviews.

The CSI team awaited her arrival, ready to analyze the footprints, fingerprints, and any clothing swatches left at the crime scene. Security camera footage would be scrutinized, and every inch of the spa would be combed for overlooked clues. Harper knew that the answers lay in the meticulous examination of the details—the threads that, when woven together, would unveil the truth behind Sophia's murder.

As the night settled over Tranquil Haven Spa, the remaining friends, unaware of the ongoing investigation, gathered for a cocktail gathering and evening dinner. The spa, now shrouded in darkness, would soon witness the convergence of its guests, each carrying the weight of their secrets. Detective Harper, driven by an insatiable need for justice, prepared to reenter the intricate dance of relationships, deception, and hidden motives that had become the backdrop of this chilling mystery. The night held the promise of revelations, and the spa's walls whispered of untold stories waiting to be unraveled.

Reflections of Guilt

As the golden hues of the setting sunbathed Tranquil Haven Spa in a warm glow, the cocktail party emerged as a lavish affair, a display of opulence against the serene backdrop. The sprawling garden, adorned with twinkling fairy lights, transformed into a realm of sophistication, inviting guests into an oasis of extravagance.

The cocktail party boasted an extravagant spread of hors d'oeuvres carefully crafted by the spa's renowned chefs. Silver platters adorned with delicacies floated through the crowd, offering a tempting array of culinary delights—smoked salmon canapés, truffle-infused bruschetta's, and miniature caprese skewers. The air carried the tantalizing aroma of exotic spices and culinary mastery.

In the heart of the garden, where the reflective pool shimmered under the moonlit sky, a live jazz band played a melodic ensemble, enhancing the ambiance with soulful tunes. Elegant tables, draped in silk and adorned with flickering candles, provided intimate spaces for conversation, adding a touch of romance to the air.

The bar, a gleaming fixture, offered an array of signature cocktails and a selection of the finest wines. Mixologists, clad in black tie attire, skillfully crafted concoctions that delighted the palate. Glasses clinked in a symphony of celebration, and the effervescent laughter of guests resonated through the spa, creating an illusion of blissful normalcy.

Attendees, dressed in a display of extravagance, showcased a spectrum of haute couture. Sequined gowns, tailored suits, and stylish ensembles adorned the guests, reflecting a blend of sophistication and individual flair. The spa's grounds transformed into a runway of luxury and elegance.

Against this backdrop of extravagance, the reflective surfaces of Tranquil Haven Spa took on a dual role—capturing the beauty of the moment while subtly mirroring the complexities within each guest. As the night unfolded, the juxtaposition of luxury and hidden motives set the stage for a dramatic unveiling of guilt and self-discovery. Amid the celebration, the shadows of truth and deceit danced, waiting for the right moment to emerge from the depths of the spa's opulent facade.

Olivia Barnes, the embodiment of elegance and success, arrived at the opulent cocktail party with an air of sophistication that seamlessly blended with the luxurious ambiance of the spa. Her silver sequined dress shimmered under the soft glow of chandeliers, reflecting the radiance of her achievements. As the first to arrive, Olivia's entrance set the tone for the evening, yet her eyes, while radiating poise, hinted at the unresolved tensions within the group. The reflective surfaces mirrored not only her flawless appearance but also the complexities of her relationships, laying the foundation for an evening that promised to unravel the intricacies concealed beneath the facade of tranquility.

Mia, draped in a gracefully crimson evening gown, entered the scene with an aura of composed sophistication. Yet, within her eyes flickered a tempest of emotions hidden behind a facade of poise. The sparkle of a diamond pendant around her neck stood out against the weighty secret she bore—the disclosed affair with Emily. By her side stood Diane, her spouse, who, fully aware of the complexities beneath the surface, provided silent support during the impending storm.

Diane, draped in a midnight blue evening gown, arrived alone, her demeanor a mix of sadness and introspection. Having previously confided in Sophia about her failing marriage to Mia, she navigated the gathering with a heavy heart. The friends exchanged furtive glances, sensing the intricate web of relationships beginning to fray.

Mark, donned in a meticulously tailored navy suit, entered the gathering with his wife, Emily. Despite their marital connection, an unmistakable chill surrounded their interactions, apparent to keen observers. Aware of the disclosed affair between Emily and Mia, Mark attempted to engage with the group. However, his eyes betrayed a sense of confusion, and as glances were exchanged among the friends, an unspoken tension permeated the air, forewarning that the evening held revelations that could strain the bonds of their once seemingly unshakeable friendship.

Emily, adorned in a flowing emerald gown, made her entrance hand in hand with her husband, Mark. Unseen by him, she carried the heavy burden of an affair with Mia. Her once lively eyes now betrayed a subtle tinge of guilt as she maneuvered through the social intricacies. The atmosphere around her crackled with palpable tension, accentuated by the covert glances exchanged between the friends, revealing an underlying coldness and distrust in her relationship with Mark.

Richard, the epitome of composure in a classic tuxedo, arrived solo, a glimmer of concern in his eyes. Unfamiliar with the unfolding drama, he keenly observed the subtle shifts in dynamics among the friends. The atmosphere crackled with unspoken revelations, each grappling with their individual secrets. Meanwhile, Richard awaited Olivia's fashionably late entrance, a hint of perturbation coloring his stoic demeanor.

As Olivia gracefully entered the cocktail party, the silver sequined dress shimmering under the ambient lights, the room took a collective breath. Her presence, though sophisticated, carried an undercurrent of tension. The nuances of her success, intertwined with unspoken judgments within the group, were reflected in the exchanged glances.

Clad in a classic tuxedo, Richard greeted her with a polite smile, but his eyes couldn't mask the glimmer of concern. Olivia sensed his unspoken questions as he subtly inquired, "You're fashionably late tonight. Everything alright?"

Olivia offered a tight-lipped smile, her gaze momentarily distant. "Just caught up in some work-related matters," she replied, her tone maintaining the composed exterior. The spa's reflective surfaces silently witnessed the strained exchange, capturing the echoes of unspoken conflicts.

Ava, the impressionist artist, made a grand entrance in a vibrant, flowing dress that mirrored her artistic spirit. The room stirred as she walked in, her presence captivating yet tinged with unresolved conflicts with Sophia. The unspoken tension she carried manifested in the charged atmosphere around her.

As Ava's eyes met those of the friends, a subtle exchange of glances unfolded. Unbeknownst to others, Ava's gaze lingered momentarily on Mark, whom she had been seen with in the spa's restaurant earlier by Detective Harper. The reflective surfaces of the spa captured this fleeting connection, adding layers to the intricate dynamics at play.

Meanwhile, Emily, dressed in a resplendent emerald gown, couldn't help but notice the exchanged glances between Ava and her husband, Mark. A palpable tension emerged as the complexities within the group heightened. Initially intended for relaxation, the evening transformed into a canvas of swirling emotions and unspoken conflicts.

As the friends mingled in the opulent setting, their uneasiness marked their interactions. The reflective surfaces, once a symbol of tranquility, now mirrored the fractures in their relationships. Each gaze, laden with secrets and guilt, heightened the anticipation of an inevitable confrontation as the night unfolded.

Amidst the elegant ambiance of the cocktail party, the clinking of glasses and murmurs of conversation enveloped the room. Mia moved through the gathering with a composed exterior that belied the storm of conflicting emotions. The revelation of her affair with Emily had cast a shadow over the tranquility of her marriage to Diane.

As Mia circled the room, the reflective surfaces of the spa mirrored the tumultuous undercurrents of her soul. Guilt and regret, hidden behind a stoic facade, emerged like ripples on a once-quiet pond.

The pivotal moment arrived when Mia's path intersected with Diane's. The air crackled with tension as the two women faced each other, their unspoken turmoil laid bare. The subtle shifts in dynamics were palpable, and the friends in attendance exchanged uneasy glances as they sensed the impending confrontation.

At the lavish cocktail party, the strains of the harpist's melody created an illusion of tranquility, masking the storm brewing between Mia and Diane. The two women locked eyes across the opulent space, their unspoken tension palpable to those closest to them. Initially, their conversation unfolded in hushed whispers, exchanging carefully chosen words like a delicate dance of swords.

Mia attempted to maintain a facade of normalcy despite the weight of guilt etched on her face. "Diane, there's something we need to address," she began, her voice barely audible over the ambient sounds of the party. Though betrayed and wounded, Diane met Mia's gaze with a stoicism that belied the turmoil beneath.

Diane, her composure momentarily unbroken, faced Mia with a measured tone. "This is not the time or place," she replied, her eyes searching Mia's for any sign of sincerity.

As the conversation progressed, the harpist's melody seemed to fade into the background, drowned out by the weight of the unresolved conflict. The whispers became more audible exchanges, their words now like daggers cutting through the strained atmosphere. Mia tried to explain the complexities of their situation and the reasons behind her choices. Still, each word seemed to deepen the wound.

Diane, no longer able to maintain her composed exterior, expressed her refusal to play along with the facade of normalcy. "I won't pretend everything's fine, Mia. Not here, not now," she asserted, her voice carrying a mix of betrayal and hurt.

The onlookers, previously engaged in their own conversations, began to notice the escalating tension between the two women. The reflective surfaces of the spa captured the shifting emotions, turning the once-tranquil setting into a battleground of exposed secrets.

Their voices echoed through the opulent space as Mia and Diane's argument reached its zenith. The friends, now drawn into the unfolding drama, exchanged uneasy glances, unsure how to navigate the fractures in their once-close-knit group.

As the intensity of Mia and Diane's argument reverberated through the abundant space, Emily, recognizing the need for intervention, hurried over to mediate. Her emerald gown swirled around her as she approached, attempting to diffuse the escalating tension between the two women.

"Mia, Diane, let's not do this here. We're at a party, trying to release some of the grief from Sophia's murder." Emily pleaded, her voice a calming melody against the discordant backdrop.

However, instead of easing the situation, Emily's presence seemed to add fuel to the fire. Her eyes ablaze with anger and hurt, Diane turned her attention to Emily. "Don't you dare try to play the peacemaker, Emily? You've already done enough damage," Diane seethed, her words cutting through the strained air.

Mia, caught in the crossfire, attempted to interject, "Diane, please, let's talk about this later." But Diane's emotions, fueled by betrayal and frustration, reached a breaking point.

"Later? No, Mia. We're going to settle this now," Diane declared, her voice rising. The onlookers, previously silent witnesses, exchanged uneasy glances as the once-elegant affair spiraled into a public spectacle.

Emily, feeling the weight of the accusations, tried to maintain composure. "Diane, we can find a more private place to discuss this," she suggested, her eyes pleading for understanding.

However, Diane, unyielding in her resolve, unleashed her pent-up emotions. "Private? Do you think you can just destroy our marriage and then suggest a private conversation? Sophia warned me about you, about both of you!" Diane's revelation hung in the air, a bombshell that shattered the fragile calm.

The revelation echoed through the room, creating a ripple effect of shock among the friends. Emily, confronted not only by Diane's anger but also by the mention of Sophia's warning, found herself at the storm's epicenter. The once-tranquil spa, now a stage for exposed secrets and shattered relationships, witnessed the aftermath of a friendship on the brink of collapse.

Mark rushed to Emily's side as the tumultuous scene unfolded, determined to quell the escalating confrontation. "Emily, come on. Let's get out of here," he urged, his tone a mix of concern and frustration.

Mia, however, intercepted Mark, her eyes flashing with defiance. "Stay out of it, Mark. This is between Emily and me," she asserted, unwilling to let him intervene in the unfolding drama.

Ava, witnessing the confrontation, recognized the need for assistance. She approached, her vibrant dress contrasting with the growing darkness of the emotional atmosphere. "Mark, let's give them some space," she suggested, grabbing his arm and attempting to guide him away from the heated exchange.

Emily, however, turned her attention to Ava, her eyes narrowing with accusation. "You too, Ava? Don't pretend to be the innocent one here. I know all about you and Mark," she declared, shoving Ava aside, adding another layer of tension to the already charged atmosphere.

The friends, now fully drawn into the chaotic spectacle, exchanged uncertain glances. The once-elegant cocktail party had transformed into a stage for the exposed wounds and unraveling relationships among the friends. As Emily and Mia's confrontation unfolded, each revelation echoed like a dissonant note, threatening to shatter the remaining fragments of their once-close-knit circle.

Amid the growing chaos, Olivia observed the scene with concern and discomfort. Richard, standing nearby, sensed the escalating tension and exchanged an uneasy glance with Olivia. The shadows of their own secrets and connections with the deceased Sophia loomed large amid the unfolding turmoil.

The confrontation took a darker turn as Emily's accusations against Ava reverberated through the room. Unable to contain her emotions, Mia lashed out with a sharp retort. "Don't act innocent, Emily. Sophia warned me about you."

The mention of Sophia's name hung like a chilling breeze, casting a solemn pall over the gathering. The friends, now entangled in a web of revelations and accusations, stood witness to a confrontation that transcended the boundaries of their individual secrets.

Attuning to the unfolding drama's nuances, Richard stepped forward, attempting to mediate. "Enough of this. Let's not forget why we're here. Sophia's gone, and we need to find out who's responsible."

The room fell into silence, the weight of Sophia's absence echoing through space. Emily and Mia, still locked in a tense stand-off, reluctantly turned their attention to Richard's words.

Olivia, realizing the gravity of the situation, took a step forward, "Richard's right. This isn't helping anyone. We need to focus on finding the truth about Sophia's murder."

As the friends attempted to regain control of the spiraling confrontation, the spa's reflective surfaces seemed to mirror the fractured relationships and unresolved conflicts. The once-tranquil haven now echoed with the dissonance of exposed secrets and the haunting specter of Sophia's untimely demise.

Detective Harper silently returned to the Spa and observed the tumultuous scene unfolding among the friends and emerged from the shadows just as the echoes of Emily and Mia's confrontation faded into a heavy silence. Her presence, previously unnoticed, cast a sobering effect on the gathering. Olivia, Richard, and Ava exchanged uneasy glances while Mark, Emily, Mia, and Diane stood awkwardly.

As Harper approached, her gaze met Emily's, acknowledging the moment's gravity. "Is everything okay here?" Harper inquired calmly, though her keen eyes hinted at the intensity of her scrutiny.

Before anyone could respond, Emily, overcome with emotion, stormed away, a gust of tension trailing behind her. Mia followed suit, leaving Mark and Diane to share a solemn look. Olivia, Richard, and Ava exchanged uncertain glances, the spa's reflective surfaces mirroring the fractured lines of their friendships.

Standing at the center of the lingering unease, Harper addressed the remaining friends. "It seems there are layers to this mystery that we've yet to uncover. Tomorrow morning, I'll need all of you back here for further inquiry. The CSI lab has provided some crucial information, and we need to get to the bottom of this together."

Harper left the group in the fading echoes of the strained evening, the reflective surfaces of the spa capturing the turmoil etched across their faces. The friends dispersed, each carrying the weight of their secrets and the looming specter of Sophia's unsolved murder.

Silent Threads Unraveled

The sterile hum of fluorescent lights cast a bright, clinical glow, illuminating the bustling scene within the CSI lab. The labyrinthine facility unfolded before Detective Harper; a domain dedicated to decoding the intricate secrets woven into the aftermath of crimes. The rhythmic tap of keyboards, the low murmur of conversations, and the occasional beep of high-tech equipment formed a symphony of investigative activity.

Detective Harper, flanked by seasoned forensic investigators, stepped into the heart of the forensic analysis hub. Sleek stainless-steel tables, each meticulously organized with evidence, stretched across the expansive room. Microscopes, DNA sequencers, and other cutting-edge instruments gleamed under the lights, ready to unveil the hidden narratives concealed within the traces left behind.

Computer monitors flickered with real-time data, displaying complex analyses and simulations. Shelves lined with labeled containers housed various forensic tools, chemicals, and evidence samples. Whiteboards adorned with case notes and diagrams outlined the ongoing investigations, resembling a detective's chessboard where every move held the potential to uncover the truth.

Forensic analysts moved with purpose in the controlled chaos, their attention divided between screens, microscopes, and evidence processing stations. The air bore the faint scent of chemicals and sterile cleanliness, a sensory reminder of the precision required to dissect a crime scene's minutiae.

The CSI lab, a nexus of scientific inquiry and investigative prowess, stood as a testament to the meticulous effort invested in unraveling the mysteries concealed within the traces left behind at Tranquil Haven Spa.

"Meet our lead forensic experts," Harper introduced, gesturing toward the team. Mary Chen, a meticulous analyst with a keen eye for detail, and Alex Rodriguez, an expert in surveillance technology, stood ready to unravel the enigma surrounding Sophia's murder.

Alex, fingers dancing over the keyboard, brought up footage from the spa's security cameras. A mosaic of images appeared on the large monitor, capturing each friend's movement in the hours leading up to the tragic discovery of Sophia's body.

"We've compiled the footage from various cameras, focusing on the area near the yoga studio," Alex explained. "Here's Olivia near the spa entrance around the time of the incident."

The screen displayed Olivia Barnes, her figure gliding past the spa entrance, her poise regal. The timestamp confirmed her presence at a crucial juncture.

"And here's Richard near the yoga studio," Mary added, pointing to another feed. Richard's composed demeanor suggested he was on his way to join Olivia.

Harper leaned in closer to the screen, her eyes fixed on the footage of Richard near the yoga studio. The forensic experts manipulated the controls, adjusting the angle and zooming in to provide a more detailed view. Richard's figure stood next to a door leading to a hallway that, according to Mary, connected to the yoga studio.

"Can we track Richard's movements before this point?" Harper asked, her focus unwavering.

The CSI team swiftly navigated through the timeline, searching for additional footage capturing Richard's path leading up to the moment near the yoga studio. The screen flickered, displaying snippets of Richard in different areas of the spa.

"He's seen in the lounge, the dining area, and the outdoor garden," Alex reported, guiding Harper through the sequence of locations. "It seems he was enjoying the facilities before heading toward the yoga studio."

Harper scrutinized the footage, assessing Richard's demeanor and interactions in the various spaces. She sought any signs of unusual behavior or encounters that might hint at a motive or connection to the crime.

"Can we trace his steps further back?" Harper inquired, her mind racing with the need to reconstruct the events leading up to Sophia's murder.

The team continued their digital journey, mapping Richard's movements with precision. However, the timeline presented a gap before he appeared near the yoga studio door.

"We don't have footage of him coming from another area," Mary explained, pointing out the limitation in their surveillance coverage.

Harper absorbed this information, contemplating the significance of Richard's presence near the yoga studio entrance. The unanswered question lingered, adding another layer of mystery to the intricate web of events surrounding Sophia's tragic demise.

As Harper scrutinized the footage, a pressing thought crossed her mind. "Did either Olivia or Richard go into the yoga studio, or did they exhibit any strange behavior?"

Mary rewound the video to the moment when Olivia neared the spa entrance. "Here's Olivia walking with a champagne glass. Keep an eye on that."

The footage rolled, and Olivia walked gracefully, holding a champagne glass. The image, frozen in time, depicted her entrance into the spa.

"Oddly enough," Mary remarked, "she's seen walking without the glass in the subsequent clips."

Harper furrowed her brows, the subtle details not escaping her detective instincts. "Any signs of Olivia or Richard entering the yoga studio during that time?"

Alex zoomed in on the relevant sections of the footage, meticulously scanning for any movements toward the yoga studio. "No direct entry into the studio. They seem to be heading elsewhere."

Mary chimed in, "It's worth noting that Olivia's actions raise questions. She had the champagne glass at one point, and then it's gone. Did she leave it somewhere or deliberately get rid of it?"

"Let's move on to the champagne glass," Mary suggested, guiding Harper to another section of the lab.

A sterile table held an array of evidence meticulously organized for scrutiny, with the champagne glass positioned at the center. With the precision of a seasoned analyst, Mary donned a pair of latex gloves and began her analysis. She carefully extracted a minute lipstick sample from the rim, placing it on a glass slide for further examination.

"The lipstick on the glass matches the one found on the spa's exterior," Mary explained, her focus unwavering. "Same brand, same shade. We can confidently link Olivia to the glass."

Detective Harper, absorbing the meticulous analysis conducted by Mary, inquired further. "Considering Olivia mentioned giving cosmetic cases to her friends, is it possible someone else might have used that glass?"

Mary, her eyes focused on the evidence before her, nodded thoughtfully. "It's a valid question, Detective. However, we have additional evidence that points directly to Olivia. We found a partial fingerprint on the glass, and when we ran it through the fingerpoint database, it matches Olivia Barnes."

She gestured toward the computer monitor displaying the results, emphasizing the scientific precision involved in the identification process. The digital image of a fingerprint glowed on the screen, a match to Olivia's known profile. Mary continued, "The likelihood of another person coincidentally having the same lipstick and leaving behind a matching partial fingerprint is highly improbable. The evidence aligns with Olivia being the one who used that particular glass."

Harper observed the process, absorbing the weight of this revelation. The connection between Olivia and the champagne glass seemed to solidify, creating a tangible link in the chain of evidence. The spa's reflective surfaces, which once seemed to conceal secrets, were now aiding in exposing hidden truths. Harper nodded, the investigation taking a turn, with Olivia's actions becoming a focal point.

Detective Harper, her curiosity piqued by the developments in the investigation, made her way to the video lab, where the surveillance footage was scrutinized. The air in the lab hummed with the low hum of electronic equipment, and the glow of multiple monitors cast an eerie glow on the investigators hunched over their workstations.

Entering the dimly lit room, Harper acknowledged the dedicated team of technicians and analysts, each engrossed in unraveling the visual narrative captured by the spa's security cameras. As she approached the lead technician, Alex, she could see the playback of the events surrounding Sophia's death.

"What have you got for me, Alex?" Harper inquired; her gaze fixed on the screens displaying different angles from within the yoga studio.

Alex adjusted his glasses and pointed at a particular monitor. "Detective, take a look at this. It's the internal camera footage from the yoga studio. Pay close attention to this moment."

As Harper focused on the screen, a shadowy figure came into view, moving deliberately toward the camera. The obscured lens transformed the scene into a murky tableau, concealing the responsible person's identity. The room descended into darkness, obscuring any further visual information, leaving only the distant sounds of obscured movements.

Harper's investigative instincts kicked into high gear. "Enhance that section," she instructed, squinting at the screen as the technicians worked their magic. The room buzzed with activity as they attempted to unveil the obscured details that held the key to understanding the events leading up to Sophia's tragic demise.

"What's this?" Harper inquired, leaning closer to the screen.

"That's where it gets interesting," Alex replied. "We found some silk threads hanging from the camera. The killer might have accidentally left them while tampering with the equipment."

Mary, meticulously studying the footage, added, "And notice the timing. This happened just before Sophia was found."

As Harper's gaze remained fixed on the screen, the atmosphere in the video lab buzzed with anticipation. The CSI team, diligently analyzing the silk threads discovered near the yoga studio's internal camera, began unraveling the intricate details that would piece together this forensic puzzle.

The lead forensic analyst, Mary, expertly dissected the composition of the silk threads. Her fingers deftly handled the delicate strands, and her expert knowledge allowed her to identify the rare fabric used in Olivia's exclusive fashion designs. The revelation was a profound link between the crime scene and Olivia, the threads of evidence weaving a connection that added complexity to the unfolding mystery.

Absorbed in the revelations, Harper watched as the forensic experts presented their findings. The video lab became a hub of revelations, each piece of evidence shedding light on the shadows that veiled the truth behind Sophia's tragic demise. The reflections of guilt, once obscured, were slowly being illuminated, creating a vivid tableau of the events that led to that fateful night at Tranquil Haven Spa. The intricacies of the investigation were becoming more apparent, but the whole picture remained just beyond their grasp.

The CSI team continued their meticulous examination of the video footage. As they sifted through the digital archives, another intriguing sequence emerged. In this particular clip, Mark and Ava were captured in a clandestine embrace in a dimly lit hallway just outside the yoga studio. Their body language spoke volumes, suggesting an intimacy that transcended the boundaries of friendship.

As the footage unfolded, Sophia, seemingly caught off guard, strolled by the amorous pair. Although the video lacked audio, the tension in the air was palpable. With a discerning gaze, Sophia spoke words that carried weight, a mixture of condemnation and a veiled threat. While silent to the viewers, her lips formed sentences that left an unmistakable impact on Mark and Ava.

The CSI team, equipped with cutting-edge technology, employed forensic lip-reading techniques and advanced audio analysis to decipher Sophia's silent dialogue.

As the words materialized on the screen, the threatening dialogue Sophia had delivered to Mark and Ava became crystal clear. The video captured Sophia's stern expression as she admonished them, her lips forming words that were both a condemnation and a promise of consequences.

Sophia's threat echoed through the silent footage. "If you don't put an end to this affair right now, I won't hesitate to tell Emily the truth. You're playing with fire, and it's time to face the consequences."

The weight of Sophia's words hung in the air, and the expressions on Mark and Ava's faces spoke volumes. The camera revealed Ava's shock as she turned toward the yoga studio entrance, where Sophia had entered, her eyes widening in realization. Before Ava could make a move, Mark stepped in, holding her back with a restraining hand.

Mark's face reflected a mix of concern and anxiety, knowing the gravity of Sophia's threat. The tension in the hallway intensified as Mark, aware of the potential fallout, tried to prevent Ava from confronting Sophia in the yoga studio. The silent exchange portrayed the unraveling dynamics, and the CSI team, with each passing frame, uncovered more threads that wove the intricate tapestry of deceit within the close-knit group of friends.

The CSI team redirected their attention to the array of monitors displaying surveillance footage from the spa's parking lot. As they sifted through the recordings, a scene unfolded on one of the screens: Diane, her expression strained, was attempting to enter a car in the parking lot. Mia rushed over, seemingly in an attempt to prevent Diane from leaving.

In the footage, Mia grasped Diane's arm, trying to pull her away from the car. Diane resisted; the tension palpable even through the silent recording. The struggle escalated, and Mia, seemingly overwhelmed, resorted to a sudden slap across Diane's face. The force of the blow left a momentary shock in its wake, capturing the attention of the CSI team.

Diane, visibly stunned, recoiled from the slap. The parking lot, now a stage for the friends' escalating conflicts, bore witness to this unsettling episode. After a moment of tense silence, Diane's expression, a mix of anger and hurt, abruptly broke free from Mia's grip.

Storming away from the car, Diane retreated into the depths of the spa, leaving Mia alone in the parking lot. The surveillance footage then shifted to reveal a secondary scene: Diane, having returned to the spa, entered the yoga studio. Simultaneously, Mia, her demeanor altered, headed towards the spa's bar. The contrast in their movements spoke volumes about the internal strife brewing within the group.

As the CSI team processed the implications of the recorded interactions, Harper pondered the significance of the confrontations between Diane and Mia, recognizing that the shadows of the past extended far beyond the confines of the tranquil spa. The unfolding revelations cast a disturbing light on the intricate dynamics within the group, hinting at a complex interplay of motives and conflicts that might hold the key to solving the mystery of Sophia's murder.

Detective Harper, absorbing the unsettling scene captured in the parking lot, turned her attention back to the CSI team. Shrouded in the sterile hum of electronic equipment, the room bore witness to the unfolding investigation.

"Any footage of Diane leaving the yoga studio?" Harper inquired; her eyes fixed on the monitors.

Mary, navigating the controls, swiftly pulled up another sequence. The screen revealed Diane emerging from the yoga studio, her expression frantic and unsettled. She took a few steps, paused, and cast a hesitant glance back into the studio before breaking into a run, disappearing from the frame.

The room fell into a heavy silence as the implications of Diane's behavior hung in the air. Harper, contemplative, recognized the significance of Diane's actions. The footage hinted at a moment of internal conflict, a decision made, or a realization that prompted her abrupt departure.

The CSI team, meticulous in their examination, continued to analyze the footage frame by frame, searching for any additional clues that might unravel the mysteries concealed within the tranquil spa. As the screens flickered with the visual tapestry of the friends' intertwined destinies, the shadows of guilt and deception cast their long reach, leaving Detective Harper poised on the brink of discovery.

Harper and the forensic team continued their meticulous examination of the surveillance footage. The monitor displayed a timestamp indicating the critical moment when Ava entered and exited the vicinity of the yoga studio upon discovering Sophia's lifeless body.

As the video played, the atmosphere in the lab became tense. Harper focused intently on the screen, observing Ava's every move. The timestamp revealed the urgency of the situation – Ava had entered shortly before discovering Sophia's body. However, the footage from inside the yoga studio was obscured, the camera having been deliberately covered with silk fabric.

The video from the hallway outside the studio presented a different perspective. The door to the yoga studio swung open, and Ava stepped into the dimly lit space. The timestamp indicated her swift entry, capturing the urgency of the moment. The camera recorded her demeanor, revealing a blend of shock and disbelief as she absorbed the grim reality.

Soon after, Ava exited the vicinity of the yoga studio, her facial expressions transitioning from shock to a mix of sorrow and concern. The timestamp indicated that Ava had moved swiftly, her exit suggesting a sense of urgency, likely to inform the friends of the tragic turn of events.

The compressed timeline, underlining Ava's swift actions, became a crucial piece in the puzzle of Sophia's demise. Absorbing the visual narrative, Harper pondered the significance of Ava's emotions during those fateful moments. The surveillance footage, a silent witness to the unfolding drama, held a key to understanding the initial reactions of one of the closest friends to Sophia.

Detective Harper's brows furrowed in contemplation as the CSI team presented their latest discovery. "We found a cosmetic case hidden in a bush on the spa grounds," Alex reported, gesturing towards the images displayed on the screen. The cosmetic case, identical to the ones distributed among the friends, lay nestled in the foliage, a clandestine repository of potential evidence.

Mia, Emily, Ava, Mark, and the rest of the group had received similar cases as part of the spa's promotional gift. The discovery of a hidden case hinted at a deliberate effort to conceal something—an unsettling revelation that added another layer to the unfolding mystery.

Harper's mind raced, considering the implications. Could the hidden cosmetic case hold clues to Sophia's murder, or was it a mere coincidence?

As the team delved deeper into the analysis, Harper prepared for the impending return to Tranquil Haven Spa, where the friends would be confronted with the threads of truth woven into the fabric of their relationships.

Shattered Reflections

As the morning sun began to ascent over Tranquil Haven Spa, its warm rays painted the picturesque surroundings with a deceptive tranquility. The pristine gardens, the reflective pools, and the serene atmosphere all seemed to belie the tumultuous events that transpired just hours before.

Detective Harper's arrival added a palpable tension to the otherwise serene ambiance. Her unmarked expression betrayed nothing, though her eyes held the weight of the revelations uncovered in the CSI lab. The early light played on the Detective's face, casting shadows that hinted at the complexities she carried. The hushed whispers among the staff and lingering glances from those who had been present the night before underscored the gravity of the situation.

Harper's footsteps echoed in the quiet halls as she made her way to the heart of the spa, a determined presence amid the spa's beauty. The morning seemed almost surreal, a stark contrast to the revelations that awaited the unsuspecting friends who had gathered there, each carrying the weight of their secrets and the consequences of the night that had shattered the illusion of tranquility.

Detective Harper, her gaze focused and demeanor unwavering, gathered the remaining friends in the spa's lounge area. The morning sunlight streamed through the large windows, casting a serene glow over the room, a stark contrast to the intensity that loomed in the air.

"I have more questions," Harper announced, her voice cutting through the uneasy silence. Harper directed everyone to take a seat, her eyes scanning the room as each person settled into the plush chairs. The lounge, usually a space for relaxation and camaraderie, now served as the backdrop for a different kind of gathering—one that would delve into the shadows of the past and the tangled relationships among the group.

The friends, seated within the spa's lounge, exchanged furtive glances as Detective Harper's directive sank in. The morning sunlight played on their faces, revealing expressions ranging from apprehension to outright discomfort. The plush chairs, once inviting, now cradled a group of individuals on edge, each anticipating the probing questions that awaited.

Mark and Emily, seated side by side, exchanged glances that conveyed both shared uncertainty and the strain of their strained relationship. Dressed in a chic ensemble, Olivia occupied a seat near the center, her poised exterior masking the complexities beneath. Ever the composed gentleman, Richard sat beside Olivia, his expression betraying the tension within.

Weariness etched across her face, Diane sought solace near the window as if the sunlit panorama could offer a respite from the encroaching shadows of their unraveling truths. Her determination, a flame still flickering within her tired gaze, hinted at an internal struggle she was yet to articulate.

Mia, the epitome of elegance, maintained her poised demeanor, occupying a chair adjacent to Diane. Her outward composure belied the tempest of emotions swirling beneath the surface. A palpable tension lingered between the two friends, a silent acknowledgment of the unspoken complexities that had strained their relationship.

As the atmosphere thickened with unresolved questions, Diane rose from her seat, feeling the weight of the moment. Determinedly, she moved to another chair on the opposite side of the room, passing by Emily and Mark. Her gaze, filled with disgust and disappointment, conveyed an unspoken message that resonated within the hushed space. The distance she put between herself and the couple hinted at a fracture in their once-close bonds, an undeniable consequence of the revelations that now cast a shadow over Tranquil Haven Spa.

Ava, the impressionist artist with a history of conflicts, took a seat further away, her eyes expressing a blend of wariness and defiance. Positioned at the forefront, Harper surveyed the assembly with a discerning gaze, aware that the spa's lounge was now a microcosm of tangled relationships and unresolved conflicts among the friends.

An unspoken tension hung in the air as the friends settled into their designated spots. The once-familiar space now felt like a courtroom, each chair a witness stand, and the looming questions about to be unleashed served as the prosecutor's argument. The stage was set for a confrontation that would either unravel the web of deception or deepen the mysteries that enshrouded Tranquil Haven Spa.

Having spent hours poring over the results from the CSI lab, Harper was armed with new insights and, more importantly, a keen awareness of the inconsistencies in certain testimonies.

"We'll continue the questioning in the yoga studio, one by one," she announced, her eyes traversing the semi-circle of faces. "I need everyone to be honest and transparent. The truth is our only way forward."

As Harper's gaze traversed the room, she caught the subtle exchange between Mark and Emily. Mark, attempting an air of nonchalance, shifted in his seat, his eyes briefly meeting Harper's before he averted them. The Detective noted the tension in his posture, a telltale sign of nervousness.

Mark's wife, Emily, sat beside him, offering a reassuring smile that didn't quite reach her eyes. Her attempt at composure was evident, yet a flicker of unease lingered beneath the surface. As Emily's eyes met Harper's, a brief moment of acknowledgment passed between them—an unspoken understanding that their facade of normalcy was under scrutiny.

At that moment, Emily's gaze subtly shifted toward Mia, seated across the room. Their connection, hidden behind layers of secrecy, added another layer of complexity to the unfolding drama. Harper, attuned to the dynamics within the group, registered the silent exchange, recognizing the intricate web of relationships that had become entangled in the tragedy at Tranquil Haven Spa.

Olivia, draped in an exquisite gown, exuded an air of composed elegance that masked the turmoil within. Her features, carefully guarded, betrayed little emotion. Richard, attuned to the subtle shifts in his wife's demeanor, exchanged a knowing glance with her. Their silent communication spoke volumes, conveying a shared understanding that eluded the rest of the group.

As Harper observed the interactions, her detective instincts homed in on Olivia's movements. She noticed Olivia's fingers fiddling with the delicate fabric of her dress, a small detail that caught the Detective's attention. It was a subtle manifestation of nerves, a physical manifestation of the underlying tension within.

The air in the room seemed to thicken as Harper cataloged these silent cues. The spa's once-tranquil atmosphere now hung heavy with anticipation, each friend, knowingly or unknowingly, contributing to the palpable sense of unease. Olivia's subtle gesture, though seemingly inconspicuous, added a layer of intrigue to the unfolding investigation.

Diane, positioned near the window, met Harper's gaze with a steely resolve. Mia, seated beside her, exuded a measured calm, though the tension in her shoulders hinted at the internal struggle.

Ava, a bit further away, displayed a mix of defiance and wariness, her eyes meeting Harper's with a challenging intensity. The Detective, accustomed to reading subtle cues, noted the distinct reactions—some faces revealing more than they intended. In contrast, others attempted to mask the truth behind practiced expressions.

The lounge, once a place of relaxation, now transformed into an arena of scrutiny. As Harper prepared to unravel the complexities that had trapped the group, the friends braced themselves for a confrontation that would lay bare the hidden truths and fractured relationships among them.

The friends exchanged uneasy glances, the weight of Harper's words settling over them. As they braced themselves for another round of probing, the Detective's decision on the location of the questioning hinted at a deliberate strategy. The yoga studio, once a haven for serenity, now stood as a potential stage for the revelation of truths and the unraveling of secrets that had been carefully concealed.

"Listen carefully," Harper's voice cut through the anticipatory silence. "We need to maintain the integrity of this investigation. From this moment forward, I don't want any of you discussing the case with each other. No sharing of information, no conferring about what was said in this room or the yoga studio. Understand?"

A collective nod passed through the group, each friend acknowledging the directive with a mix of compliance and unease. The realization that the walls of camaraderie were crumbling under the weight of suspicion settled in, and the once close-knit circle felt the strain of the investigation.

Harper's gaze lingered on each friend, assessing their reactions and commitment to the directive. Satisfied with the acknowledgment, she pointed a stern finger toward the distant entrance of the yoga studio.

"Mark, you're up first. Follow me."

Mark hesitated for a moment, his eyes searching Harper's face for any signs of the impending conversation. "Why me first?" he questioned, a defensive edge creeping into his tone. "What do you want to talk to me about?"

Harper met his gaze evenly, revealing nothing. "We'll discuss that in the studio. Just follow me, Mark."

As they walked through the quiet spa, the air thick with tension, Mark couldn't shake the feeling that the eyes of his friends were drilling into his back. Uncomfortable with the scrutiny, he quickened his pace to match Harper's determined stride.

Upon reaching the yoga studio door, Mark took a deep breath. The room loomed before him; a sanctuary violated by a heinous act. He hesitated, his hand hovering above the door handle. "Why here?" he asked, his voice barely above a whisper.

Harper turned to face him, her expression unyielding. "We need to revisit the scene, Mark. I have questions, and I need your cooperation."

Mark's reluctance was palpable, but he pushed the door open, revealing the serene yet haunting space within. The muted hues of the room seemed to intensify the gravity of the situation. The yoga mats lay in somber silence, and the echoes of that tragic night reverberated through the air.

As Mark entered, the weight of the room pressed down on him. His eyes darted around, avoiding the mat where Sophia's life had been extinguished. The room seemed to pulse with disquieting energy, and Mark couldn't shake the feeling that the air held the secrets he wished to keep buried.

Harper, adopting a measured tone, began her questioning. "Mark, we've reviewed the footage from the security cameras, and certain inconsistencies have come to light. You were seen with Ava in the hallway near the yoga studio the night of the incident. Can you explain the nature of your encounter?"

Mark's eyes darted nervously, the realization sinking in that there was no escaping the scrutiny. "Ava and I were just talking. Nothing more. I didn't even know the cameras were there."

Harper raised an eyebrow, her gaze steady. "Talking about what, Mark? The nature of your conversation becomes significant when it aligns with Sophia's threat towards you and Ava. What was said?"

Mark shifted uncomfortably, choosing his words carefully. "It's personal. Ava and I have our issues, and we were trying to work through them."

Harper pressed on, her knowledge extending beyond the immediate situation. "Sophia's threat suggested a secret between you and Ava. Care to elaborate on what she might have been referring to?"

Mark hesitated, his gaze avoiding Harper's. "Look, we've had some issues, but it's nothing criminal. Just personal stuff that doesn't concern anyone else."

Harper, undeterred, continued her line of inquiry. "The video also captures your interaction with Emily during the party. It seems there's tension between you two. Care to shed some light on that?"

Mark's jaw tightened, his discomfort evident. "Emily and I have our problems, but they're unrelated to what happened to Sophia. We're working on our issues."

Harper, maintaining a scrutinizing gaze, probed further. "Mark, the video footage indicates more than just a casual conversation between you and Ava. There's a level of intimacy that raises questions. How do you explain the closeness captured on camera, especially considering Sophia's threat to expose a secret between you and Ava?"

Mark sighed, his discomfort escalating. "Fine, there's more to it. Ava and I, we had dinner together. It was a moment of weakness, and Sophia found out. She threatened to tell Emily if we didn't stop whatever we were doing."

Harper noted the admission, delving deeper into the dynamics of their relationships. "How did Emily feel about your closeness with Ava? Did she know about the dinner and Sophia's threat?"

Mark's shoulders slumped, a sense of resignation in his voice. "Emily and I have our problems. She's aware that things aren't great between us, but she didn't know about the dinner. Sophia's threat complicated everything. I didn't want Emily to find out that way."

Harper continued to navigate the delicate web of emotions and secrets. "How did you feel about Sophia's threat? Did it influence your actions or feelings towards her?"

Mark's expression tightened, reflecting a mix of frustration and regret. "Sophia knew how to hit where it hurts. Her threat made me uneasy, but I never thought it would lead to... this." He gestured vaguely to the yoga studio, the weight of the situation settling heavily on his shoulders.

Harper nodded, absorbing the information. "We'll discuss that further, Mark. For now, let's move on to the CSI findings." She presented the evidence, showcasing the silk threads found in the studio and linking them to a fabric used in Olivia's designs.

Mark's brow furrowed in confusion. "What does Olivia's fabric have to do with all this?"

Harper clarified, "The silk threads from the crime scene match the fabric used in Olivia's designs. We found traces of it near the yoga studio. Can you think of any reason why Olivia's fabric would be present there?"

Mark's eyes widened with realization. "Oh, Olivia. She's made clothes for almost everyone in the group. Maybe it got there through some of our clothing."

Harper considered the possibility. "We'll explore that angle, but we need to account for every detail. Now, about your relationship with Emily and Ava—who knew about it?"

Mark hesitated, glancing away. "Only Emily and Sophia. We kept it discreetly, or at least, I thought we did."

Harper continued her meticulous questioning, unraveling the intricate connections within the group, each revelation bringing them one step closer to the truth behind Sophia's murder.

Harper released Mark from the intense questioning, directing him to return to the group and sending him on his way with a purpose. "I need Emily in the yoga studio next. Please let her know."

Mark, a mix of relief and uncertainty in his expression, nodded and returned to the group, leaving Harper to prepare for the next round of inquiries.

Mark reentered the main room, his face betraying the gravity of the situation. The group's eyes flickered toward him, each friend wondering what transpired in the sacred confines of the yoga studio. Emily, seated beside Mia, met Mark's gaze, and a subtle tension settled over her features.

"Harper wants to see you next," Mark conveyed in a low voice, his eyes holding a mixture of concern and caution. Emily, momentarily caught off guard, nodded, acknowledging the summons. The atmosphere in the room seemed to tighten as the friends exchanged uneasy glances, aware that each passing moment brought them closer to the heart of the mystery that shrouded Sophia's tragic end.

As Emily rose to follow Mark's directive, her gaze instinctively sought out Diane and Mia, the two women entangled in the complex web of emotions that defined their relationships. A flicker of apprehension danced across Emily's features as she shot a brief, searching glance at Diane, who met her eyes with a stoic reserve that hinted at an underlying current of conflict.

Mia felt Emily's gaze and reciprocated with a fleeting connection. The weight of their shared life loomed between them, intensifying the charged atmosphere in the room. Unspoken words lingered in the air, entangled with the unspoken tensions that surrounded the group.

As Emily walked past Mark, she yearned for a reassuring touch, a connection to ground her in the storm of uncertainty. However, Mark, perhaps grappling with the previous night's revelations, turned away, denying her that comfort. The subtle rejection added another layer to the complex dynamics that unraveled within the group, setting the stage for the next chapter in Harper's meticulous quest for the truth.

Feeling the weight of Mark's rejection, Emily hesitated in the hallway just outside the yoga studio. She took a deep breath, attempting to compose herself before facing the impending questions from Detective Harper. The muted ambiance of the spa corridor contrasted sharply with the tumultuous emotions swirling within her. As she slowly moved toward the open door, Emily's mind replayed the events of the cocktail party, the confrontations, and the unsettling revelations that had fractured the once-close-knit circle of friends.

The door to the yoga studio creaked open, and Emily stepped into the dimly lit space, the hallowed grounds where Sophia's life had taken a tragic turn.

The mats beneath her feet seemed to hold the echoes of the past, and the air carried an almost palpable weight of secrets waiting to be unraveled.

The door swung shut behind her, muffling the sounds of the hallway and enveloping her in the confines of the room where truth and deception coexisted in an intricate dance.

Detective Harper stood near the center of the room, her gaze steady and unreadable. The room's muted colors and calming ambiance juxtaposed with the intensity of the investigation. As Emily approached, she attempted to maintain a façade of composure, her expression blending curiosity and anxiety.

Harper nodded to Emily, gesturing for her to take a seat. The yoga studio, once a haven for peace and introspection, now served as an interrogation room, a stark reminder of the shattered tranquility that had gripped Tranquil Haven Spa.

"Emily," Harper began, her voice measured, "we've been reviewing the CSI findings, and some aspects demand clarification. Take a seat, and let's go through this together."

As Emily settled onto a yoga mat, Harper delved into the details uncovered by the CSI team. The silk threads found in the studio, the lipstick on the champagne glass, and the unsettling footage from various cameras began to weave a narrative, each piece of evidence contributing to the intricate tapestry of the investigation.

Harper's gaze bore into Emily's eyes, her questions cutting through the charged air like a knife. "Emily, the video evidence places you near the yoga studio at a crucial time. Care to explain your presence there?"

Emily hesitated, her eyes flickering for a moment before she composed herself. "I was nearby, but I didn't go inside. I didn't even know what was happening until later."

Harper continued her meticulous probing, unfazed by Emily's initial response. "The footage shows you walking towards the studio. Can you clarify your movements during that time?"

Emily bit her lip, a subtle sign of internal conflict. "I... I might have been heading that way, but something caught my attention, and I changed course. I didn't enter the studio."

Harper raised an eyebrow, her skepticism evident. "The video doesn't lie, Emily. We also have footage of you near the bar. What were you doing there?"

Emily sighed, her composure slipping. "I needed a moment to myself, away from the tension in the group. I didn't realize something terrible was happening until later."

As Harper pressed on, delving deeper into the intricacies of the video evidence, Emily's carefully measured responses began to unravel. The air in the room became charged with the weight of unspoken truths, and each word exchanged between Detective and Emily brought them closer to the heart of the mystery.

Harper, her expression unwavering, shifted the focus of her questioning. "Emily, we're aware of your affair with Mia. Can you tell me when it started and how it might be connected to the events leading to Sophia's death?"

Emily's eyes widened slightly, a mix of surprise and resignation crossing her face. "It's true. Mia and I, we got involved. It started a few months ago. Our marriages were struggling, and we found solace in each other."

Harper nodded, acknowledging the admission. "Now, regarding your relationship with Mark. How would you describe your marriage? Were there conflicts, and did they play a role in your involvement with Mia?"

Emily sighed, her gaze momentarily falling to the floor. "Mark and I had our issues. We drifted apart, and I found myself seeking connection elsewhere. Mia understood, or at least, I thought she did."

Harper pressed on, her questions navigating the complex web of relationships entwined within the group. "How did you feel about the closeness between Mark and Ava, and how much did Sophia know about your affair?"

Emily's eyes darted between Harper's, revealing the weight of guilt. "I knew about Mark and Ava getting close. Sophia warned me, but I never expected it to lead to this. As for my affair, I never thought Sophia knew. It could have added another layer of tension to everything if she did."

Harper leaned forward, her gaze steady. "Sophia's warning—can you elaborate on that? What exactly did she say?"

Emily hesitated, her fingers nervously tracing the edge of the yoga mat. "She told me about Mark and Ava, said she'd expose everything if they didn't stop. I warned her to mind her own business, that my relationships were not hers to meddle with."

The admission hung in the air, revealing a moment of confrontation that had taken place before the tragedy unfolded.

Emily, sensing the weight of her own words, tried to backtrack. "I didn't mean it like that. I was just frustrated, and I never thought it would lead to something like this."

Harper, her intuition honed by years of investigation, continued to peel back the layers of the complex dynamics that had festered within the group. The threads of guilt and resentment began to weave a more intricate tapestry, bringing the friends closer to the heart of Sophia's mysterious demise.

Harper shifted her focus, her gaze unwavering. "Emily, we found a cosmetic case near the crime scene. Do you know anything about it, and where's yours located?"

Emily's eyes flickered with uncertainty, her voice stammering slightly. "Uh, I don't remember where I left mine. I have a few of them, you know, and they kind of get misplaced sometimes."

Harper noted the evasion but continued with her line of inquiry. "And the lipstick container inside? Can you account for its whereabouts?"

Emily's fingers absentmindedly traced the edge of her silk dress, a subtle gesture that did not escape Harper's keen observation. "I... I'm not sure. I switch them around, and I don't keep track."

Harper made a mental note of Emily's response, the cosmetic case potentially holding the key to unraveling more secrets concealed within the threads of the investigation. The labyrinth of deception within the once-close-knit group was becoming more intricate with each revelation.

The yoga studio's serene atmosphere now echoed the confessions and revelations of Emily's tangled relationships. The room, once a sanctuary for self-discovery, bore witness to the unraveling of secrets that had long remained hidden beneath the surface of friendships.

As Emily rose from the yoga mat, Detective Harper nodded and acknowledged her cooperation. "Thank you, Emily. We might need to follow up later if there are further questions."

With that, Emily exited the yoga studio, the door creaking softly as it closed behind her. A sense of unease lingered as she returned to the group in the main room. Emily's eyes scanned the room, seeking out Mark, but he had vanished without a trace, leaving behind a noticeable void. No one noticed his departure, and Emily's attempt to sit next to him went unnoticed.

With that, Emily approached Ava, who was still seated in the main room with the group. "Ava, you're next," she said, indicating the direction of the yoga studio.

As Ava stepped into the yoga studio, the atmosphere seemed to shift, the hallowed space bearing witness to the unfolding drama. Detective Harper, her expression neutral yet probing, gestured for Ava to take a seat on one of the mats. The room retained a quiet tension, each breath echoing the gravity of the situation.

Harper pressed on, her questions methodical. "Let's start with the cosmetic case. We found one hidden in a bush on the spa grounds, the same type everyone received. Any idea how it ended up there?"

Ava hesitated, her composure momentarily faltering. "I... I don't know. Maybe I misplaced it. It's been chaotic lately."

Harper studied Ava's reactions, the subtle nuances that betrayed emotions beneath the surface. Harper observed Ava's unease but chose not to disclose that she hadn't explicitly mentioned the case belonging to Ava. Instead, Harper maintained a neutral expression and acknowledged, "It's understandable that things can get a bit disorganized. If you remember anything or find it later, let me know. We're just trying to piece together the puzzle." Ava nodded, still visibly perturbed.

"Let's talk about the events captured by the security cameras," Harper began, presenting the evidence unveiled by the CSI team. "There's footage of you and Mark in a hallway, which appears more than just a casual conversation. Care to explain what was happening?"

Ava's eyes flickered with a mix of surprise and concern. "Mark and I were just talking," she replied, her voice steady. "There's nothing inappropriate about that."

Studying Ava's reaction, Harper raised an eyebrow as she questioned further. "Mark mentioned there might be more to your relationship than just a conversation. Is that true?"

Ava's gaze wavered momentarily, and a fleeting expression of uncertainty crossed her face. She took a breath before responding, "We've had some disagreements, but it's nothing more than that. We were just trying to sort things out."

Harper observed Ava closely, detecting a subtle nuance in her response. "When you say, 'sort things out,' do you mean Mark might have misunderstood the nature of your relationship and the dinner you had?"

Ava hesitated, her fingers lightly grazing the edge of her dress. "It's possible," she admitted, her voice softening. "I think Mark may have misread things. Our dinner was about closure, not rekindling anything."

Detective Harper, her keen intuition ever at play, leaned forward slightly, her eyes narrowing as she probed deeper into Ava's words. "Closure? That's an interesting choice of words. Care to elaborate on what kind of closure you were seeking with Mark?"

Ava shifted uncomfortably in her seat, the weight of unspoken history lingering in the air. "Mark and I had some unresolved issues from the past. We needed to address them, put them to rest, for the sake of moving forward."

Harper, not one to let vague explanations pass, pressed further. "Unresolved issues? Could you be more specific? It might help in understanding the dynamics at play here."

Ava hesitated, a fleeting moment of vulnerability crossing her features. "We had an affair years ago. It was a mistake, but it happened. I wanted to ensure we had no lingering feelings or misconceptions. We needed closure."

Harper's eyebrows raised subtly, recognizing the complexity introduced by this revelation. "So, you and Mark were romantically involved in the past. And this dinner was to ensure there were no misunderstandings about your current relationship?"

Ava nodded; her gaze fixed on a distant point as if retracing the steps of her tangled history. "Exactly. I wanted to clear the air and move forward with a clean slate. Nothing more."

Detective Harper filed away this new piece of information, recognizing its potential significance in the intricate web of relationships that had woven itself around the tragic events at Tranquil Haven Spa.

As Harper delved deeper into the intricacies of Ava's connection with Mark, the layers of their story began to unfold, revealing more complexities beneath the surface. The room retained an air of anticipation, waiting for the next revelation to shed light on the shadows surrounding Sophia's tragic end.

Harper shifted the focus of her questioning, her tone measured. "There's another aspect we need to discuss, Ava. The video showed Sophia walking by you and Mark outside the yoga studio. Can you tell me what she said to you during that encounter?"

Ava responded with a forced smile, "Oh, she just said hello and wished us a good night. Nothing more."

Harper's gaze remained steady, "I appreciate your honesty, Ava. However, our CSI team was able to analyze the audio, and it seems Sophia's words were quite different from what you've just shared."

Ava's composure cracked, replaced by a mix of frustration and anger. "I don't have to sit here and be accused of things I didn't do. If you have any more questions, talk to my lawyer." With that, Ava stood abruptly and stormed out of the room, leaving an atmosphere of tension and unanswered questions.

Ava stormed out of the yoga studio, her swift and purposeful strides carrying her through the room where the remaining friends waited anxiously. She didn't utter a word, and the air seemed to thicken with tension in her wake. The friends exchanged uneasy glances, uncertainty lingering like a cloud.

As Ava disappeared down the hall, Harper exited the yoga studio with a measured expression and entered the room where the remaining friends waited.

As Harper entered the room, the friends turned their attention toward her, expressions marked with concern and anticipation. The atmosphere was charged with an unspoken tension, the recent events leaving them on edge.

Amid the tumultuous scene, Olivia's voice sliced through the chaos like a sharp blade. "Harper, what the hell happened with Ava? You can't just let her storm off without an explanation!" Her eyes bore into Harper, demanding answers that were yet to be provided.

Mia, standing beside Olivia, added to the growing chorus of voices. "This is ridiculous! We need to know what's going on. Ava can't just leave like that!" Her words carried a mix of urgency and frustration, reflecting the shared sentiment of the group.

Richard, usually composed, found himself swept up in the rising tide of emotion. "Harper, we deserve to know the truth. What's going on with Ava, and why is this investigation causing such chaos?" His inquiries were pointed, his eyes narrowing as he awaited a response.

Diane, losing her patience with the unfolding mystery, shouted across the room, her voice cutting through the clamor. "Enough of this secrecy, Harper! Tell us what's happening, or we'll have no choice but to find out on our own!" The frustration in her voice mirrored the growing tension in the room.

In the midst of the cacophony, Emily's voice rose above the others, expressing a blend of frustration and concern. "We came here to relax, not to be interrogated and torn apart. What's the point of all this, Harper?" Her words echoed the sentiments of those who felt the weight of the investigation bearing down on them.

Harper, facing the barrage of questions and demands, held up her hands in an attempt to restore order. "I understand your concerns, but I need your cooperation. I will explain everything in due time.

Right now, I must continue the investigation. Please be patient, and we'll get to the bottom of this together." Despite Harper's attempt to calm the storm, the friends remained on edge, their emotions swirling in the face of the unfolding mystery.

The room buzzed with tension as friends shouted over one another, each desperate for information, their emotions running high in the face of the unfolding mystery. In the eye of the storm, Harper tried to maintain order amid the clamor, ready to resume the investigation and untangle the web of secrets within the group.

"I can't discuss the details at the moment," Harper asserted, her gaze sweeping across the room. "Each of you will have your turn. Right now, I need to continue the questioning." The room fell into a hushed silence, the friends left to grapple with their own thoughts and anxieties, the weight of the investigation pressing down on them.

As the friends exchanged uneasy glances, Harper's attention shifted to the next phase of her meticulous quest for the truth. She needed to continue the questioning, pulling the threads of their interconnected lives tighter, unraveling the intricate tapestry of their relationships, secrets, and, ultimately, the events that led to Sophia's tragic end.

With a determined nod, Harper turned to Olivia and beckoned Olivia to follow her to the yoga studio for the next round of questioning. The friends, still reeling from the abrupt departure of Ava, awaited Olivia's turn, unaware of the revelations that would unfold and the shadows that would be brought into the harsh light of scrutiny.

Detective Harper led Olivia into the yoga studio, the once serene space now transformed into a stage for revelations and interrogations. The echoes of the past lingered in the air, and Olivia couldn't escape the palpable tension that gripped the room. The yoga mats beneath her feet seemed to harbor secrets, and the walls, witnesses to the unfolding drama.

As Olivia settled onto a yoga mat, Harper delved into the details uncovered by the CSI team. The silk threads, the lipstick on the champagne glass, and the unsettling footage began to paint a vivid picture. Harper's questions probed the depths of Olivia's involvement, her connections with other friends, and the motivations that might have influenced her actions.

The air in the room crackled with tension as Harper navigated the labyrinth of her inquiries. Olivia, usually composed, felt the weight of scrutiny. The polished titanium cosmetic case that Olivia had gifted each friend became a focal point. Harper inquired about

Olivia's intention behind the extravagant gifts, the choice of cosmetics, and the underlying dynamics at play.

"And the silk garments?" Harper asked, her gaze unwavering. "Why the elaborate silk wraps, Olivia?"

Olivia, momentarily taken aback, composed herself before responding. "I wanted to create a sense of luxury, a unique experience for each of them. The silk wraps were my way of expressing appreciation for our enduring friendships."

Harper continued, focusing on the champagne glass found near Sophia's body. "The lipstick on this glass matches the one on the spa's exterior. Same brand, same shade. Care to explain how it ended up there?"

Olivia, her features betraying a hint of uncertainty, explained, "I might have used it earlier. It's not uncommon for me to freshen up before an event. As for the glass, I don't recall leaving it anywhere near where Sophia was found."

The discussion circled back to the cosmetic cases. Harper's questions probed deeper into Olivia's relationships within the group, particularly with Sophia.

"What was your relationship with Sophia?" Harper asked, her gaze piercing.

Olivia's response carried a mix of emotions. "Sophia and I had our differences, but I respected her talent. We were friends, but like any friendship, it had its complexities."

Unyielding in her pursuit of the truth, Harper probed deeper into the intricacies of Olivia's relationship with Sophia. Once a haven of serenity, the yoga studio now bore witness to the unraveling dynamics hidden beneath the surface.

Olivia's admission of their differences hung in the air, a tacit acknowledgment of the underlying tensions that had colored their interactions. Harper, keenly observant, sensed there was more to their connection than Olivia was willing to reveal. The lines of Olivia's composed exterior seemed to fray, revealing glimpses of vulnerability.

"And these differences," Harper pressed on, "can you elaborate on what they were? Any specific incidents or disagreements?"

Olivia hesitated, her eyes flickering with a mixture of guardedness and introspection. "Sophia had a way of challenging everyone, pushing boundaries. It sometimes led to clashes of opinions. We had our share of disagreements, especially when it came to creative decisions and the direction of our projects."

The mention of creative differences hinted at a more profound discord, an unspoken struggle for control or influence within their shared endeavors. Harper, attuned to the nuances of human relationships, prodded further, seeking to uncover the layers obscured by Olivia's carefully crafted facade.

"Did these disagreements ever escalate? Was there tension beyond the professional realm?" Harper's questions, like delicate instruments, sought to dissect the complexities of emotions that lingered beneath the surface.

Choosing her words with measured precision, Olivia replied, "At times, the tension spilled over into personal matters. We had clashes of personalities, but I always believed it was part of the creative process. Our friendship weathered those storms."

Noting the evasiveness in Olivia's responses, Harper continued to peel away the layers of their relationship. The air in the studio crackled with unspoken sentiments, and the yoga mats beneath Olivia seemed to bear the weight of unresolved conflicts.

"You mentioned complexities in your friendship," Harper remarked. "Can you elaborate on what those complexities were? Any unresolved issues or lingering resentments?"

Olivia's gaze wavered for a moment, revealing the vulnerability that lay beneath her composed exterior. "Friendships are intricate, Detective. We had our share of ups and downs, moments of camaraderie, and moments of tension. It's the nature of any long-standing relationship."

Detective Harper, sensing there was more to Olivia's connections with both Richard and Sophia, decided to delve into the personal dynamics that could be crucial to understanding the events leading to Sophia's death.

"In the spirit of transparency, Olivia, let's address the personal relationships within the group. Specifically, the dynamics between Richard and Sophia," Harper asserted, her tone measured but probing.

Olivia, now facing the prospect of revealing a concealed chapter from their shared history, took a breath before responding. "Before Richard and I were married, yes, he and Sophia were involved. It was brief, and they decided to end it. However, I always suspected that Sophia wasn't entirely over Richard when we got together."

Harper, recognizing the significance of Olivia's admission, pressed further. "You believed Sophia might still have feelings for Richard even after they ended their relationship?"

Olivia nodded; her gaze fixed on a point in the distance. "It was a hunch, a gut feeling. Sophia was private about her emotions, but I couldn't shake the feeling that she harbored lingering sentiments for Richard. Even after we married, I couldn't shake the suspicion that something between them wasn't entirely resolved."

Detective Harper, now armed with this newfound information, considered the implications of the tangled relationships within the group. The revelation added a layer of complexity to the dynamics between Olivia, Richard, and Sophia, painting a more intricate picture of the emotions that simmered beneath the surface.

Harper, sensing there was more to be unraveled, probed deeper, her questions designed to expose the nuances that Olivia might be reluctant to share. The yoga studio, once a sanctuary, now became the stage for the disclosure of hidden truths, and Olivia found herself navigating the delicate dance between revelation and concealment.

Detective Harper, recognizing the intricate web of emotions within the group, homed in on the personal interactions that had the potential to unravel hidden truths.

"Olivia, did you ever confront Sophia about your suspicions? About her feelings for Richard?" Harper inquired; her gaze unwavering.

Once compelled to reveal a chapter marked by confrontation and warning, Olivia hesitated before responding. "Yes, I did. Sophia and I had a conversation about it. I made it clear that I expected her to stay away from Richard. I warned her in no uncertain terms that any lingering feelings needed to be put to rest. Sophia insisted that she wasn't interested in Richard anymore, but my gut told me otherwise."

Harper absorbed this revelation, recognizing the depth of Olivia's concerns and the tensions that simmered beneath the surface of their friendships. The yoga studio, where revelations unfolded like petals, held echoes of past confrontations and unspoken warnings.

The dynamics between Olivia, Richard, and Sophia were now laid bare, revealing a landscape fraught with complexities, suspicions, and confrontations. Armed with this understanding, Detective Harper continued her meticulous journey through the tangled threads of friendships, hoping to untangle the mysteries surrounding Sophia's tragic demise.

The interrogation turned to Olivia's own silk garment, and Harper inquired about its location. Olivia, subtly fidgeting with the fabric of her dress, struggled to recall its whereabouts.

"I don't remember exactly where I left it. It's been chaotic lately with everything going on," Olivia stammered.

Noting Olivia's unease, Harper pressed on, unraveling the intricate threads connecting Olivia to the unfolding mystery. The yoga studio, once a sanctuary, now bore witness to unraveling friendships and exposing hidden truths. The chapter unfolded as Harper meticulously peeled back the layers, one question at a time, weaving a narrative that would either exonerate or implicate Olivia in the tragic events at Tranquil Haven Spa.

Detective Harper, unwavering in her pursuit of the truth, shifted the focus of her inquiry to the intricacies of Olivia's personal life, honing in on her relationship with Richard. The yoga studio, once a place of tranquility, now echoed with the tension of unanswered questions.

Harper's gaze bore into Olivia's eyes as she posed her next question, "Let's talk about your relationship with Richard. How did he feel about Sophia, and how did Sophia feel about him?"

Olivia, momentarily caught off guard by the shift in the line of questioning, composed herself before responding. "After the early affair, Richard and Sophia had a professional relationship. They collaborated on projects, and while I can't speak for his feelings, I believe it was purely business. As for Sophia, she respected his work but wasn't particularly close to him personally."

Harper, experienced in deciphering the nuances of human relationships, delved deeper, aiming to uncover any layers of sentiment that Olivia might be concealing. "And between you and Richard, were there ever any issues or tensions related to Sophia's involvement in your projects?"

Choosing her words carefully, Olivia replied, "Like any couple working together, we had our challenges. But Sophia was a professional, and her contributions were valuable. There were no significant issues related to our collaborations."

Harper, noting Olivia's composed responses, continued her probing. "Were there any conflicts between you and Richard regarding Sophia's creative input or decisions?"

Olivia's features revealed a fleeting hint of contemplation before she responded, "There might have been disagreements on creative matters, but it was never personal. We all shared a commitment to our projects."

Detective Harper, perceptive to the nuances of Olivia's responses, continued her line of questioning, determined to unearth the buried secrets that connected Olivia, Richard, and Sophia.

"In your collaborations, Olivia, did you and Richard ever encounter situations where Sophia's influence became a point of contention?" Harper inquired, her gaze unwavering.

Despite her composed exterior, Olivia sensed the gravity of Harper's inquiry. She hesitated momentarily before responding, "Our collaborations were generally smooth. Any professional disagreements were managed within the scope of our work. Richard never explicitly expressed discomfort with Sophia's influence."

Harper, noting the carefully chosen words, pressed further. "What about outside the professional realm? Were there any personal dynamics that could have contributed to tensions within the group?"

Olivia, aware that Harper was delving into a delicate territory, chose her words cautiously. "Richard and Sophia had their differences, as any colleagues might. However, these differences never interfered with our collaborations. Our group dynamic was always a balance between personal and professional relationships."

Harper, sensing there was more beneath the surface, shifted her focus to Olivia's interactions with Sophia. "Let's discuss your relationship with Sophia. Were there any unresolved issues, conflicts, or secrets between you two that might shed light on the events leading to her death?"

Olivia's facade wavered, a flicker of vulnerability crossing her features. "Sophia and I had our share of disagreements, but we were friends. There were no lingering issues that would explain what happened at the spa."

Detective Harper, adept at reading between the lines, persisted. "And Richard? Did he ever confide in you about any concerns or conflicts he might have had with Sophia outside the professional realm?"

Olivia, her guard momentarily down, responded with a hint of hesitation, "Richard and Sophia had their differences, but he never explicitly shared personal conflicts with me. Our friendships within the group have always been built on trust and discretion."

As the questioning unfolded, Harper recognized the delicate dance of secrets and alliances within the group. The answers provided by Olivia hinted at concealed tensions and unspoken dynamics, leaving the Detective determined to unravel the threads that bound Olivia, Richard, and Sophia in a complex web of intertwined relationships. The investigation was far from over, and the revelations within the yoga studio promised to expose the hidden truths that lay beneath the surface of their seemingly idyllic friendships.

Detective Harper, with a discerning intuition, recognized the need to delve into Richard's perspective to further unravel the intricate web of relationships surrounding Sophia's tragic demise. She excused Olivia from the yoga studio, instructing her to send Richard in for questioning.

As Olivia returned to the room where the friends were anxiously awaiting their turn, she approached Richard with a subtle urgency. The other friends, curious by Olivia's mysterious demeanor, exchanged speculative glances as the two engaged in a hushed, whispered conversation.

The room buzzed with muted speculation as the friends observed Olivia and Richard in their clandestine exchange. Diane leaned into Emily, his voice low, "What do you think Olivia's telling him? This whole thing is getting weirder by the minute."

Diane, ever observant, shot a concerned look in their direction. "Whatever it is, Olivia seems intent on controlling the narrative. This isn't adding up."

Meanwhile, Mia, who had been quietly watching from a distance, shared a questioning glance with Diane. "Do you think Olivia is trying to influence Richard's statement? This investigation is putting a strain on all of us."

As the friends exchanged wary glances and speculated about the whispered conversation between Olivia and Richard, the tension in the room escalated. Little did they know that Harper's meticulous questioning in the yoga studio was slowly unraveling the threads of deception, bringing them closer to the truth they all sought and feared.

Having received Olivia's whispered reassurance, Richard took a deep breath to steady himself. He cast a calming glance her way, silently conveying that everything would be okay. With an air of newfound confidence, he made his way to the yoga studio, where Detective Harper awaited his turn for questioning.

As Richard entered the room, the once serene space seemed to pulse with the weight of impending revelations. The yoga mats beneath his feet held the echoes of those who had preceded him, each leaving behind a trail of secrets and uncertainties. Richard's demeanor exuded a composed assurance, a facade carefully crafted to conceal any apprehensions or guilt that might lie beneath the surface.

Harper, seated and ready to continue her meticulous inquiry, observed Richard's entrance with a measured gaze. The air in the room crackled with tension as the Detective prepared to unravel the threads of Richard's involvement in the complex tapestry of Sophia's tragic demise.

"Richard," Harper greeted, her tone neutral but probing. "Please, have a seat. We need to discuss some aspects related to Sophia's case."

Maintaining his calm exterior, Richard took a seat, ready to face the questions that would dissect his connections, knowledge, and the web of relationships that defined their tight-knit group. The chapter unfolded as Harper's inquiries delved into Richard's perceptions, shedding light on the dynamics between him, Olivia, and Sophia. Little did Richard know that the unraveling mystery would bring him to a crossroads, where the choices he made during this interrogation would determine his place in the intricate dance of loyalty, deceit, and betrayal.

Detective Harper's gaze lingered on Richard as he settled into the chair, the calm facade he presented doing little to dissuade her keen scrutiny. The yoga studio, now a theater of revelations, awaited the next act in the unfolding drama.

"Richard," Harper began, her tone measured, "let's discuss your relationship with Sophia. How would you characterize it?"

Choosing his words carefully, Richard responded, "Sophia and I had a professional relationship. We worked together, and I admired her talent. Beyond that, we were acquaintances in the group, as friends tend to be."

Richard maintained his calm demeanor but couldn't entirely conceal a flicker of discomfort. "There might have been disagreements, but it wasn't anything out of the ordinary. People have differences. It doesn't mean there's foul play involved."

Harper, undeterred, shifted the focus to the gifts Olivia had presented to each friend. "Olivia's extravagant cosmetic cases—what's your perspective on that? Did it seem like a mere gesture of goodwill, or was there an underlying motive?"

Richard hesitated before responding, "Olivia has a way of showing off her success. It's her nature. The cosmetic cases, though ostentatious, were just her way of sharing her achievements with the group."

Harper, drawing on CSI findings, addressed the silk garments. "The silk wraps accompanying the cosmetic cases—can you shed light on their significance? Did they hold any particular meaning in your understanding?"

Richard, attempting to maintain transparency, explained, "Olivia often includes luxurious items in her gifts. The silk wraps were likely meant to enhance the overall experience. I don't think there was any hidden agenda."

The Detective's inquiries navigated through the intricacies of Richard's relationships within the group, emphasizing Olivia and Sophia's dynamic. The chapter unfolded as Harper meticulously peeled back the layers, probing Richard's perceptions, exposing potential conflicts, and setting the stage for revelations on the horizon. Little did Richard realize that his choices during this interrogation would be crucial in determining the role he played in the labyrinthine narrative of friendships surrounding Sophia's tragic fate.

Detective Harper, her gaze unwavering, leaned forward slightly as she continued her questioning of Richard in the yoga studio. The atmosphere was charged with anticipation, and the echoes of Olivia's whispered concerns lingered in the air.

"Richard," Harper began, her tone measured, "there's something I need to discuss with you. Olivia mentioned a shared past, secrets you both believed were buried. Care to elaborate on that?"

Richard's composure faltered, his eyes meeting Harper's with a mix of surprise and trepidation. The Detective, armed with her thorough investigation and a keen understanding of the dynamics within the group, had unraveled a thread that connected Olivia and Richard to a hidden chapter of their shared history.

"We all have secrets, Detective," Richard replied cautiously, attempting to downplay the significance of their past. "What Olivia and I went through is personal. It has nothing to do with Sophia's death."

Harper, however, persisted. "I beg to differ, Richard. Our investigations sometimes lead us to unexpected places. Olivia and your shared secret might be key to understanding the events that transpired at Tranquil Haven Spa. Can you provide some context? What secrets were you two trying to keep buried?"

Knowing that the revelation was inevitable, Richard took a deep breath before responding. "Sophia and I were romantically involved before, during the early years of our friendship. It was a complicated time, and we decided to end things to preserve our friendships within the group."

The Detective, with a nod of acknowledgment, continued her probing. "Do you believe this past relationship might have played a role in Sophia's death? Any lingering tensions or repercussions from that time?"

Richard, though visibly uncomfortable, asserted, "No, Detective. Our past is just that—past. It has no bearing on what happened to Sophia. We've all moved on."

Detective Harper, recognizing the delicate nature of the situation, delved deeper into the past, seeking to uncover any hidden tensions or repercussions that might have contributed to the tragic events.

"Richard," Harper began, her tone measured, "were you aware that Olivia confronted Sophia about her suspicions regarding your past relationship? Olivia used the words 'In no uncertain terms' when warning Sophia to stay away from you. Were you aware of the extent of Olivia's feelings about this?"

Richard, caught off guard by this revelation, hesitated before responding, "I knew Olivia had reservations about Sophia, but I wasn't aware of the specifics. Our past with Sophia was complicated, and I thought we had put it behind us. Olivia never mentioned the exact nature of her conversation with Sophia."

Detective Harper, sensing the importance of untangling the emotional web within the group, pressed further, her questions probing the heart of the matter.

"Richard, Olivia hinted at her suspicions that Sophia might not have been entirely over you. Can you shed more light on that? Were there any indications that Sophia might have reciprocated those feelings, or was it solely Olivia's perception?"

Grappling with the weight of his admission, Richard sighed before answering, "Olivia's suspicions weren't entirely unfounded. I... I was still pursuing Sophia. I couldn't shake my feelings for her even after Olivia and I got together, even after Sophia and I ended things. It was a complicated time, and I found myself torn between the past and the present."

Harper, recognizing the significance of Richard's revelation, probed further. "So, Olivia's suspicions were rooted in reality. How did this impact the dynamics between Olivia, you, and Sophia?"

Richard, a mix of guilt and regret etched on his face, replied, "It strained our relationship, obviously. Olivia warned Sophia to stay away, and I was caught in the middle, unable to let go of my feelings for Sophia fully. It created an undercurrent of tension that persisted despite our efforts to move forward."

Richard's admission hung in the air, a confession that unraveled the carefully woven threads of their relationship. As he spoke of his lingering feelings for Sophia, Detective Harper delved into the specifics, seeking to unravel the intricacies of the emotional tug-of-war that had played out among Olivia, Richard, and Sophia.

"Can you elaborate on how you tried to maintain contact with Sophia despite Olivia's warnings?" Harper inquired, her tone measured but insistent.

Richard, hesitant but determined to provide a full account, admitted, "I tried to keep in touch with Sophia, subtly at first. Casual conversations, friendly gestures. I told myself it was harmless, that I could navigate the complexities. But Olivia saw through it. She became increasingly angry and frustrated, warning Sophia to stay away from me."

As Richard spoke, the atmosphere in the yoga studio thickened with the weight of unresolved emotions. Harper, keenly observant, noted the impact of Richard's actions on the dynamics between the three friends. Olivia's anger, rooted in the perceived betrayal, had intensified, creating an undercurrent of tension that had lingered, unspoken but palpable.

"And how did Sophia respond to Olivia's warnings?" Harper probed, her gaze unwavering.

Richard sighed, acknowledging the complexity of the situation. "Sophia insisted that there was nothing between us, that she had moved on. But deep down, I think she enjoyed the attention, the validation. It became a source of conflict between Olivia and me."

Detective Harper, navigating the complex web of relationships, probed further into Richard's actions and their impact on the unfolding tragedy. The question lingered in the dimly lit yoga studio, casting a shadow over the trio's tangled dynamics.

"Richard, did your attempts to maintain contact with Sophia extend to the weekend at Tranquil Haven Spa?" Harper asked, her gaze intent on his reaction.

Richard hesitated, the weight of his admission evident in the furrow of his brow. "I did," he admitted, his voice tinged with regret. "The first night at the spa, I went to Sophia's room. I knocked, hoping to talk. But she refused to let me in."

The air in the room grew heavier as Harper probed deeper. "Did Olivia find out about this?" she asked, her keen perception honed on the subtleties of Richard's response.

A moment of hesitation passed before Richard spoke again. "Yes, she saw it from a distance. I wasn't aware Olivia was watching. It escalated our tensions even further."

Detective Harper, recognizing the significance of Olivia's reaction to Richard's attempt to contact Sophia, probed further into the aftermath of that pivotal moment. The room held its breath as Harper inquired, "Richard, what transpired between you and Olivia after she witnessed you knocking on Sophia's door?"

Richard admitted, "Olivia was furious. She confronted me and warned me that she'd take care of it once and for all. I thought she meant she would talk to Sophia, resolve the tension. I never imagined..." His voice trailed off, leaving the unsaid hanging in the air.

Harper, absorbing this piece of the intricate puzzle, nodded in acknowledgment. "Thank you for your honesty, Richard. You may return to the group but be aware that we might have more questions as the investigation progresses."

With that, Richard, burdened by the weight of his own actions and the revelation of Olivia's ominous words, left the yoga studio. Detective Harper remained, her mind a tapestry of clues and emotions, weaving together the threads that would unveil the truth behind Sophia's tragic demise.

After Richard's conversation with Detective Harper, he returned to the room where the friends were anxiously awaiting updates. The air was thick with tension, and the weight of suspicion lingered, casting a shadow over the group. Olivia, with a subtle nod toward the corner, indicated for Richard to join her away from the prying eyes of their friends.

As they moved to a more secluded part of the room, Olivia's eyes bore into Richard's, a silent demand for answers. The subdued hum of whispered conversations surrounded them, creating a veil of privacy within the larger gathering.

"What did Harper ask you?" Olivia inquired, her voice a hushed murmur that betrayed a mix of concern and urgency.

Knowing that his response could have far-reaching consequences, Richard said, "She was asking about us, Liv. Our history with Sophia, the conflicts. She wanted to understand our connections."

Olivia's expression remained unreadable as she processed his words. The web of their shared history and the intricate dynamics with Sophia had become a focal point of the investigation. The revelation of their past, now intertwined with a tragedy, threatened to expose vulnerabilities and hidden truths.

"I told her what she needed to know," Richard continued, attempting to reassure Olivia. "That our past is just that—past. It doesn't have anything to do with what happened to Sophia."

A flicker of uncertainty crossed Olivia's features; her thoughts stormed beneath a composed exterior. The web of connections within their group had become more tangled than ever, and the weight of suspicion pressed down on each friend, straining the bonds that had once seemed unbreakable.

"What did she say?" Olivia pressed further, her gaze unwavering.

Richard exhaled, choosing his words carefully. "She didn't reveal much. Just that she's continuing the questioning and that we should be prepared for more tomorrow."

Olivia's eyes narrowed as Richard tried to ease her concerns. The unspoken weight lingered, and her intuition prodded her to dig deeper. She couldn't shake the feeling that there was more, that perhaps Richard had left out crucial details about his feelings for Sophia.

"What exactly did you tell her, Richard?" Olivia's voice carried a steely edge, a subtle warning that she expected complete transparency.

Richard, sensing Olivia's suspicion, maintained a measured composure. "I was honest, Liv. I told her about our history, about Sophia, and that we had moved on. There's nothing more to it."

A flicker of frustration crossed Olivia's face. The unease that had lingered since the spa retreat now blossomed into a torrent of suspicion. She pressed on, her tone tinged with impatience, "Did you tell her about your lingering feelings for Sophia, Richard?"

Richard's gaze faltered, a subtle admission that there was more to the story. Olivia's eyes widened in disbelief. The revelation hung in the air like a crack in their carefully constructed facade.

"Olivia, it's not like that," Richard began, attempting to diffuse the tension. "Sophia and I had something in the past, but it's over. I love you, and I chose you."

Olivia's expression hardened, a storm brewing beneath the surface. "Chose me? You should have chosen me without any hesitation or lingering attachments, Richard. How am I supposed to trust that you've truly moved on?"

Richard's attempt to downplay the significance of his lingering feelings only fueled Olivia's anger. The fractures in their relationship widened, and the trust that had once been their bedrock eroded with each passing moment.

As their conversation reached an impasse, Olivia's voice carrying a sharp edge said, "You've jeopardized everything, Richard. If there's even a hint of deceit, I won't be a part of it." With that, she turned away, leaving Richard standing in the wake of her fury. The once unbreakable bond between them now hung in the balance, a casualty of the tumultuous events that had unfolded at Tranquil Haven Spa.

The gravity of the situation hung in the air between them. The retreat, meant for relaxation and reflection, had morphed into a crucible of secrets and uncertainty. Olivia nodded slowly, her eyes reflecting the turmoil within, acknowledging the storm that awaited them.

As they rejoined the group, the unspoken tension lingered, each friend grappling with their own suspicions and fears. The retreat, once a sanctuary, had transformed into a battleground of hidden truths, leaving the friends to navigate the treacherous terrain of their tangled relationships.

Detective Harper, unraveling the layers of secrecy and deceit, considered the implications of Richard's actions. The shadows of the past cast long over the present, and the revelations in the yoga studio became vital pieces in the puzzle that Harper sought to solve.

As Harper left the room, she couldn't shake the unsettling feeling that something crucial had eluded her. The question of how the killer had slipped away from the yoga studio without being seen gnawed at her. It was a detail that, if overlooked, could unravel the entire investigation.

With a determined resolve, Harper ascended to the main area where the friends anxiously awaited her return. The atmosphere in the room was tense, the trust among friends fractured by the revelation of hidden secrets and the looming threat of a killer still among them.

"I appreciate your cooperation today," Harper began, her gaze sweeping across the room. "I'll be back tomorrow with more questions. In the meantime, I urge each of you to reflect on anything that might help us understand what happened in that yoga studio."

The friends exchanged wary glances, their sense of security shattered by the reality that the killer remained at large. The bonds of trust that once held them together now strained under the weight of suspicion and fear.

As Harper left the room, she carried with her a cacophony of conflicting emotions and unresolved questions. The retreat meant for tranquility, had transformed into a battleground of hidden truths and exposed vulnerabilities. The friends, now scattered in unease, grappled with the uncertainty of the killer's identity, questioning the very foundation of their relationships.

In the quiet solitude of the CSI lab, Harper reviewed the evidence once more, searching for any overlooked detail that could provide a breakthrough. The strands of silk, the lipstick-stained champagne glass, the cosmetic cases—each piece of the puzzle held a story, waiting to be deciphered.

Harper couldn't escape the gnawing realization that she might have missed a crucial detail, a misstep that allowed the killer to evade capture. The urgency of solving the case weighed heavily on her, pushing her to delve deeper into the shadows of the past and unravel the intricacies that had woven the fabric of this complex mystery.

Shadows in the Sanctuary

In a dimly lit corridor, Emily trailed after Mark, her gaze fixed on his retreating form. The atmosphere between them had grown strained, and she needed answers. With determination etched on her face, Emily finally caught up with Mark.

"Mark, why did you leave the room earlier?" Emily's voice was low but charged with curiosity.

Mark hesitated, the weight of secrecy palpable in the air. "I needed some air, Em. It's been intense, and I just needed a moment."

Emily's eyes narrowed, her suspicion evident. "Is that all it was, Mark? We're supposed to be a team, especially in times like this. You can't just disappear."

In the quiet corridor of Tranquil Haven Spa, Mark felt the weight of unspoken words settle heavily between him and Emily. His sigh, laden with guilt and frustration, escaped into the silent night, dissipating like a secret carried away by the wind.

"I didn't want to involve you," Mark confessed, his eyes avoiding Emily's searching gaze. "There are things I need to figure out on my own."

The air hung heavy with tension as Emily's eyes bore into him, demanding more, demanding the truth. Yet, Mark, shrouded in his own uncertainties and entangled in the web of his complex emotions, couldn't summon the courage to reveal the full extent of his thoughts. His admission lingered in the air, a heavy silence that neither dared to break.

With a tense nod, Emily turned away, leaving Mark standing alone in the dimly lit corridor. He watched her retreating figure, a knot tightening in his chest. The unspoken words echoed in the space between them, and Mark grappled with the turmoil that churned within. The corridor, once a pathway to serenity, now bore witness to the fractures in their connection, shadows that seemed to lengthen with every step Emily took away from him.

Emily walked away from Mark, each step a resounding echo of the unspoken tension that lingered in the air. The dimly lit path became a metaphor for the shadows encroaching upon the sanctuary of their relationship.

As Emily retreated into the solitude of her thoughts, a whirlwind of emotions churned within her. The knot in her chest tightened with each replay of Mark's words. She couldn't escape the gravity of his confession, the admission that there were things he needed to figure out on his own. The corridor, once a symbol of tranquility, now mirrored the fractures in their connection.

In the hushed stillness, Emily grappled with her own secrets, the weight of her clandestine affair with Mia pressing down on her.

The affair, a dance originally hidden from Mark, cast a long shadow over her conscience. She replayed the stolen moments with Mia, their shared glances, and the intoxicating allure of a connection kept in the shadows.

As Emily reached her room, she found herself on the precipice of an emotional crossroad. The corridor had become a threshold between her past's familiarity and her future's uncertainty. The fractures in her relationship with Mark had cracked wider, exposing the vulnerabilities that lay beneath the surface.

The room, once a retreat within the tranquil haven, now served as a canvas for Emily to confront her own truths. The echoes of Mark's unspoken words reverberated, intertwining with the unspoken questions about her own actions. The corridor, the silent witness to their unraveling, held the remnants of a connection that seemed to fray with every passing moment.

Mark watched Emily's retreating figure, a sense of unease settling over him. The corridor, once a pathway to serenity, now felt fraught with tension. He decided to give her some space, to let the emotions cool, hoping that time would lend a perspective that words couldn't.

Minutes stretched into an eternity as Mark stood alone in the dimly lit corridor. The distant hum of activity from other parts of the spa provided a dissonant soundtrack to the turmoil within him. He couldn't shake the feeling that the foundations of their relationship were shifting, and the corridor, once a familiar passage, now seemed like uncharted territory.

After a while, Mark returned to the door of the room Emily had entered. He hesitated, his hand hovering over the handle. The anticipation in the air was palpable, and the weight of unspoken words seemed to press against the door.

Summoning a reservoir of courage, Mark turned the handle and stepped into the room. Emily, facing away from him, seemed engrossed in her thoughts. The silence between them hung like a heavy fog, and Mark struggled to find the right words to bridge the growing chasm.

"Emily," he began tentatively, his voice breaking the stillness.

She turned to look at him, her expression a mixture of vulnerability and determination. The room felt like a pressure cooker, emotions simmering beneath the surface, threatening to boil over.

"I didn't mean to upset you," Mark continued, his words carefully chosen. "There are things I need to figure out, but I want you to know that you're important to me."

"I need to tell you something," Mark began, his voice carrying the weight of the difficult revelation he was about to make. The air in the room seemed to thicken, and Emily's eyes narrowed, a mix of anticipation and apprehension clouding her expression.

The words lingered, a silent promise of forthcoming truths that had the potential to reshape the delicate fabric of their relationship. In the charged atmosphere of the room, Mark and Emily faced the daunting task of navigating the uncharted territory of their emotions, uncertain of the impact these revelations would have on the foundation they had built together.

Emily's gaze bore into him, a silent challenge. The room, a witness to the intimate moments of their shared history, now held its breath as if bracing for the impact of the words that hung in the air.

As the tension escalated, Mark and Emily stood on the precipice of a pivotal moment, unsure whether their connection could withstand the storm that had descended upon them.

Meanwhile, Ava Turner stared at her phone in her room, contemplating whether to reach out to Mark. The recent divorce had left her seeking solace and connection in the midst of the friends' tumultuous night. She dialed Mark's number, hoping for a reprieve from the brewing storm.

"Mark, it's Ava," she said, her voice carrying a subtle invitation. "Care to join me in the bar? I could use some company."

Ava's voice carried a subtle invitation through the phone, an undertone of insistence that Mark found hard to ignore. The allure of a distraction, a brief escape from the complexities of his personal life, tugged at him. After hesitating, he declined with a polite excuse, citing the need to sort things out with Emily.

"I appreciate the offer, Ava, but I need to sort things out with Emily. Maybe another time," Mark explained, his voice holding a mix of regret and determination.

As Ava hung up, a palpable sense of disappointment settled over her. Once promising solace and camaraderie, the evening now felt lonelier than ever. However, Ava couldn't easily accept rejection, especially when she believed there were pressing matters to discuss.

Frustration coursed through Ava as she paced back and forth in the lounge, her impatience growing with each passing moment. The ambient hum of conversations and the soft clinking of glasses provided a backdrop to her internal turmoil. Glancing at the entrance, she clung to the hope that Mark might reconsider, that he would emerge from the shadows and join her to address the pressing matters at hand.

Unable to contain her frustration any longer, Ava retrieved her phone and redialed Mark's number. As the phone rang, her determination rang true in her voice when he answered.

"Mark, we need to talk. I don't care if you're busy with Emily; this can't wait," Ava asserted, her tone unyielding.

Mark, torn between the conflicting demands of Emily and Ava, hesitated but eventually relented, "Fine, Ava. I'll be down in ten minutes."

Ava hung up, a triumphant glint in her eyes. However, as the minutes ticked by, Mark found himself wrestling with the decision he had just made. The weight of his obligations to Emily clashed with the allure of avoiding a confrontation with Ava. As he stood in the quiet of his room, contemplation gave way to a subtle sense of defiance.

Mark decided not to go to the bar. He rationalized that Ava's urgency might be a ploy to manipulate him. Perhaps she hoped to catch him off guard, extracting information that could be used against him. The prospect of facing Emily's wrath weighed heavily on him, but the fear of Ava exposing his secrets pushed Mark into a reluctant stance of defiance.

As Ava waited in the bar, growing increasingly impatient, Mark's decision to stand her up intensified the brewing storm of emotions within her. The friends, each grappling with their own secrets and resentments, teetered on the edge of a precipice, unaware that the fragile threads holding their relationships together were fraying with each passing moment.

Minutes passed, and as Mark failed to materialize, Ava's initial disappointment morphed into a simmering anger. She felt stood up, dismissed in a way that stoked the flames of her indignation. Ava found herself muttering to herself, her words laced with a determination to make Mark understand the gravity of the situation.

"If he thinks he can just walk away, he's got another thing coming," Ava whispered, a fiery resolve in her eyes. "There are things that need to be discussed, and if he won't face them voluntarily, maybe it's time everyone knew the truth about Sophia."

Ava, fueled by frustration and a desire for retribution, contemplated revealing the secrets she had been holding onto. The bar, once a haven for relaxation, now bore witness to Ava's internal turmoil, setting the stage for revelations that could shatter the fragile balance among the friends.

In Olivia's penthouse, the air crackled with tension. Olivia, seething with anger from her confrontation with Richard, paced the sleek, modern space.

Olivia's stiletto heels echoed against the marble floor as she paced the penthouse suite, her frustration radiating like waves through the room. The sleek, modern space, a testament to her success, seemed to amplify the tension between her and Richard. The trust that had once been the bedrock of their relationship was now marred by the echoes of their recent confrontation.

"Richard, you need to understand," Olivia began, her voice laced with condescension. "This penthouse, our lifestyle—it's all because of my success. You should be grateful for what I've achieved."

Richard, already simmering with his own frustrations, bristled at Olivia's thinly veiled attempt to assert dominance. "Success doesn't give you the right to belittle me, Olivia. We built this life together."

The exchange escalated as Olivia vented her grievances about the murder of Sophia, the disruption of her carefully planned gifts of silk wraps and cosmetic cases, and Harper's relentless investigation that threatened to expose the cracks in their friendships.

"The murder has ruined everything!" Olivia exclaimed, her hands gesturing emphatically. "My thoughtful presents, the spa retreat—

all of it tainted by that woman's death. And now Harper is poking into our lives, making accusations. It's truly infuriating!"

Richard, unable to contain his frustration any longer, snapped, "Enough, Olivia! Sophia's death is a tragedy, not an inconvenience for your perfect plans. Harper is doing her job, trying to find out what happened. We should be focused on supporting each other, not fighting among ourselves."

Once momentarily taken aback by Richard's outburst, Olivia glared at him with anger and disbelief. The penthouse, once a symbol of their success and shared accomplishments, now bore witness to the fractures in their relationship, a microcosm of the disintegration unfolding within their group of friends.

Olivia, recovering quickly from her momentary shock, straightened her posture and met Richard's gaze with a cold, calculating expression. The glint in her eyes hinted at a shift from surprise to a strategic mode, as if she had found a new angle to assert control.

"If you can't handle the reality of our success, Richard, maybe you should reflect on why you're here," Olivia retorted, her tone devoid of the warmth that had once defined their interactions. "You want to talk about Sophia? Fine. Go cry to Sophia about it, oh wait, you can't, she's dead!"

The words hung in the air, a vicious reminder of the raw emotions that simmered beneath the surface. Olivia's calculated attack struck at the heart of Richard's unresolved feelings, exploiting the vulnerability that Sophia's death had stirred within him.

Richard, momentarily stunned by Olivia's coldness, felt the weight of her words settle like a heavy stone in the pit of his stomach. The penthouse, once a haven for their shared success, now became a battleground for unspoken tensions and resentments. As the echoes of their heated exchange lingered, both Olivia and Richard stood on opposite sides of a growing divide, the fractures in their relationship widening with each passing moment.

Diane sat alone in her hotel room, the echoes of the confrontation with Mia in the parking lot still reverberating in her mind. She couldn't shake the image of Mia's hostility, the physicality of the encounter contrasting sharply with the intricate tapestry of their friendship.

The room, once a haven of tranquility, now felt suffocating. Diane sought solace in the muted ambiance, attempting to unravel the complexities of Mia's unexpected outburst. They had weathered storms together, navigated the peaks and valleys of life's challenges, but today's clash was unlike anything Diane had experienced.

The question lingered, haunting her thoughts: Was Mia capable of such unbridled anger elsewhere? Diane's mind darted to Sophia, the intricate web of relationships connecting them all. Had Mia unleashed that torrent of fury on Sophia, too?

Diane's fingers drummed nervously on the edge of the hotel bed as she pondered the implications. Mia, usually composed and calculated, had shown a side of herself Diane hadn't known existed. The raw intensity of the confrontation hinted at a depth of emotion and unresolved issues that Diane struggled to comprehend.

With a heavy sigh, she began to piece together fragments of their shared history. Mia's meticulous planning for the spa retreat, her desire for control, and the unspoken complexities of their relationship—all wove into a narrative that now bore the stain of uncertainty.

As Diane delved into her memories, she wondered if Mia's anger had deeper roots, if there were hidden layers to their connection that had yet to be exposed. The room, enveloped in shadows, became a sanctuary for reflection, a space where Diane grappled with the disquieting revelations that unfolded beneath the tranquil surface of their friendships.

In hushed solitude, Diane resolved to seek answers. The tangled threads of their relationship had unraveled, and the Spa, once a retreat of solace, now held the weight of secrets that threatened to reshape the very foundation of their shared history.

Diane sank onto the bed, her emotions a tumultuous sea. The decisions she had made all weighed heavily on her. The retreat, meant for tranquility and reflection, now mirrored the turbulence in her heart. The threads of connection and secrecy that bound the group were fraying, and Diane found herself at the center of the unraveling tapestry.

In the silence of her room, Diane wrestled with conflicting emotions. The choice to distance herself from Mia was a protective measure, a way to shield their connection from the prying eyes and judgmental whispers of their friends. However, as the implications of Sophia's death reverberated through their group, Diane couldn't shake the feeling that their shared secret might unravel in ways she hadn't anticipated.

Diane's mind churned with a tumultuous mix of emotions as she sat alone in the hotel room. The remnants of Mia's confrontation lingered, casting a shadow over her thoughts. Doubt crept in, and Diane couldn't help but wonder if she had pushed Mia to the point of hostility.

"What could I have done differently?" she mused, questioning her own actions and choices. The weight of responsibility bore down on her, and Diane grappled with the possibility that she might have driven Mia away. Their once unshakeable bond now felt fragile, frayed at the edges.

Diane's internal monologue took a darker turn as she replayed the events leading up to the confrontation. The focus shifted from self-reflection to suspicion. Her thoughts, tinged with anger, turned toward Emily, the coworker entangled in a clandestine affair with Mia.

Diane couldn't shake the sense of betrayal, and a surge of resentment bubbled within her. The tendrils of doubt wove a narrative that painted Emily as a potential catalyst for the upheaval in Mia's life. She wondered if Emily harbored a darker side, a facet of her personality that had ensnared Mia in a web of secrets and deception.

A simmering anger rose within Diane as she considered the possibility that Emily's influence had driven a wedge between her and Mia. Once a sanctuary for reflection, the hotel room became a battleground for conflicting emotions. Diane grappled with the complexity of her feelings—betrayal, guilt, and a gnawing suspicion that there was more to Emily than met the eye.

Mia's room, down the hall from Diane, once a sanctuary shared with Diane, felt unfamiliar and cold as Mia entered. The echoes of their laughter, the shared secrets, and the intimacy they once reveled in had been replaced by a palpable sense of solitude. Mia couldn't escape the gravity of her emotions, each vying for dominance in the confined space.

The affair with Emily, once a clandestine escape, now loomed large, casting a shadow over the room's every corner. The warmth of their shared moments seemed distant, replaced by the reality of betrayal. Mia paced the room, grappling with the tangled threads of her own decisions, questioning the choices that had led her down this treacherous path.

The fight with Diane in the parking lot replayed in Mia's mind like a relentless loop. The physical confrontation, witnessed by Harper, now added another layer of complexity to the unraveling weekend. Mia's relationships, both romantic and platonic, stood on shaky ground, and the weight of her actions bore down on her shoulders.

The spa retreat, meticulously planned to be a haven of tranquility, had crumbled into chaos. Mia's efforts to create a seamless experience for her friends had been overshadowed by personal turmoil and the exposure of her secrets. The weekend meant to be a respite now became a crucible of emotions, a testing ground for the bonds that once held the group together.

As Mia stared at the space she used to share with Diane, the gravity of the situation settled over her. The room, a witness to the highs and lows of their friendship, now felt haunted by the ghosts of fractured connections. Mia's emotions, a tempest of guilt, regret, and longing, swirled around her, leaving her in the center of a storm that showed no signs of abating.

As the night settled over Tranquil Haven Spa, each friend found themselves alone with their thoughts, grappling with the weight of the revelations and tensions that had surfaced throughout the day. The air in their individual spaces felt heavy with uncertainty, mirroring the unspoken fears that lurked within.

In Olivia's penthouse, the sleek surroundings couldn't mask the fractures in her relationship with Richard. The once harmonious symphony of shared successes now resonated with discord, leaving Olivia to ponder the shadows that had cast their ominous presence over their friendship.

Diane, in her room, contemplated the physical confrontation with Mia, questioning the depth of their connection. The memories of their shared moments, once filled with laughter and whispered confidences, now seemed fragile, hanging in the balance.

Ava ruminated on Mark's absence in the bar and the frustration that accompanied the solitude. The promises of a distraction had turned into a solitary struggle, and Ava was left with echoes of unanswered questions.

The space in Emily and Mark's room bore witness to the unresolved tension between her and Mark. Once a sanctuary, the room now felt like uncharted territory, with the unknown awaiting on the other side of the door.

As the friends settled into the solitude of their respective spaces, a collective unease lingered, fueled by the unsettling knowledge that the killer was still among them. Tomorrow loomed with the promise of more questions, revelations, and the ever-present fear that the bonds tying them together might unravel completely. In the quiet of the night, Tranquil Haven Spa held its breath, anticipating the storm that awaited on the horizon.

Unveiling Shadows

Detective Harper sat in the dimly lit CSI lab, surrounded by the hum of machinery and the soft glow of computer screens. The videos from the yoga studio played in an endless loop as she meticulously scrutinized every frame, determined to uncover the elusive details that had eluded her so far.

The subtle dance of shadows on the walls taunted Harper as she replayed the footage, each pass revealing nothing more than what she had already seen. Frustration bubbled within her, a relentless itch to find the missing link in the chain of events that led to Sophia's demise.

The room, typically a sanctuary for analysis and revelation, now felt like a labyrinth of unanswered questions. Harper's eyes darted across the screens, searching for the minutest anomaly—a flicker, a movement, any sign that might lead her to the truth.

The silence in the lab was oppressive, broken only by the occasional tap of Harper's fingers on the keyboard. The images on the monitors flickered as she zoomed in, dissecting each frame with surgical precision. Her mind raced, grappling with the weight of the investigation and the urgency to bring justice to Sophia.

A distant memory flashed in Harper's mind, the echo of Ava's voice earlier, questioning why the killer was still among them. Harper couldn't shake the feeling that time was slipping through her fingers, leaving her standing on the precipice of a mystery she was determined to unravel.

As the night deepened, Harper continued her solitary quest for answers. The yoga studio footage became a kaleidoscope of movements, each frame examined under the unforgiving gaze of the investigator. Shadows intertwined with the reality of the crime scene, and Harper strained her eyes, hoping to catch a glimpse of what had eluded her so far.

The metallic tang of frustration lingered in the air as Harper toggled between screens, her focus unyielding. Every sound and every visual cue became a potential clue. Yet, the elusive truth remained just beyond her grasp, teasing her with its intangibility.

With a heavy sigh, Harper leaned back in her chair, the glow from the screens casting shadows across her face. The room held a quiet intensity, mirroring the storm within her mind. The answers, she knew, lay hidden in the intricate dance of details, and Harper was determined to unveil them, even if it meant plunging deeper into the shadows of Tranquil Haven Spa.

Focusing her gaze on a specific set of frames, Harper isolated the critical moments when the murder unfolded in the yoga studio. The rhythmic play of light and shadow on the screens revealed a subtle shift, an anomaly that could be easily overlooked.

Her trained eyes narrowed as she homed in on a particular sequence. The faintest hint of a sound, imperceptible to an untrained ear, echoed through the speakers. Harper replayed the frames, her concentration unwavering. There, amidst the ambient noise of the studio, was a soft, almost muted click—a sound she had initially dismissed.

A spark of realization ignited within Harper. She rewound the footage, scrutinizing the frames preceding the click. As she pieced together the fragments, a revelation unfolded—the sound coincided with a slight distortion in the air, a minute disturbance that suggested more than met the eye.

Harper's mind raced as she contemplated the implications. The click, she concluded, was not a random noise but the subtle confirmation of a concealed door. Her hypothesis gained momentum, and she cross-referenced the sound with her mental map of the yoga studio.

The Detective's fingers danced over the keyboard, enhancing the frames and isolating the sound. It wasn't just a door; it was an exit, a clandestine passage that had eluded both the initial crime scene analysis and her subsequent reviews. The hidden door, she believed, was the key to understanding how the killer had slipped away unnoticed.

The revelation sparked a renewed sense of determination in Harper. She knew she had uncovered a vital piece of the puzzle—a secret door that opened the possibility of a second escape route. With a decisive nod, Harper prepared to delve further into the shadows of Tranquil Haven Spa, armed with newfound knowledge and an unwavering resolve to unmask the killer.

Suddenly, the door creaked open, and a forensic analyst stepped into the room, holding a folder. Harper glanced up, her eyes reflecting the exhaustion that came with the weight of an unsolved case.

"Detective Harper, we've made a significant discovery regarding Sophia's cause of death," the analyst announced, her tone conveying a mix of urgency and anticipation.

Harper leaned forward, her interest piqued. "What did you find?"

The analyst handed over the folder, and Harper quickly scanned the contents. The revelation hit her like a jolt of electricity. "Sophia wasn't killed by the blow to her head. She was already dead by the time she sustained that injury."

Harper's brow furrowed, her mind racing to comprehend the implications. "What are you saying?"

The forensic analyst pointed to the detailed report. "Sophia's cause of death was strangulation. The blow to her head was post-mortem."

The Detective's eyes widened as the realization sank in. "Strangulation? But how—"

Detective Harper's brow furrowed in contemplation as the CSI analyst delivered the unsettling revelation about Sophia's cause of death. The mention of ligature marks hinted at a deliberate act, a systematic approach that added a layer of cruelty to the already heinous crime.

"Any idea on what could have been used for the strangulation?" Harper inquired, her mind already racing through the possibilities.

The analyst, scrutinizing the detailed findings, responded, "We found traces of silk threads embedded deep within the ligature marks. It's unusual, but it suggests that the material might have been a silk scarf or something similar."

Harper's eyes narrowed as she considered the implications. Silk, a luxurious and seemingly inconspicuous material, now took on a sinister role in Sophia's demise. The choice of such an item raised questions about the killer's intent—was it a deliberate selection, a calculated move to add a layer of symbolism or personal significance to the act?

The Detective's thoughts spiraled, contemplating the significance of the silk threads entwined with the ligature marks. Each detail, no matter how minute, carried the weight of potential clues that could unravel the mystery surrounding Sophia's death. As Harper absorbed the information, a sense of urgency compelled her to explore this new lead, to follow the silk threads that now intertwined with the intricate web of deception surrounding Tranquil Haven Spa.

The CSI investigator continued, "There's another intriguing detail. The silk threads we found on Sophia's neck match those discovered on the camera in the yoga studio. It appears that the killer used a piece of the silk scarf to tamper with the camera, attempting to obstruct any recording of the crime."

Harper's eyes widened at the revelation, the puzzle pieces falling into place. The deliberate attempt to manipulate the surveillance equipment suggested premeditation and sophistication. The killer wasn't just seeking to commit a crime; they were methodically covering their tracks, weaving a tapestry of deception that extended beyond the physical act of murder.

As the implications of the silk threads on both Sophia's body and the camera unfolded, Harper realized that she was dealing with an adversary who not only understood the art of concealment but also possessed a level of cunning that elevated this investigation into a complex game of strategy and hidden motives. Determined to untangle the threads of this mystery, Harper steeled herself for the challenges ahead, ready to navigate the intricate maze of Tranquil Haven Spa's dark secrets.

Harper's mind raced, connecting the dots. "So, the killer wanted us to believe that was the cause of death."

"Exactly," the analyst confirmed. "The ligature marks tell a different story, and we're running tests on the silk threads we have. It might lead us to the murder weapon or provide more insight into the killer's method."

A CSI investigator re-entered the room, holding a small evidence bag containing a carefully preserved silk thread. "Detective Harper, we've made another discovery," the analyst announced. "We found tiny particles on the silk threads, and preliminary tests indicate that they match the lipstick we recovered from the champagne glass."

Harper's eyebrows furrowed in concentration. The intricate connection between the silk threads, the ligature marks on Sophia's neck, and the lipstick particles added complexity to the investigation. The killer's meticulous efforts to erase any trace of their involvement were unraveling, leaving behind a trail of clues that Harper was determined to follow.

Harper knew that each revelation brought her one step closer to unmasking the perpetrator and understanding the motives lurking in Tranquil Haven Spa's shadows. With a renewed sense of purpose, she continued to piece together the puzzle, determined to bring justice to Sophia and unveil the truth that had been carefully concealed.

Harper sat back as the forensic analyst left to attend to her duties, grappling with the new information. The puzzle had taken an unexpected turn, and she realized the case's complexity had deepened. Once a source of frustration, the videos now held a renewed significance. Harper resumed her examination, determined to uncover the elusive details that would lead her to the killer and bring justice to Sophia.

As the clock ticked past 3 a.m., the dimly lit CSI lab seemed to echo with the weight of Harper's determination. The discoveries made in those late hours had opened new avenues in the investigation, each thread of evidence leading her closer to the elusive truth.

Harper knew the upcoming meeting with the friends at Tranquil Haven Spa was crucial. It was the moment she would connect the dots, lay bare the intricacies of the murder, and unveil the identity of Sophia's killer. Time pressed against her, a relentless force urging her to finalize her findings and prepare for the confrontation that awaited in the morning.

With a final glance at the screens displaying the evidence, Harper rose from her chair. The exhaustion of relentless scrutiny hung on her shoulders, but the fire of determination burned bright in her eyes. She gathered the files, evidence bags, and her notes, creating a tangible representation of the investigation's progress.

The journey back to Tranquil Haven Spa loomed ahead, and Harper felt a sense of urgency. The tangled web of secrets, lies, and betrayals would soon be exposed, and the friends would confront the harsh reality that had been concealed beneath the surface of their seemingly idyllic retreat.

As Harper left the CSI lab, the city outside slept, oblivious to the impending storm of revelations. The quiet streets contrasted with the tumult within her mind, where pieces of the puzzle started to align, forming a mosaic that would soon reveal the face of the killer. The friends, still unaware of the storm about to break, awaited Harper's return, their fates intertwined with the impending truth.

Unraveling Ties

The friends had gathered in the elegant restaurant, expecting Detective Harper to meet them there. The aroma of fresh coffee and the delicate clinking of utensils against porcelain created a deceptive veneer of normalcy. However, the uneasy undercurrent that flowed through their conversations betrayed the tension within.

Emily glanced nervously around the table, her eyes seeking reassurance from the familiar faces of her friends. Ava fidgeted with the edge of her napkin, a knot of apprehension tightening in her stomach. Mark exchanged cautious glances with anyone looking around, grappling with the unspoken understanding that their secrets were no longer safe.

As the minutes ticked away, an uncomfortable silence settled over the group. Olivia, usually the one to command attention effortlessly, found herself subdued by the weight of the pending conversation. Though attempting to maintain a composed exterior, Richard felt the subtle tremors of unease.

The friends exchanged speculative glances, each nursing their individual fears and uncertainties. The restaurant, bathed in the soft morning light, held an incongruity—the calm facade at odds with the storm brewing within.

Suddenly, the door swung open, and a pair of officers, accompanied by another detective, entered the restaurant. Their authoritative presence caused heads to turn, and a hush fell over the table.

"Good morning, everyone," the Detective addressed the group. "I'm Detective Simmons. Detective Harper has requested that you move to the yoga studio. She'll meet you there shortly."

The friends exchanged bewildered looks. Questions lingered on their lips, but the stern expressions of the officers silenced their inquiries. With a collective nod, they rose from the table, the unease deepening as they exited the restaurant and made their way to the yoga studio.

As the door closed behind them, the restaurant retained its serene facade, masking the turbulence of emotions lingering in the air. The morning shadows played on the walls, concealing the secrets that awaited revelation in the tranquil haven of Tranquil Haven Spa.

The soft morning light bathed Tranquil Haven Spa in a gentle glow as the friends filed into the familiar yoga studio. A palpable sense of unease clung to the air, threading through the subtle whispers and shifting glances exchanged among them. Detective Harper, positioned at the front of the room, cast a discerning gaze over the group, a blend of determination and gravity etched on her features.

Minutes stretched into an anxious silence as the friends took their places, the uncertainty mounting with every passing second. The muted rustle of clothing and the occasional clearing of throats were the only sounds that echoed in the room. Once a sanctuary for relaxation and reflection, the yoga studio now held an undercurrent of tension.

Harper, still absent, left the friends to their own contemplations. Ava stole a glance at Emily, a mixture of curiosity and anxiety in her eyes. Richard exchanged a cautious look with Olivia, both wondering about the revelations that hung in the air.

The door creaked open, and Harper entered the room, breaking the uneasy stillness. Her arrival prompted a collective shift in the atmosphere, an acknowledgment that the moment of reckoning had drawn near.

"Thank you for gathering here," Harper began, her tone measured but carrying the weight of impending revelations. The friends, their nerves on edge, turned their attention to the Detective, waiting for the shadows to unfurl in the morning light.

Harper began, her voice cutting through the hushed whispers that circulated among the friends. "We need to talk about what happened to Sophia, and I believe this room holds some crucial answers."

The atmosphere tensed as the friends exchanged uneasy glances, acutely aware of the shadows that clung to their connections. With a subtle sense of theatricality, Harper began to unravel the intricate web of relationships within the group. She delved into the affairs, the clandestine moments that had woven threads of deceit through the fabric of their friendships.

As Harper continued her relentless unraveling of the intricacies within the group, she focused her piercing gaze on Emily and Mia, the storm's epicenter that had disrupted the tranquil haven of their spa retreat.

"Emily and Mia," Harper's voice echoed in the room, the weight of her words tangible. Emily, who had once exuded confidence, now shifted uncomfortably in her seat, a visible crack in her composed demeanor. Mia, whose stoicism was a shield against the impending storm, allowed a glimpse of turmoil to surface.

"Emily, your involvement in this affair has been portrayed as a catalyst," Harper stated, her tone measured. "Can you shed light on how this affair began and its impact on the relationships within the group?"

Her composure was shaken by the revelations; Emily took a deep breath before responding. "Detective, I won't deny my mistakes, but I'm not the sole catalyst here. Mia and I were both involved, and it's unfair to lay the blame solely at my feet. I love Mark, and I never intended for any of this to happen."

The room, caught in the crossfire of emotions, held a collective breath as Emily defended her actions. The fractures in the once-solid friendships were now exposed, and Emily's attempt to justify her role in the affair hung in the air.

Mia, her stoic façade replaced with simmering anger, interjected, "Don't pretend you're the victim here, Emily. You knew exactly what you were doing. This affair didn't just happen to you; you actively participated. And let's not forget, Sophia warned you about my manipulative nature."

Emily's eyes widened at the mention of Sophia's warning, a revelation that added another layer of complexity to the narrative. She stammered, "Sophia warned me about you, yes, but that doesn't excuse your actions. We are all responsible for our choices, Mia."

Mia, visibly angered by the suggestion that she had manipulated Emily, retorted, "Sophia had her own issues. She couldn't stand to see others happy when she couldn't find happiness herself. Don't use her warnings as an excuse for your own choices, Emily."

The room, now a battleground of conflicting emotions, echoed with the tension that had been building over the years. The friendships that had weathered numerous storms were now facing their most challenging test yet, and as Harper continued to guide them through the labyrinth of secrets, the truth threatened to shatter the foundations of their intertwined lives.

Emily and Mia, held captive by the exposure of their transgressions, exchanged glances that oscillated between defiance and vulnerability. Each word from Harper cut deeper into the foundations of their friendships, unraveling the delicate web that had bound them together.

Unrelenting in her pursuit of the truth, Harper recounted the explosive confrontation between Mia and Diane in the parking lot. She painted a vivid picture of the physicality that had marred their usually harmonious relationships, the clash of emotions erupting in a place meant for serenity.

"As we delve deeper into the intricacies of your relationships," Harper continued, her gaze moving between Mia and Diane, "we must confront the incident that unfolded in the spa's parking lot."

The room, already tense, grew quieter as Harper narrated the untold chapter of conflict. The friends, unaware of the confrontation, exchanged puzzled glances.

"During this affair, emotions reached a boiling point between Mia and Diane. It was a moment of raw intensity that shattered the tranquility of this place," Harper explained, her words carrying the weight of unspoken revelations.

Sitting with a mix of discomfort and apprehension, Diane cast a fleeting glance at Mia. The Detective's words transported her back to that tumultuous encounter.

"During this confrontation," Harper continued, focusing on Diane, "Mia, can you explain the aggression displayed in the parking lot? Diane, how did you experience that moment?"

Diane hesitated for a moment before responding, "It's true, Detective. Mia and I had a heated argument, and things escalated. I was frightened by Mia's actions." She paused, gathering her courage, and then pointed to a bruise on her upper arm. "She grabbed me, and it left a mark."

Mia's expression shifted from defiance to a flicker of guilt. The revelation of the physical altercation added a new layer of complexity to the unfolding drama. The friends, witnesses to the unraveling of their once-solid bonds, absorbed the impact of the revelations, their shared haven now marked by the scars of hidden conflicts.

Attempting to defend her actions, Mia stammered, "It was just a moment of passion, Detective. People say things they don't mean in the heat of the moment." The words hung in the air, a feeble attempt to downplay the severity of the rift that had formed within their once unbreakable circle. The room, now a canvas for the unraveling drama, held its breath, awaiting the next revelation that would further redefine the dynamics of their friendships.

Sitting on the periphery of the revelation, Ava observed the unfolding drama with a mix of empathy and judgment. Her eyes, keenly attuned to the nuances of the room, flickered between Emily and Mia, searching for the threads that connected their past actions to the present turmoil.

Mark, Emily's husband, sat with a tense posture, absorbing the impact of the revelations. His eyes flitted from Harper to Emily, a silent plea for an explanation lingering in his gaze. Once discreetly hidden, the fractures in their marriage now cracked wide open for all to see.

The air in the yoga studio grew heavy with the weight of revelations. Grappling with the newfound knowledge, Mark couldn't contain the turmoil within. His jaw clenched as he turned to Mia, concern across his face.

"What the hell, Mia?" Mark's voice was laced with a mix of anger and genuine worry. "You grabbed Diane? What's going on with you?"

Momentarily taken aback by Mark's directness, Mia shot back with a defensive retort. "Oh, spare me your concern, Mark. Maybe if you paid a little more attention to Emily, she wouldn't be seeking comfort elsewhere."

The room fell silent, the tension escalating with Mia's brazen accusation. The friends exchanged uneasy glances, the unraveling dynamics of their relationships now exposed in the harsh light of truth.

Now on the defensive, Mark couldn't let Mia's words stand unchallenged. "This isn't about Emily. This is about your violent outburst with Diane. What the hell is going on with you?"

Undeterred, Mia said, "Maybe if you weren't so preoccupied with Ava, Emily wouldn't be looking for something more."

The revelation of Mark's connection with Ava, previously veiled in secrecy, hung in the air like an unspoken truth. The friends, once bound by trust, now found themselves entangled in a web of revelations, their shared haven transformed into a battlefield of exposed secrets.

Emily's world tilted on its axis as Mia's words reverberated through the room. The revelation of Mark's past affair with Ava hit her like a sucker punch, the air suddenly heavy with the weight of betrayal. She turned her gaze towards Mark, a mix of shock and anger contorting her features.

"You and Ava? Is this true?" Emily's voice trembled with a blend of disbelief and hurt.

Mark, caught in the unforgiving spotlight, hesitated before nodding solemnly. "It was a mistake, Emily. Something that happened a long time ago. It's over."

But Mia, fueled by her own agenda, seized the opportunity to further destabilize the group. "Oh, it's over, Mark? Just like that? Maybe you should've thought about that before cozying up to Ava again."

Sophia's earlier threat to Emily about Mark and Ava flashed through her mind, a cruel irony now manifesting itself in the unraveling of her own marriage. The room crackled with tension as Emily's emotions boiled over, her voice rising in a tumultuous crescendo.

"Get away from me, Mark! Just get away!" Emily's command cut through the air, leaving an echo of shattered trust in its wake.

As Mark recoiled, Ava, ever the provocateur, couldn't help but smirk. The subtle satisfaction in her expression added fuel to the fire, a silent acknowledgment of the chaos she had managed to sow among the friends. The delicate threads of their relationships now frayed, and the once tight-knit group teetered on the edge of irreparable rupture.

Emily's restraint shattered like glass as the smirk on Ava's face became the catalyst for an explosive outburst. The room, already charged with tension, witnessed the unraveling of civility. Emily's eyes blazed with fury, her fists clenched at her sides.

"You think this is amusing?" Emily's voice, now a seething torrent of anger, echoed through the room. "I'll wipe that smirk off your face, Ava. You don't get to revel in destroying our lives and walk away unscathed."

Without a second thought, Emily lunged towards Ava, her hands outstretched as if to grab hold of the source of her anguish. The once-calm haven of the yoga studio transformed into a battleground of emotions, the air thick with the acrid scent of betrayal.

Mark, caught in the crossfire, tried to intervene, his hands reaching out to separate the two women. "Emily, stop! This won't solve anything."

But Emily, fueled by a volatile cocktail of rage and hurt, paid little heed. Sophia's warning about Ava echoed like a rallying cry in her mind. "If Sophia were alive, she'd help me put you in your place!" Emily's words were a poignant reminder of the absence of the one person who could have quelled the storm that now raged within their midst.

Initially taken aback by the sudden physical confrontation, Ava quickly composed herself. The smirk transformed into a cold, defiant expression. She held her ground, prepared to weather the storm she had helped unleash upon the once-harmonious group of friends.

Watching the escalating confrontation with disdain and disbelief, Olivia finally decided she had seen enough. As the chaos unfolded, she rose from her seat with an air of superiority, her eyes casting judgment on the friends who seemed to have lost all sense of decorum.

"Enough!" Olivia's sharp and commanding voice cut through the room like a whip. "This behavior is utterly disgraceful. We are not children throwing tantrums. Pull yourselves together!"

The friends, momentarily stunned by Olivia's intervention, stepped back from the brink of physical conflict. Emily, still seething, shot a resentful glance at Ava, while Mark, caught between guilt and frustration, retreated.

Olivia's gaze turned towards Mark, and her tone became sharper. "Mark, you should be ashamed of yourself. An affair with a friend? This is beneath you. We're here to find out who killed Sophia, not to indulge in petty fights."

The rebuke hung in the air, a stark reminder of the gravity of their situation. The once-close-knit group, now fractured by secrets and betrayals, stood in the aftermath of a storm that threatened to tear apart the fabric of their friendships. Olivia's disapproval lingered, a bitter taste in the air, as the friends grappled with the consequences of their own actions.

Richard, who had been seething silently, could no longer contain his frustration. Olivia's mask of pretense, her judgmental tone, and the constant charade of sophistication grated on his nerves like sandpaper.

"Oh, spare us the theatrics, Olivia!" Richard's voice edged with pent-up annoyance, cutting through the room's lingering tension. He stepped forward, no longer willing to play by Olivia's rules. "Your pretentious act is getting old. We're not characters in one of your high-society dramas."

Olivia's eyes flashed with indignation, but Richard wasn't done. He directed his frustration at her and the entire façade that had defined their friendship.

Richard's declaration hung in the air, challenging the carefully curated world Olivia had woven around herself. The room, once a haven of shared laughter, was now charged with the electric intensity of confrontation.

Accustomed to maintaining control, Olivia squared her shoulders and shot Richard a withering glance. "I don't see how my standards should be lowered just because you all can't keep your lives together."

Richard, undeterred, met her gaze with a steely resolve. "Standards? You mean the ones you use to judge everyone? Your elitism isn't fooling anyone, Olivia."

A murmur of agreement rippled through the room, some friends nodding in reluctant acknowledgment of the tensions that had long simmered beneath the surface.

"Maybe if you dropped the act for a moment, we could actually get to the bottom of what happened to Sophia," Richard continued, his voice cutting through the tension. "But you're too busy pretending to be above it all."

Olivia's eyes narrowed, her composure cracking under the weight of Richard's accusations. "I don't need to explain myself to you. Sophia's death is tragic, and your baseless accusations won't change that."

Richard scoffed, the frustration evident in his tone. "Tragic, indeed. But let's not pretend you cared about her the way you're pretending now. You never liked Sophia, and everyone here knows it."

The room, caught in the crossfire of this verbal clash, held its breath. Once united by shared experiences, the friends found themselves navigating uncharted territory. The cracks in their relationships widened, and the façade of unity shattered in the face of harsh truths.

"And let's talk about your friendship with Sophia, shall we?" Richard continued, his tone biting. "You never liked her. You were always condescending, acting like she was beneath you. Now, all of a sudden, you play the grief-stricken friend, pretending like you care? It's insulting."

Olivia, usually composed and collected, was taken aback by Richard's sudden outburst. Still reeling from the previous confrontation, the friends watched the exchange with curiosity and discomfort.

"Your fake concern and judgmental attitude have done enough damage," Richard concluded, his words hanging in the air like an unspoken challenge. The pent-up frustration that had simmered beneath the surface had erupted, leaving Olivia seething with fury. The once-impenetrable façade that Olivia meticulously maintained crumbled, revealing the fractures in their friendships that went beyond the immediate turmoil.

Her face flushed with anger; Olivia glared at Richard, her composure slipping away like sand through her fingers. The room, already fraught with tension, braced for the storm that Olivia was about to unleash.

"You want to talk about damage?" Olivia's voice dripped with venom as she turned her attention to Richard. "Let's not forget about your little affair with Sophia. Or was that over, just like you claim it was?"

The revelation landed like a bombshell, sending shockwaves through the room. The friends, already grappling with their secrets, were blindsided by the sudden exposure of a clandestine affair that had remained hidden until now.

Richard, caught off guard, tried to regain his composure. "That was a long time ago, and it's irrelevant to what's happening now."

Olivia, however, wasn't ready to let him off the hook. "Irrelevant? How convenient that you conveniently forget about it."

The friends exchanged uneasy glances, the weight of this new revelation sinking in. The once-stable ground of their friendships had turned into a quagmire of betrayals.

Richard, his face a mask of frustration, shot back, "That's ancient history. Sophia and I moved past it."

But Olivia, fueled by a combination of anger and desperation, pressed on. "Moved past it? You were still seeing each other when Sophia died. Don't think everyone is oblivious to your ongoing affair."

The room fell into a stunned silence. The air, thick with accusations and unspoken tensions, hung heavily around the group. The friends, now confronted with the harsh reality of their intertwined lives, struggled to grapple with the unraveling of their relationships.

As Harper delved into the intricacies of the affairs, the atmosphere thickened with an unspoken acknowledgment of the collective betrayal that had festered beneath the surface. The tranquility of the yoga studio, disrupted by the echoes of concealed truths, seemed to pulse with the weight of unresolved emotions.

Harper, however, was merely laying the foundation. She transitioned seamlessly as the atmosphere thickened and the friends grappled with the revelation of long-buried emotions.

Detective Harper, observing the turmoil within the group, stepped forward, her voice cutting through the charged atmosphere like a knife. "Enough of this. We're here to discuss a murder, not your personal grievances."

The friends, momentarily diverted from their internal conflicts, turned their attention to Harper. Olivia, still seething, shot a disdainful glance at Richard before focusing on the detective.

Harper, with a stern expression, continued, "I've been meticulously combing through evidence—video surveillance, fingerprints, DNA, footprints—piecing together the puzzle that is Sophia's death. The crime scene suggested an initial attempt to mislead investigators."

As Harper paused, the tension in the room heightened, and then, with a subtle nod to her CSI team, the door creaked open, revealing a small group of investigators carrying large easels covered with white sheets. Harper's gaze lingered on each friend, watching for the subtle shifts in their expressions.

With a dramatic unveiling, the investigators revealed large, detailed pictures of Sophia's lifeless body, capturing the brutal reality of her demise. The images, splashed across the easels, depicted the gruesome aftermath—the blood, the contorted posture, the lifeless gaze. The once-serene yoga studio was now transformed into an eerie gallery of death.

The friends, now confronted with the visceral evidence of Sophia's murder, gasped in shock. The room echoed with a collective intake of breath as the haunting images bore into their consciousness. Harper's unyielding gaze lingered on each face, searching for the slightest tremor, a flicker of guilt, or any reaction that might betray the killer in their midst.

The silence that followed was deafening, broken only by the faint echoes of emotions held in check. The friends, bound by shared secrets and fractured alliances, stood in the shadow of the macabre display, their internal turmoil mirroring the gruesome scene prepared to expose the truth buried within the tangled web of their connections.

As Harper pointed to a close-up image of Sophia's fractured skull, she began, "This shows where Sophia was bludgeoned in the head..."

Richard's voice cut through the heavy air, his tone filled with disbelief. "Bludgeoned?"

A collective gasp swept through the room, some friends turning away from the gruesome image as others stared, transfixed by the horrific sight before them.

"Who could do such a thing?" Richard's voice trembled with a mix of shock and horror.

The friends grappled with a collective sense of disbelief and horror as the shocking revelation unfolded. The air grew thick with tension, and uneasy glances darted between them, each person silently questioning the others. Still visibly shaken, Richard sought solace in his friends' faces.

Ava, her expression a blend of shock and concern, exchanged a glance with Mark, their shared history suddenly cast under a suspicious light. Her eyes wide with disbelief, Emily shot a wary look at Mia, remembering the tumultuous affair that had unraveled their friendship. Olivia, usually composed, struggled to maintain her poise, her gaze flickering between each friend, evaluating the potential guilt written on their faces.

Harper, observing the reactions, understood the weight of the revelation. The carefully woven tapestry of their friendships had been torn apart, revealing the hidden fractures beneath. The images displayed were a grim depiction of Sophia's tragic end and a mirror reflecting the darker shadows that lurked within the bonds that once seemed unbreakable.

As Richard's question hung in the air, the room became a silent battlefield of glances and unspoken suspicions. The detective, keenly aware of the undercurrents of their relationships, pressed forward, determined to unravel the truth that remained elusive among the tangled threads of betrayal and deceit.

Harper, maintaining her composure, responded with a calm but resolute tone. "Sophia's body," she revealed, "initially appeared to have been bludgeoned. A deliberate attempt, it seems, to divert suspicion toward someone with a potential motive for violence. But upon closer examination, the true cause of death emerged."

The revelation hung in the air, a weighty truth that forced the friends to confront the chilling reality of Sophia's murder. The once-clear lines of their friendships blurred, overshadowed by the specter of a killer among them. Harper, her unwavering gaze, continued to dissect the layers of deception, determined to unveil the hidden secrets beneath the surface of their seemingly idyllic lives.

Harper, with a solemn expression, moved to a second picture, revealing marks around Sophia's lifeless body. A collective hush fell over the room, the friends held captive by the impending revelation.

"The forensic analysis points to strangulation as the actual cause of Sophia's death," Harper declared, her words reverberating through the once-harmonious yoga studio. The friends exchanged glances, absorbing the chilling implication that someone among them had orchestrated a meticulous cover-up to obscure the true nature of Sophia's demise.

The stark images on the easel painted a grim portrait of betrayal and violence, the fractures in their relationships mirroring the fractures in Sophia's body. The weight of the truth settled heavily upon the group, forcing them to confront the horrifying reality that the killer was not only among them but had taken deliberate steps to manipulate the investigation.

As the friends grappled with the revelation, Harper continued her meticulous unraveling of the case, determined to expose the layers of deception and deceit that had woven a web around the tragic end of their once-unbreakable friend. Once a sanctuary of serenity, the yoga studio had transformed into the epicenter of a storm that threatened to shatter the bonds of trust and friendship forever.

Harper began, her tone commanding attention. "The murder weapon used on Sophia involved a ligature. We found traces of it on her neck. But that's not all."

The friends, still reeling from the revelation of strangulation, shifted uncomfortably in their seats, their eyes fixed on Harper as she continued to unravel the intricacies of the crime.

"While the actual garment used for the strangulation hasn't been recovered, the killer left behind threads of a very specific fabric embedded in the strangulation marks. Through rigorous testing, we've identified it as a unique type of silk—rare and distinctive."

A heavy silence settled over the room as the implications of Harper's words sank in. The killer had not only taken Sophia's life but had left behind a subtle, damning signature, a trace of their actions that would become a pivotal clue in the pursuit of justice. The once tight-knit group of friends found themselves entangled in a web of secrets, their alliances fractured by the shocking revelation of the murderer's deliberate and calculated methods.

As Harper pressed forward with her investigation, determined to expose the truth, the yoga studio became a crucible where friendships were tested and loyalties strained under the weight of a dark and evil force that had infiltrated their lives.

A collective murmur swept through the room as the friends exchanged puzzled glances. The mention of silk threads was a revelation none of them had anticipated.

Harper continued, "These silk threads match those found in the camera strategically covered in the yoga studio. Someone in this room was aware of the murder and tried to conceal evidence."

The friends, still reeling from the shock of the affair revelations, now faced the unsettling prospect that the killer standing among them was manipulating events to their advantage.

Sensing the gravity of the situation, Ava exchanged a furtive glance with Mark. Emily, her anger momentarily set aside, listened intently as Harper unraveled the layers of the murder mystery.

A tense murmur swept through the friends as they exchanged wary glances. Harper gestured to one of the CSI experts, who carefully extracted silk threads from a bag, unfolding hem with deliberate precision. The silk, an exquisite piece that mirrored the luxurious gifts bestowed upon each friend by Olivia, held a damning secret.

The room fell into an uneasy hush as the silk wrap was unveiled. Gasps of shock rippled through the group as the intricate details of the fabric became apparent. The friends, eyes wide with horror and realization, faced a disturbing truth—they all possessed identical wraps.

Emily, her voice quivering with disbelief, was the first to speak, her gaze fixed on Olivia. "Those look like threads from the wraps you gave us, Olivia. We all have them."

Ava, Mark, and Diane exchanged incredulous looks, the weight of the revelation sinking in. The once-thoughtful gifts from Olivia now transformed into potential instruments of betrayal. The room seemed to contract, its confines echoing with the unsettling revelation that someone among them had used the very tokens of friendship to commit a heinous act.

Olivia, usually composed and assured, staggered back from the group. The realization of her unwitting involvement in this macabre affair left her stunned. She stammered, attempting to find words to explain or deny the damning connection between the luxurious wraps and the crime scene.

Regaining a semblance of composure, Olivia faced her friends' accusatory gazes with a mixture of defiance and disbelief. "This is absurd," she retorted, her words laced with a defensive edge. "Someone is clearly trying to frame me for this murder. I had no idea those wraps would be used in such a horrific way."

Her eyes darted around the room, seeking validation or support, but the expressions of her friends remained a mosaic of suspicion and concern. The once-trusted gesture of gifting silk wraps had now become an unwitting entanglement in a sinister plot.

"You were all happy with these wraps at first," Olivia continued, her tone tinged with frustration. "Now you're just ungrateful for my wonderful gesture of friendship. I had no reason to harm Sophia."

Ava, her patience worn thin, interjected with a biting remark. "Ungrateful? Olivia, we're not ungrateful. We're shocked and disgusted by the fact that the murderer used these wraps to strangle Sophia, and they all lead back to you."

The room crackled with tension as Olivia, cornered by the weight of evidence and the suspicion of her friends, attempted to salvage the remnants of her dignity. The once-opulent silk wraps now stood as silent witnesses to a crime threatening to expose the darkest corners of their seemingly idyllic friendships.

Harper, seizing the moment to maintain control of the situation, addressed the group sternly. "These silk threads match those threads found in the camera that was strategically covered up in the yoga studio. Someone in this room tried to conceal the murder."

The air grew heavier with tension as the friends grappled with the chilling implications of their once-thoughtful gifts becoming tools in a murder mystery that now threatened to unravel the very fabric of their friendships.

"This particular silk wrap," Harper declared, her words cutting through the charged atmosphere, "was found in Sophia's room at the spa. It matches the fabric used in the strangulation, linking the killer directly to this group."

Now confronted with tangible evidence, the friends felt the weight of suspicion pressing upon them. The once-familiar yoga studio, a sanctuary for serenity and shared moments had transformed into a battleground where the truth would be revealed, no matter how deeply it was buried.

Harper, with a steely resolve, continued to unravel the threads of deception that had trapped the group, determined to expose the killer and bring justice to Sophia's memory. The friends, still grappling with their own secrets, faced the harsh reality that the bonds they once cherished had become fragile threads threatening to unravel at the hands of a murderer in their midst.

"In addition," Harper continued, "lipstick traces were found on the silk ligature threads. Sophia's lipstick. The same lipstick that matches the one on the champagne glass she drank from that night."

Always poised and assertive, Olivia couldn't hide the unease that flickered across her face. Sensing an opportunity to deflect attention, she spoke with a hint of skepticism, "Lipstick traces could be from anywhere. It doesn't necessarily implicate anyone here."

Unfazed by Olivia's attempt to cast doubt, Harper calmly reached into a folder and produced a detailed CSI analysis report. She turned it towards Olivia, revealing the conclusive findings. "Actually, Olivia, the lipstick traces on the silk ligature match the compound of the lipstick found in the cosmetic cases you gifted to everyone."

A collective gasp echoed through the room as the friends absorbed the revelation. Olivia's confident facade wavered, replaced by a stark silence. The once-untouched bonds of trust were strained to their limits, and the realization that one of their own had meticulously orchestrated a murder, framing others in the process, hung heavily in the air.

Harper, seizing the moment, pressed on, determined to unravel the web of deceit and bring the elusive killer to justice. The room, once a sanctuary for shared moments and laughter, now stood as a haunting testament to the fractures within their once-unbreakable friendships.

Harper's gaze swept across the room, her words hanging like an ominous fog. "That champagne glass," she said, her tone unwavering, "was found just outside the yoga studio, strategically placed to divert attention. The lipstick on it, upon DNA testing, contains Sophia's genetic material."

Harper continued, her eyes focused on the friends, each of whom was now caught in the intricate web of the investigation. "The silk threads on the ligature, the same threads found in the camera, link back to Olivia's gift—the silk wraps. But it doesn't end there."

She paused for effect, letting the gravity of her revelation sink in. "Sophia's silk scarf, the one Olivia gifted her, was the murder weapon. The killer used it to strangle her and then cunningly replaced it in Sophia's room to divert suspicion. We have evidence that the scarf was deliberately taken from her belongings and substituted after the murder."

A collective gasp echoed through the room, the friends grappling with the realization that a seemingly thoughtful gesture of friendship had been transformed into a deadly instrument. Olivia, in particular, stood frozen, her gift unwittingly implicated in a crime that had shattered their lives. The once-cordial silk wraps now symbolized a macabre betrayal, forever tarnished by the tragedy unfolding within Tranquil Haven Spa's walls.

Diane, her eyes filled with confusion and suspicion, directed her question at Harper. "Why would the killer place the champagne glass outside? What purpose does that serve?"

With a thoughtful expression, Harper responded, "It seems like an attempt to mislead us, to create a false narrative. But as we've established, that was a deliberate diversion."

Diane's gaze darted around the room, landing on the familiar faces of her friends. Harper, seizing the moment, posed a question. "Who among you is always associated with champagne? Someone frequently seen with a glass in hand."

The friends exchanged glances, a palpable tension lingering in the air. It didn't take long for the collective realization to dawn on them. Olivia, often the hostess of their gatherings, was known for her affinity for champagne, a detail that had become evident during the planning event at her penthouse.

Ava, breaking the uneasy silence, commented, "Olivia, you're always drinking champagne. I remember it from the planning event at your place."

The group turned towards Olivia, whose usual air of composure was now clouded by the mounting suspicion. The champagne glass, initially thought not to be a key piece of evidence, was revealed to be yet another intricately placed puzzle piece in the elaborate game orchestrated by the killer.

Grabbing the edge of her seat, Ava exchanged uneasy glances with Emily. Mark's brow furrowed in contemplation while Olivia's expression shifted from anger to a more somber acknowledgment of the gravity of the situation.

"As you can see," Harper continued, "this goes beyond personal disputes and affairs. There's a calculated effort to conceal the truth. Someone here knows more than they're letting on."

Harper, ever the meticulous detective, directed the group's attention back to the images of Sophia's head, the forensic evidence becoming the focal point of their grim discussion.

"Upon closer examination of the bludgeoning marks," Harper explained, her voice measured, "we were able to identify the type of instrument used. The CSI team determined that the force and pattern of the blows were consistent with a hard metal object."

A hushed silence settled over the room as the friends absorbed the chilling revelation. The implication — someone among them had used a metal object to bludgeon Sophia. Harper continued, "This brings us to the metal cases each of you received as a gift from Olivia. The design and weight of those cases match the characteristics of the murder weapon."

The friends exchanged uneasy glances; the once-appreciated cosmetic cases now transformed into potential instruments of death. The room, once a sanctuary for yoga and camaraderie, had become a crime scene filled with shadows of suspicion and betrayal.

Mark's gaze, heavy with accusation, fixed on Olivia. "You gave us those cases, Olivia. The same cases that match the murder weapon. You knew Sophia criticized you, and you took it to this extreme?"

Emily's eyes, reflecting anger and disbelief, joined Mark in confronting Olivia. "We all knew Sophia's words got under your skin, Olivia. But murder? I never thought it would come to this."

Olivia, her composure shaken, raised her hands in a defensive gesture. "I would never hurt Sophia. Yes, I gave you the cases, but they were personalized for each of you. Anyone could have taken advantage of that and used them for this... this terrible act."

Ava, who had been silent until now, interjected with a pointed remark. "Not anyone, Olivia. You're the only one who created those cases, the silk wraps, and the lipstick. This isn't a coincidence. You're the common thread in all of this."

Olivia's attempts to deflect blame faltered as Ava's words resonated in the room. The friends, once bound by trust and shared secrets, now found themselves at the precipice of a chilling revelation, their lives entwined with the sinister threads of murder and betrayal.

Determined to prove her innocence, Olivia declared, "I can settle this right now. I'll bring down my cosmetic case, and we can see that there are no bloodstains on it. You'll all see that I had nothing to do with this."

The room fell into a tense silence as Olivia, with a mix of defiance and desperation, left to retrieve her cosmetic case. The friends exchanged wary glances, unsure of what the examination might reveal. Harper, ever watchful, observed the unfolding drama, knowing that the answer to this mystery might lie within the seemingly innocuous details of Olivia's cosmetic case.

Detective Harper, keen on getting to the bottom of the mystery, spoke with authority. "I suggest we temporarily leave the room and retrieve our cosmetic cases. We'll then return here for a thorough examination to determine if any of them bear traces of blood or any other evidence related to the crime."

The friends, gripped by anxiety and curiosity, reluctantly nodded in agreement. The once-cozy yoga studio, now a crime scene, echoed with the shuffling of feet as they filed out, each contemplating the impending revelation that awaited them.

The friends returned to the yoga studio, each clutching their personalized cosmetic cases except for Ava, who had earlier informed Harper that she couldn't locate hers. The atmosphere in the room had intensified, anticipation and suspicion hanging in the air.

Olivia, typically composed as the group gathered, took a defiant stance. "Well, where's Ava's case?" she questioned, her tone accusatory. "It seems like she conveniently 'lost' it to avoid scrutiny."

The friends exchanged glances, and a collective murmur of suspicion enveloped the room. Aware of the accusatory eyes fixed upon her, Ava stood her ground, her expression a mix of defiance and innocence. Harper, observing the dynamics, decided to address the mounting tension.

"Calm down, everyone," Harper urged, her voice cutting through the charged atmosphere. "Let's approach this systematically. We'll examine each case individually to determine if there's any evidence linking them to the crime."

The friends reluctantly agreed, their eyes narrowing on Ava as she became the focal point of their scrutiny. Aware of the delicate balance, Harper prepared to unveil the truth hidden within the contents of those cosmetic cases.

As the tension in the yoga studio escalated, Harper decided to take control of the situation. She signaled to one of the CSI team members, who stepped forward holding a familiar-looking cosmetic case. The atmosphere in the room shifted as the friends focused their attention on the case in the CSI team member's hands.

"Is this Ava's case?" Harper asked, her gaze piercing through the room. The friends exchanged uneasy glances, their suspicions turning towards Ava. As the CSI team member nodded, Ava's eyes widened in disbelief.

"Where did you find that?" Ava demanded, her voice a mix of surprise and confusion. The friends, now distancing themselves from Ava, watched with growing suspicion. Harper maintained her composure, ready to provide the answers that would unravel the mystery surrounding Ava's missing cosmetic case.

The yoga studio seemed to contract, the air thick with accusations as the friends turned their collective gaze toward Ava. Mark's disbelief was palpable, his eyes searching Ava's face for any sign that this was a misunderstanding.

"Ava, how could you?" Mark's voice wavered with a mix of betrayal and confusion. "We trusted you."

Ava, though met with the accusing stares of her friends, stood defiantly. "I didn't do this. I don't know how my cosmetic case ended up outside, but I swear, I'm innocent."

Emily, consumed by a torrent of anger and betrayal, lunged towards Ava, her hands outstretched with the intention of reaching Ava's throat. Mark, reacting instinctively, intercepted Emily, pulling her back to prevent any physical altercation.

"You've destroyed us, Ava!" Emily's voice trembled with rage. "You were supposed to be our friend."

As Mark struggled to restrain Emily, the atmosphere in the room became charged with an almost tangible tension. The accusations hung in the air, and Ava, though steadfast in her claims of innocence, found herself isolated in the center of the storm. Now unraveling at the seams, the group faced the harsh reality that someone among them was capable of unspeakable actions.

Amidst the turmoil and accusations, Olivia found a renewed sense of confidence. The air of smug satisfaction returned to her features, and she seized the opportunity to assert her dominance again. Richard, already on edge, couldn't help but feel a surge of irritation at Olivia's demeanor.

"Oh, how the mighty have fallen," Olivia remarked with a sly smile, her eyes locking onto Richard's. "Seems like our little detective work is paying off. It's quite the spectacle, isn't it?"

Richard, grappling with his own emotions and the unraveling events, shot Olivia a disdainful look. "This isn't a game, Olivia. Someone died. Sophia is dead."

But, seemingly unfazed, Olivia continued to revel in the chaos surrounding them. "And yet, here we are, unraveling the web of secrets. Isn't it fascinating? Who would've thought that beneath the facade of friendship lurked such darkness?"

Richard, exasperated by Olivia's taunting tone, chose not to engage further. Now more fractured than ever, the friends struggled to navigate the treacherous waters of suspicion and betrayal. For the moment, Olivia reveled in her apparent vindication, leaving a bitter taste in the mouths of those who once considered her a friend.

Diane's world crumbled around her, the weight of the accusations and revelations pressing down on her like a suffocating force. As the truth unfolded and suspicion cast its shadow over their once tight-knit group, Diane felt a surge of panic rising within her. Once a haven for shared laughter and camaraderie, the room transformed into a battleground of broken trust and shattered friendships.

Her hands trembled as she clutched at the fabric of her dress, the material offering little solace in the face of the emotional upheaval. Tears welled up in her eyes, blurring her vision as the reality of the situation sank in. The friendship that had once provided comfort and stability was now tainted by deceit and betrayal.

Sensing Diane's unraveling, Mia moved closer, extending a hand in a gesture of comfort. "Diane, we'll figure this out together. Trust me."

But Diane, lost in the tumult of her emotions, recoiled from Mia's touch. "No, no, no!" she cried, her voice laced with hysteria. "This can't be happening. Sophia is gone, and now everything is falling apart. How did it come to this?"

Mia persisted, her concern evident in her eyes. "Diane, please, let me help you. We need each other now more than ever."

But Diane, overwhelmed by the avalanche of revelations, pushed Mia away, stumbling backward. "Stay away from me!" she exclaimed, her voice a desperate plea. The unraveling of their friendships and the dark secrets laid bare left Diane teetering on the edge of despair.

As Diane stumbled backward, the weight of her emotions driving her into the unknown, her back collided with what seemed to be an unyielding wall. To her surprise, the wall gave way, revealing a hidden door – a concealed passage reserved for staff. The unexpected discovery momentarily shifted the focus from the turmoil within the group to the clandestine depths of the spa.

The door swung open, revealing a dimly lit back hallway that snaked through the spa's hidden recesses. Still grappling with her tumultuous emotions, Diane found herself in a realm veiled from the prying eyes of the friends gathered in the yoga studio.

Mia, her concern deepening, rushed to Diane's side. "Diane, are you okay?"

Diane, dazed and disoriented, glanced around at the secret passage. "I... I didn't know this was here. What is this place?"

Mia, recognizing the corridor as a staff-only area, furrowed her brow in contemplation. "This must be a part of the spa restricted to the staff."

The commotion drew the attention of the friends, who rushed over to Diane to ensure she was unharmed. Harper, sensing the urgency, joined the group to assess the situation.

"Diane, are you okay?" Mark inquired, concern etched across his face. Diane, shaken but physically unharmed, nodded. "I'm fine, just startled. I didn't expect the wall to give way like that."

Harper, taking charge, called the friends back into the yoga studio. "Let's regroup. We need to stay focused on the investigation." Turning to the CSI team, she added, "Explore that corridor, see if there's anything relevant to the case."

As the friends reluctantly left the mysterious hallway behind, the CSI team ventured into the hidden depths of Tranquil Haven Spa in pursuit of clues that might unravel the enigma surrounding Sophia's tragic demise. Little did they know, the secrets concealed within the spa's walls began to unfurl, weaving a complex tapestry that connected the past to the present.

Unveiling Shadows

Detective Harper, her gaze unwavering, brought the attention of the friends back to the heart of the investigation—the cosmetic cases that had become both a gift and a potential instrument of death.

"I'll get back to Ava's case in a moment, but first, the forensic analysis on the cosmetic case we found outside revealed something significant," Harper began, her tone measured but filled with gravity. "Despite attempts to clean it, we discovered blood residue in the corner of the case. The DNA analysis confirms it matches Sophia's blood type."

The friends exchanged uneasy glances, the weight of this new revelation sinking in. The once-stable ground of their friendships had turned into a quagmire of betrayals, and now, the very gifts meant to symbolize unity held a darker truth.

Harper continued, "Now, let me demonstrate how the blow could have been delivered."

She motioned for one of the CSI team members to step forward, holding the cosmetic case found outside. With calculated precision, Harper mimicked the motion, showing how the case could have been wielded as a weapon after Sophia was already dead. The stark image unfolded before the friends, illustrating the cold and deliberate nature of the crime.

"The blow was post-mortem, a calculated move to mislead us into thinking Sophia's cause of death was due to a head injury," Harper explained, her words echoing through the once-harmonious yoga studio.

Detective Harper, the room tense with anticipation, turned her attention to the unresolved mystery of Ava's missing cosmetic case. The friends, still reeling from the revelation of the stained case, now braced themselves for another twist in the unraveling drama.

"I know many of you have assumed that the case we found outside belonged to Ava," Harper began, her eyes scanning the group. "But in a surprising turn of events, it seems we were mistaken."

Gasps echoed through the room as the friends exchanged bewildered glances. Mark, his anxiety palpable, spoke up, "How do you know this isn't Ava's case?"

Before Harper could respond, Olivia, her demeanor regaining a smug confidence, stepped forward. "I can answer that question," she declared, her gaze locking onto Harper.

The room fell into a stunned silence as Olivia's words hung in the air. The friends, each grappling with their own fears and suspicions, now faced the realization that the true owner of the blood-stained case had yet to be revealed. The once tight-knit group, torn apart by secrets and betrayals, stood on the precipice of a revelation that would expose the darkest corners of their intertwined lives.

Olivia's tone dripped with smug self-assurance as she asserted her dominance in the room. She stepped forward, a triumphant glint in her eyes, relishing the opportunity to showcase her design prowess.

"I don't expect all of you to notice the finer details, but I took the liberty of adding a touch of sophistication to the cases," Olivia remarked, her words laced with a subtle arrogance. Her gaze swept over the friends, emphasizing the exclusivity of her revelation. "Each case bears the mark of its owner—an exquisite monogram discreetly placed in the top inside corner."

The friends, already grappling with a myriad of revelations, now faced Olivia's unabashed display of self-congratulation. Her smug demeanor, a stark contrast to the tension in the room, left the group in a momentary state of disbelief. The once-harmonious haven of Tranquil Haven Spa had transformed into a battleground of egos, where Olivia's claim to design supremacy overshadowed the darker truths that lurked within their midst.

Harper, acknowledging Olivia's claim, decided to confirm the authenticity of Olivia's design features. She approached the case thought to be Ava's, which had sparked a wave of accusations, and carefully opened it for all to see. The room fell silent, anticipation hanging like a heavy veil in the air.

As the lid lifted, revealing the subtle monogram inside, Harper announced, "Emily Rodriguez."

A collective gasp echoed through the room. The friends, who had assumed the case belonged to Ava, were now faced with the unsettling revelation that the mix-up had occurred within their own circle. Wide-eyed and stunned, Emily looked at her case, realizing the truth that had eluded them all.

Harper, not wasting a moment, walked over to Emily, who was now holding her case with a mixture of confusion and disbelief. Harper gently took the case from her hands and opened it, unveiling the initials for Ava.

"There seems to have been a misunderstanding," Harper declared, her voice steady. "This case actually belongs to Ava."

The room buzzed with tension as the friends processed the unexpected turn of events. The accusations and suspicions that had been hurled at Ava hung in the air, leaving the group in disarray. The once-solid ground of their friendships had now become a shifting landscape of uncertainty, and the search for Sophia's killer had taken an unforeseen twist.

A heavy silence settled over the room as the friends stared at Emily, their eyes filled with shock and suspicion. The revelation that the cosmetic cases had been mistakenly swapped created an unsettling atmosphere, and Emily found herself at the center of the scrutiny.

"I swear, there must be some mistake," Emily insisted, her voice shaky but determined. "I never realized it wasn't my case. I've had it all weekend."

Mark spoke up with a blend of confusion and concern, "Emily, this doesn't look good. We need an explanation. Why do you have Ava's case?"

Emily turned to Olivia, searching for answers. "Olivia, are you sure you gave each of us the right case? Maybe there was a mix-up when you handed them out."

Olivia, her composure returning, shook her head. "I didn't personally distribute them. Mia took charge of that. She insisted on overseeing every detail, and when you all arrived, she handed me the cases to pass out."

The room buzzed with a renewed sense of bewilderment. The attention turned to Mia, who had been silent until now. Her eyes darted around the room as she sensed the weight of the collective gaze.

"I don't understand," Mia finally spoke, her voice defensive. "I handed Olivia the cases I thought belonged to each of you. There shouldn't have been any mix-up."

Mia's voice held a note of indignation as she defended herself, her eyes scanning the faces of her friends, searching for support. "Don't lay the blame on me. I did my part in organizing everything. Olivia, after all, designed the wraps, the cosmetic cases, and everything else. If there's a mistake, it's on her."

She turned towards Olivia, her demeanor challenging. "You were the one who insisted on making everything so personalized as if the rest of us are beneath your design standards. Maybe you made a mistake when you handed them to me, and I simply followed your lead."

Tight with restrained annoyance, Olivia's features responded sharply, "I didn't personally hand out the cases, but I trusted you to do it correctly. I designed them to be unique for each person, and the monograms were clear. This mix-up is on your shoulders, Mia."

The tension in the room escalated as the blame bounced back and forth between Mia and Olivia. The once-solid foundation of their friendships now seemed shaky, and doubts about each other's intentions began to surface. The weight of Sophia's murder hung over them, and the unraveling of trust made it even more challenging to uncover the truth.

The door to the hidden hallway swung open, and the CSI team returned, carrying a red wrap that matched the design of the ones Olivia had created for her friends. The air in the room grew thick with anticipation as Harper accepted the piece of evidence. The friends watched, their expressions a mix of anxiety and curiosity, as Harper examined the red wrap.

Detective Harper meticulously examined the red wrap, her gloved fingers delicately handling the fabric as if searching for hidden clues. As she did, the CSI team members engaged in hushed conversations, providing additional context.

One of the CSI technicians leaned in to share crucial information. "We found it stuffed into a garbage can down the hidden corridor. Someone tried to dispose of it, but our team intercepted it."

The revelation sent a collective shiver through the room. The friends now faced the stark reality that someone had tried to hide the damning evidence, and the concealed corridor echoed with the secrets that had been unearthed. As the friends grappled with the shocking twists of the investigation, they anxiously awaited the next piece of the puzzle to fall into place.

After receiving the information from the CSI technician, Detective Harper took a step back and assessed the situation. The red wrap, a potential key to solving the mystery, was carefully bagged for further analysis. She clearly instructed the CSI team, "Take it back to the lab. I want a thorough examination, and I need to know if this is one of the wraps Olivia designed for the group."

Olivia, usually composed and confident, stepped forward as the CSI team began to leave. "That won't be necessary," she declared, a self-assured glint in her eyes. Harper turned her attention to Olivia, who continued, "I can positively identify it right here."

Intrigued by Olivia's certainty, Harper handed her the red wrap bag. Olivia studied it meticulously, her eyes narrowing in concentration. The friends watched in suspense as Olivia examined the fabric, running her fingers over the familiar design. After a tense pause, Olivia spoke with unwavering confidence, "This is one of mine. I designed and crafted this wrap."

Harper, curious and determined, probed further. "How can you be so sure, Olivia?" she asked, her eyes fixed on the red wrap that held the key to unraveling the mystery.

Olivia explained with an air of arrogance, "I spared no expense in creating these wraps. The silk is imported from Italy, exquisite and unparalleled. But the true mark of my craftsmanship is more subtle yet distinctive." Olivia's fingers delicately traced the edge of the wrap. "Just like the cosmetic cases, each wrap has the initials of its owner woven into the fabric."

She held the wrap up for Harper to inspect. "Look here," Olivia directed, pointing to a section near the edge. Harper focused on the spot, and as her gaze sharpened, the faint initials of someone in the room emerged. Olivia's tone dripped with a mix of confidence and arrogance. "This particular wrap belongs to someone here. I'm sure you can see whose initials these are."

The room fell into silence as Harper and the friends strained to see the tiny, intricate detail that Olivia claimed would identify the owner of the red wrap. Heavy with anticipation, the air crackled with the weight of impending revelation.

Harper's gaze shifted from the red wrap to the faces of the friends, her expression inscrutable. The room, caught in a moment of suspended tension, waited for her following words.

"Mia," Harper finally said, her tone measured yet pointed, "do you have anything you'd like to tell me?"

The friends turned their attention to Mia, the air thick with anticipation as they awaited her response. Mia, seemingly caught off guard, met Harper's gaze with surprise and apprehension. The red wrap, now a damning piece of evidence, had cast a shadow over the once-trusted bonds of their friendship.

Mia's demeanor shifted from surprise to defiance, her eyes ablaze with anger. She shot a scowl in Harper's direction, her tone dripping with resentment.

"You should have just minded your own business, Harper," Mia spat, her voice laced with defiance. "Then nobody would have caught on. But, yes, I killed Sophia. And, you know what? I'm glad I did it."

As Mia's chilling admission reverberated through the room, the friends instinctively recoiled, creating a palpable distance between themselves and the defiant murderer in their midst. Horror and disbelief etched across their faces; the group now stood as fragmented individuals, united only by the shock of Mia's revelation.

Mark, Emily, Diane, Richard, and Ava—each friend stepped back, their eyes wide with fear, confusion, and a profound sense of betrayal. The room, once filled with shared secrets and laughter, now echoed with the weight of Mia's ominous confession, casting a dark shadow over the fractured bonds of their friendships.

Amid Mia's shocking confession, Olivia stood stoically by Harper's side, her expression a curious blend of superiority and smugness. While the others recoiled in horror, Olivia remained unmoved, seemingly reveling in the unfolding drama.

Her cold and calculating gaze surveyed the friends' reactions with an air of detachment. The smug curve of her lips hinted at a satisfaction derived from knowing the intricate details before they were laid bare. Olivia's posture exuded a sense of control, as if she had anticipated this moment and was now witnessing the culmination of her insights.

Mia's eyes, filled with defiance, locked onto Olivia's smug expression. "You always thought you were so superior, Olivia," she spat out, her tone laced with bitterness. "So smug and certain of yourself. I could manipulate you easily because of it."

As Mia confessed to her manipulations, the room hung heavy with a sense of betrayal. Mia admitted to deliberately taking Ava's cosmetic case, orchestrating a scheme to shift suspicion onto her. She went on to reveal that the case she used in the murder belonged to Ava, intending to frame her for the crime. If that failed, Mia cunningly planted the initials pointing towards Emily, creating a web of deception that now unraveled before the horrified eyes of her former friends.

The revelation left the friends in shock, grappling with the realization that the killer had been among them all along, manipulating the intricate bonds of trust and friendship to serve their dark agenda. Still standing beside Harper, Olivia maintained her composed demeanor, seemingly untouched by the chaos she had indirectly contributed to. The enigma of Olivia's involvement in this twisted tale deepened, leaving the friends questioning the extent of her knowledge and influence.

Mia continued, "I took Ava's cosmetic case while she was out of her room. Being in charge of this weekend, it was easy to convince a maid to let me in the room on the pretense of putting in fresh flowers. Why do you all think I insisted on being in charge? Fools…Ava, you never even knew it was gone because you were preoccupied chasing Mark."

Mark's face contorted with shock and disbelief as Mia callously admitted to her manipulative actions. The weight of Mia's words hung heavily in the air, and the once-solid ground beneath Mark's feet seemed to crumble.

"You did what?" Mark's voice trembled with a mixture of anger and hurt. He looked at Mia, the person he once considered a friend, with eyes that now questioned everything. "You framed Ava and used her feelings for me to distract her? How could you be so cold, Mia?"

Mia met Mark's gaze with a defiant smirk, unapologetic for the chaos she had wrought. "It's a game, Mark, and I played it well. Ava was too blinded by her own desires to notice, just like you were."

Mark's fists clenched at his sides, struggling to contain the anger that surged within him. The betrayal cut deep, and Mia's callous admission only intensified the emotional storm brewing within him, and Mark found himself standing at the epicenter of the storm wreckage.

Ava, her eyes filled with shock and hurt, looked to Mark for an explanation. The revelation had blindsided her, and the weight of Mia's manipulation bore down on her like a heavy burden.

Ava's eyes widened in a mix of disbelief and realization. The weight of Mia's revelation crashed down on her, leaving her momentarily speechless. Ava's mind replayed moments of friendship tainted by manipulation as the truth unfolded.

The words hung like a toxic cloud, and Ava's gaze shifted between Mark and Mia. Her once-trusted friend had callously used her feelings, exploiting vulnerabilities for a twisted game. The pain of betrayal cut through Ava, leaving her heart raw and exposed.

"You used me?" Ava finally spoke, her voice a mixture of hurt and anger. "All this time, Mia, you were playing games with us? With me?" Her hands trembled with the weight of realization as the puzzle pieces fell into place.

Mark's eyes softened with empathy, recognizing the pain etched across Ava's face. He reached out, placing a comforting hand on her shoulder. "Ava, I had no idea. None of us did. This is on Mia, not you."

Ava, however, pulled away, a fire kindling in her eyes. The hurt transformed into determination, and she turned her attention back to Mia. "You think this is a game, Mia? Using my feelings for Mark to frame me? That's not a game; it's a betrayal. I trusted you, and you exploited that trust."

Mia's defiant smirk wavered as Ava found her voice, confronting the friend who had hidden behind a façade of camaraderie. The once-solid friendship between Ava and Mia now lay shattered, and Ava grappled with the harsh reality that someone she considered a friend had orchestrated such a cruel charade.

Mia's smirk twisted into a sneer as she retorted, "Ava, you were never cut out for a man like Mark. Just like you could never handle someone like Emily. It's no wonder you were oblivious to my little game." The disdain in Mia's voice cut through the air, adding another layer of cruelty to the unfolding revelation. Stung by the words, Ava felt the weight of Mia's manipulation intensify, each remark designed to wound and humiliate.

Mia's words cut through the air like a blade as she turned her attention to Emily. "Emily," Mia declared with a cold detachment, "you were never anything more than a pawn in my game. I never loved you. I used you, manipulated you, just like I used Ava and everyone else in this charade. You were a means to an end, a tool to help me cover up Sophia's murder and watch the lives of these so-called friends crumble. I despised them all, and you were just another piece on the board." The room fell silent, the weight of Mia's deception casting a shadow over the broken relationships. Betrayed and wounded, Emily felt the sting of Mia's calculated cruelty.

Emily's world crumbled around her as Mia's callous words sank in. Mark reached out to comfort her, but she recoiled, screaming, "Don't touch me! Don't any of you touch me!" The air thickened with the acrid scent of betrayal.

Through tears, Emily turned her anguished gaze toward Mia. "How can you say that? We shared so many good times, and I did everything for you, both personally and at work. How could you not love me after all we've been through?" Her voice quivered with a mix of disbelief and pain.

Helplessly standing nearby, Mark felt the weight of Emily's sorrow but knew that words alone couldn't heal the wounds inflicted by Mia's deception. The room, once a haven for friendship, now echoed with the shattered remnants of trust and the bitter taste of manipulated emotions.

While the room still reeled from Mia's shocking confessions, she turned her attention to Diane, her tone dripping with malice. "While I'm admitting stuff, Diane, you were next on my list to kill." Mia began weaving a narrative of Diane's perceived faults, emphasizing her neediness and emotional fragility. Mia seethed at Diane's habit of confiding in Sophia about every detail of her life, viewing it as a betrayal that had driven a wedge between Mia and their once-close friend.

Diane, already on edge from Mia's revelations, crumbled to the floor in hysterics, her anguished sobs echoed through the room, a haunting soundtrack to the chaos that had unfolded. Her trembling hands clutched at her chest as if trying to contain the emotional storm raging within. The once vibrant and composed Diane had been reduced to a shattered version of herself.

Reveling in the turmoil she had wrought, Mia looked on with a chilling detachment. Still reeling from Mia's earlier confessions, the others stood frozen, watching the devastation unfold. The yoga studio, once a sanctuary of peace and camaraderie, had transformed into a battleground of emotions.

Mark, sensing the fragility of the moment, moved toward Diane, his eyes filled with concern. He knelt beside her, attempting to offer comfort, but Diane recoiled from his touch. Her tear-streaked face bore the weight of Mia's revelations, each word a dagger plunging into the core of their once-unbreakable friendship.

Ava, Olivia, and Richard exchanged uneasy glances, grappling with the harsh reality of Mia's actions. Emily, still processing the revelation about her own manipulation, stood numbly, torn between the anguish of betrayal and the desperate need for answers.

As Mia continued her venomous tirade, the room pulsated with tension. The air crackled with unspoken accusations, each friend grappling with their own guilt, pain, and disbelief. The bonds that had once tied them together now hung by a thread, strained beyond recognition.

Mia's laughter, a bitter and mocking sound, reverberated through the room as she fixed her gaze on Richard. The revelation of an old secret buried deep within the shadows of their intertwined lives hung in the air like a sinister specter.

"Oh, Richard," Mia taunted, her words dripping with disdain. "I've known your little secret for quite some time. The affair with Sophia, the clandestine whispers, and stolen moments. And yet, I could never fathom what Sophia saw in a man like you."

Richard's face tightened, a mixture of shock and embarrassment etched across his features. Standing beside him, Olivia shot Mia an evil glance, her composure momentarily shaken by the unexpected revelation.

Mia continued her assault, her words slicing through the air like a well-aimed blade. "A weak man, clinging to the success of his wife. How pathetic. You're nothing more than a sponge, Richard, sucking the life out of Olivia's accomplishments."

The tension in the room escalated as Mia's calculated words struck at the heart of Richard's pride. The friends, already grappling with the wreckage of their friendships, were now confronted with the exposure of yet another hidden truth.

Olivia, normally composed and unyielding, felt a surge of anger at Mia's audacity. Their bonds strained to the breaking point; the friends stood on the precipice of a revelation threatening to shatter the remnants of their once-unshakeable camaraderie.

A volatile charge surged through the room as Mia's words hung in the air. Olivia, usually the epitome of composure, lost control. The revelation of her long-held secret and Mia's taunts triggered a visceral reaction. Fueled by rage, Olivia lunged forward with a singular intent—to confront Mia head-on.

Quickly reacting, Richard moved to restrain Olivia, his hands firm but gentle as he sought to prevent her from reaching Mia. Sensing the escalating tension, Harper also stepped in, creating a barrier between the two women. Olivia, however, was relentless, her eyes ablaze with fury as she struggled against the restraint.

"I'll kill you!" Olivia spat out, her voice a raw expression of the anger that surged within her. The once-steadfast friendships now teetered on the edge of irreparable rupture.

Unfazed by Olivia's threat, Mia met her gaze with a cold smirk. "I always knew you were a fraud, Olivia. Thinking you're better than everyone else, but deep down, you're just like me. We all have the capacity to kill when pushed far enough."

The room, caught in the crossfire of revelations and accusations, descended into chaos. The thin veneer of civility that had masked the friends' darker truths shattered, leaving behind a fractured tableau of discord and desperation.

Speaking with anger and desperation, Ava confronted Mia with a demand that echoed through the tumultuous atmosphere, "Why, Mia? Why Sophia? What did she ever do to deserve this?"

Mia, unfazed and seemingly reveling in the attention, met Ava's gaze with a steely resolve. With a sly grin, she took a moment to let the tension linger before responding, "I'll tell you exactly what she did."

The room fell silent, all eyes now fixed on Mia as she began to weave a tale of perceived slights and imagined wrongs. Mia's narrative unfolded with calculated precision, each word aimed at dismantling the pedestal on which the friends had placed Sophia.

"Sophia," Mia began, her tone dripping with disdain, "meddled in everyone's business, especially mine and Diane's. I couldn't stand her."

Mia's accusations continued to pour forth, painting a picture of a woman who, in Mia's eyes, had manipulated and undermined her at every turn. Mia wove a tapestry of grievances as she spoke, portraying Sophia as the orchestrator of her own demise.

"And then," Mia added, her voice lowering to a sinister whisper, "Sophia had the audacity to try and control me, to dictate how I should live my life. It was unbearable. Killing her became the only way to escape from her suffocating influence."

The friends, still reeling from Mia's previous confessions, now grappled with the unsettling revelation of a motive rooted in resentment and perceived injustice. The air in the room, heavy with the weight of truth and betrayal, bore witness to the unraveling of the dark secrets that had long lain dormant among this once-tight-knit group.

Mia, the architect of her own distorted reality, continued her narrative, attempting to rationalize her heinous actions in the eyes of her bewildered friends.

"Ava," she said, fixing her gaze on Ava's incredulous expression, "you knew Sophia never appreciated your so-called 'artistic expressions.' She couldn't see the beauty in it, the way it spoke to your soul. I did you a favor, liberating you from her judgment."

Turning her attention to Emily, Mia continued her sinister attempt at justification, "And you, Emily, Sophia never forgave you for exposing those personal details. She held a grudge, and it was poisoning our friendships. I simply removed the source of your torment."

Mia's words, a perverse attempt to paint her actions as a twisted form of benevolence. Now grappling with Mia's delusional reasoning, the friends exchanged uneasy glances. The once-solid foundation of their friendships had crumbled, leaving behind a landscape of betrayal and fractured trust.

Ava and Emily, each burdened by the weight of their own guilt and grief, struggled to reconcile Mia's warped perspective with the reality of the heinous act she had committed. The room, once filled with camaraderie and shared secrets, now stood as a chilling testament to the darkness that lurked within the hearts of those who had once called each other friends.

Reclaiming control of the chaotic scene, Harper fixed her gaze on Mia with unwavering resolve. "Mia," she began, holding up an evidence bag containing a worn journal, "would you like to tell them the real reason?"

Mia's eyes narrowed, confusion and trepidation etched across her face. "What is that?" she demanded, her voice edging with curiosity and defiance.

"This, Mia," Harper responded, her tone cutting through the tension, "is Sophia's journal. She documented the last five years of these retreats, capturing every moment, every emotion, and every secret shared among you. As a journalist, she kept meticulous records."

Mia's face paled, a wave of realization washing over her. "Give that to me!" she demanded, her voice escalating to a yell. The friends, still reeling from Mia's revelations, now turned their attention to the journal, the physical embodiment of the secrets they had entrusted to Sophia over the years. Harper, however, held it just out of Mia's reach, determined to reveal the truth hidden within its pages.

Mia's desperation intensified as she demanded to know where Harper had found Sophia's journal. With a steady gaze, Harper replied, "It was in the bottom of Sophia's cosmetic case, the one Olivia gave to everyone. You should have looked more thoroughly, Mia."

Undeterred, Harper opened the worn journal, its pages filled with Sophia's handwritten thoughts and observations. The friends leaned in, a mix of anticipation and dread in the air. Harper's eyes scanned the entries until she found a revealing passage.

"Listen to this," Harper declared, her voice cutting through the charged atmosphere. "Sophia wrote, 'Mia confessed her growing resentment towards the group. She feels stifled, overshadowed, and unappreciated. She's contemplating something drastic to break free.'"

Mia's face contorted with a mixture of anger and panic, realizing that her motives had not gone unnoticed by Sophia. The room fell silent, the weight of the revelation stiffilng. The journal, now a testament to the unraveling of friendships, held the key to understanding the darkness that had taken root among the once-close-knit group.

Harper continued, her voice somber, "This entry was made just days ago, indicating that Sophia was aware of Mia's growing resentment and her contemplation of something drastic to break free from the perceived constraints of the group."

The friends exchanged uneasy glances, absorbing the gravity of Sophia's words. Mia, cornered by the damning evidence from the journal, felt the walls closing in on her. The revelation exposed Mia's true intentions and underscored the tragic reality that Sophia had sensed the impending storm but was unable to prevent it.

With a grave expression, Harper continued, "I want you all to understand the depth of Mia's long-standing grudge. This entry is from three years ago." She began reading from the journal, detailing Sophia's internal struggle with her intimate relationship with Diane, a secret Mia had discovered.

In the intimate pages of Sophia's journal, the emotional struggle and turmoil were laid bare for all to witness. The words danced with a poignant mix of love, fear, and the yearning for acceptance. Sophia grappled with the complex emotions of being deeply in love with Diane while navigating the societal challenges that came with unconventional relationships.

The entries spoke of their stolen moments, the secret rendezvous where they found solace and comfort away from prying eyes. Sophia detailed the agony of suppressing their love in public, the constant fear of judgment, and the anguish that Diane endured in the shadows.

Sophia's hopes for a more inclusive and accepting future were evident in the passages, as was her desire for a world where love wasn't bound by conventional norms. However, these dreams were tainted by the looming threat of Mia, who had discovered their secret and used it as a weapon to manipulate and control.

As Harper read, the room fell into a heavy silence, each word echoing with the weight of the revelations. The friends, now fully aware of the depth of Mia's vindictiveness, were left grappling with the unsettling truth about the hidden dynamics within their once-close-knit group.

As Harper's voice filled the room with the raw emotions captured in Sophia's journal, Diane's world crumbled around her. Her eyes, once filled with anxiety and guilt, now overflowed with tears as the weight of her hidden truth surfaced. The revelation of Sophia and Diane's intimate relationship, long kept concealed from their friends, hung like a heavy fog.

Diane's breath caught in her throat as the words unfolded, painting an intimate portrait of the love she shared with Sophia. The secrecy and the pain of concealing their true selves all laid bare for everyone to witness. The burden that Diane had carried in silence, the fear of judgment and rejection, now spilled over in the form of tears.

As the last words of the journal entry echoed in the room, Diane's grief erupted. With a heart-wrenching sob, she crumbled to her knees, the weight of her emotions too much to bear. "I loved her so much, so much..." she wept, the cathartic release of years of concealed passion and sorrow pouring out in the presence of her friends.

Once filled with tension and accusations, the room was now saturated with a profound sense of empathy. The friends, witnessing Diane's emotional unraveling, were drawn into the depths of her pain, their own grievances momentarily forgotten in the face of a shared tragedy.

Mia's defiance persisted amidst Diane's emotional unraveling. As tears streamed down Diane's face, Mia stood resolute, convinced of the righteousness of her actions.

"Don't you all see?" Mia's voice cut through the heaviness in the room. "I did you all a favor. One day, you'll thank me, one day. Sophia couldn't be trusted. She was the reason Diane drifted from me; it was her fault. She needed to pay, and she did."

Her words, a twisted justification for the heinous act she committed, hung in the air like a toxic cloud. The friends, torn between empathy for Diane's pain and repulsion at Mia's callousness, struggled to comprehend the depths of the deception that had festered within their once-tight-knit group.

Mia's attempt to frame her actions as a self-righteous retribution unveiled a distorted reality shaped by jealousy, betrayal, and a misguided sense of justice. The room remained cloaked in heavy silence, the weight of the truth settling over the friends as they grappled with the shattered remnants of their friendships.

The room was thrust into chaos as a team of police officers entered, directed by Detective Harper to apprehend Mia. The atmosphere crackled with tension as Mia was handcuffed, her defiance undiminished.

"I'd have gotten away with this if it wasn't for you, Olivia, and your monogrammed silk wrap. I'll get you one day for this; you will never be safe," Mia spat venomously as the officers escorted her out of the room.

Still reeling from the revelations and emotional turmoil, the friends watched in shock and relief as Mia was led away. The weight of her threats a haunting reminder of the darkness that had infiltrated their lives. The room, once a sanctuary for friendship and camaraderie, now bore witness to the aftermath of betrayal and tragedy.

Though successful in unraveling the twisted web Mia had woven, Detective Harper wore a solemn expression as she surveyed the scene. The wounds inflicted upon the group ran deep, and rebuilding trust and healing would be challenging. The friends, bound by a shared history of joy and sorrow, faced an uncertain future where the echoes of Mia's malevolence still reverberated.

Fragments and Farewell

The friends, emotionally drained and forever changed by the tumultuous events at the retreat, gathered in the now-empty bar for a final meeting. The atmosphere was heavy with the weight of revelations, betrayals, and the lingering aftermath of Mia's hateful actions. Harper, a steady presence in the face of chaos, joined them, ready to offer closure and address any lingering concerns.

As they settled into the quiet space, the remnants of their friendships lay scattered like broken fragments. The air was thick with unspoken words, apologies, and the remnants of tears shed in solitude.

Mark and Emily: Mark and Emily, once the epitome of a loving couple, found themselves grappling with the echoes of Mia's revelations. Emily struggled to reconcile the truth about Mia's manipulations while Mark attempted to provide the support she needed. The strain on their relationship was evident as they exchanged hesitant glances.

Olivia and Richard: Olivia, standing with a regal demeanor, reveled in the collapse of her friends' facades. Richard, grappling with the exposure of his past affair with Sophia, struggled to maintain composure. Olivia's victory was bittersweet, as she pondered the cost of her pyrrhic triumph.

Diane: Diane, the unwitting victim of Mia's vengeance, grappled with the public revelation of her private life. Mia's manipulations had laid bare a secret Diane had kept hidden from her friends, and the emotional toll was evident in her tear-streaked face.

Ava: Ava, who had faced accusations and physical threats, contemplated the shattered remnants of trust among her friends. The weight of Mia's deception lingered, leaving Ava to wonder if the fragments of their friendships could ever be pieced back together.

Harper: Harper, the steadfast detective, offered a final word to the group. She acknowledged their challenges but urged them to find solace in the truth. Harper promised continued support in the investigation and hoped the healing process would begin for the group.

The dimly lit bar served as the backdrop for the friends' somber farewells. The clinking of glasses being collected and the soft murmur of distant conversations emphasized the gravity of the moment. The realization hung in the air that this retreat, meant for renewal and connection, had morphed into the final chapter of their shared escapades.

Mark and Emily shared a lingering gaze, which forever changed the unspoken acknowledgment of a relationship. Their connection, once unwavering, now navigated uncharted waters. They left the bar, trailing uncertainties that mirrored the stormy emotions within.

Olivia, always poised, made a regal exit, flanked by Richard. Despite the apparent triumph over her friends, the cracks in Olivia's facade hinted at the cost of her strategic maneuvers. In the crossfire of past and present, Richard walked beside her with a weighty silence.

Diane, emotionally raw and vulnerable, took a moment to reflect in the empty bar. The exposure of her hidden life left her grappling with the aftermath, and the uncertainty of what awaited her outside the sanctuary of the spa weighed heavily on her shoulders.

Ava, surrounded by the fragments of trust and understanding, contemplated the shattered remains of her friendships. The retreat, meant to be a respite, had become a crucible, testing the bonds that once held the group together. She departed with a mix of relief and melancholy.

As they stepped out into the cool night, the friends acknowledged that this retreat marked the end of an era. Once a sanctuary, the spa now held memories of betrayal and revelation. The uncertainty of the future loomed large, and the friends dispersed into the night, their paths diverging with heavy hearts and the knowledge that their shared history had forever altered the course of their lives.

About the Author

Arthur Patterson is a debut author whose passion for storytelling has led him on a journey to craft engaging narratives that captivate readers. Born and raised in a small town, Arthur developed an early love for literature and spent countless hours immersed in the world of books.

After earning a degree in English literature, Arthur ventured into various professions while nurturing his dream of becoming a published author. Inspired by his fascination with the human psyche and the intricacies of relationships, he found his niche in crafting suspenseful mysteries that explore the complexities of human nature.

"Beneath the Retreat's Veil" marks Patterson's foray into the world of fiction. Drawing from his experiences and observations, Arthur weaves a tale of suspense, betrayal, and the hidden truths beneath the surface of seemingly idyllic relationships.

As a storyteller, Arthur is committed to delivering narratives that resonate with readers, inviting them to ponder the intricacies of the human experience. With his debut novel, Arthur invites readers into a world where secrets unfold, friendships are tested, and the true cost of deception is revealed.

www.ingramcontent.com/pod-product-compliance
Ingram Content Group UK Ltd.
Pitfield, Milton Keynes, MK11 3LW, UK
UKHW021708190726
13853UKWH00001B/456

9 798869 156747